The Duck Springs DEFIANCE

A Novel of the Next Civil War

PETER S. ADLER

Paperback ISBN 978-1-63226-166-3
eBook ISBN 978-1-63226-167-0

Published by All Night Books
An imprint of Easton Studio Press
PO Box 3131
Westport, CT 06880
www.allnightbooks.com

Book and cover design by Alexia Garaventa

You may not be interested in war, but war is interested in you.

—Leon Trotsky

AUTHOR'S NOTE

This novel is set in the near future. The story centers on a man escaping from an unhappy past and how he is drawn into the rhythms of a quirky, out-of-the-way rural community just as a violent coup d'état throws America into a second civil war. And how his spirit revives and his community succeeds, but not without costs.

A second civil war? A small town called Duck Springs? A rear-guard resistance? Take it all as a work of fiction, but at the moment, it doesn't feel so far-fetched. If you really want to understand the dynamics of how a homegrown conflict like this might start in the United States, read *How Civil Wars Start* by Barbara F. Walter and *On Tyranny* by Timothy Snyder.

And if you believe places like Duck Springs are just a myth of some golden past, read *Our Towns: A 100,000-Mile Journey Into the Heart of America* by journalists Deborah Fallows and James Fallows. The Fallowses bought a single-engine Cirrus SR22, and over four years flew into towns and small cities across the country to see what was going on beneath the harsh enmities dominating our national headlines.

It was pretty simple, actually. They landed, headed for local libraries, cafés, and coffee shops, introduced themselves, made friends and asked, "What is the town dealing with and who makes things happen here?" They spoke with shopkeepers, public officials, and plenty of ordinary people. Unlike our persistently grumpy national mood, they found lots of vibrant, locally focused, and civically engaged people intent on getting things done for their communities. Not everywhere, of course, but more than you might assume.

I am alarmed by what Walter and Snyder predicted, loved what the Fallowses did, and remain profoundly worried about our nation's discontents. This novel is my cautionary tale.

I hope it never happens this way.

PROLOGUE

In a forest, near a river, in the little town of Duck Springs on the eastern slope of the Cascade Mountains in Washington State, Clover Fiffe opens up the café she jointly owns with Pops and Thelma Thornton. The morning is chilly and overcast.

She unlocks the door, hangs her red fleece jacket on a hook near the kitchen, and turns on the large coffee pot. She flips all the light switches in the dining areas on, heads to the pantries, and pulls out a box of oranges, cartons of eggs, loaves of bread, and packages of bacon and link sausages. Then she turns on the neon OPEN sign outside for the breakfast regulars who will be trooping in soon.

At that exact moment, 2,168 miles east, the four senior men planning America's next civil war convene again around a magnificent oak conference table in the executive suites of Hammond Brothers Industries three blocks off DuPont Circle. Travis and Casper Hammond, two of the richest people in America, are talking with Retired General Eugene Brody when Senator Remus Willard comes in from Oklahoma.

"Weather. Delayed flight," he says. "Is this place secure?"

"Waterproof. Tighter than a frog's ass," Casper replies. "The room is impenetrable, swept for bugs hourly, and men are posted downstairs by the elevator and at the door."

Willard loosens the belt on his size fifty-three pants. His words are slightly slurred, and his shirt is stained with some kind of sauce. On the plane he had downed a rib eye steak, potato salad, french fries, a large slice of pecan pie, and three stiff drinks.

"We can talk freely," Travis says.

"Good," says Brody. The general, a compact man with jet-black hair, is focused on the fight ahead. "Security, secrecy, and timing are everything now," he says. "No surprises. No leaks. We are on countdown."

It is a paperless, computer-less, and record-less meeting. Nothing will ever be traced. Brody presides and the conversation moves quickly.

Travis reports they have just over $884 million available and is confident more is coming.

"Money won't bring you happiness," quips Willard, "but it always calms my nerves."

Then he reports on the names they have been discussing for months. He has an encrypted list in his home safe with the top 750 government, business, and civic leaders in the United States targeted for elimination.

"POTUS, VPOTUS, and SCOTUS will disappear, and the Speaker, Attorney General, and others will have accidents," he says with a wink.

A discussion of others who are slated to disappear ensues until Brody stops them. "Listen," he commands, "the militias are now organized into a pyramid of cells that ensure operational security and cells that don't know each other. Each cell leader reports anonymously. Meanwhile, we have teams ready in a dozen places."

"What about Pharaoh?" asks Casper.

Brody nods and says, "In three months Pharaoh moves to Level Three and automatically inserts itself into every major social media platform. Our preliminary messaging will be everywhere and amplify as we get closer. Plus, we have people who can hack their way through anything."

"Bravo!" Remus claps his hands.

Brody frowns. "Let's not get ahead of our skis and forget why we are doing all this. It has to be a complete reboot of the United States. Nothing else will work. America is in a death spiral. If we don't act now, we lose the moment."

"Once this starts," says Willard, "we have to deal with all the Blacks, spics, and slants in the United States who will oppose us."

Casper Hammond adds, "Don't forget the kikes. They control the big banks and investment funds."

The conversation about who they need to eliminate keeps coming back but Brody cuts it off. It is repetitious and he is far more absorbed with weapons, ammunition, militias, geography, and logistics.

While Brody talks, Travis ruminates on their fungible assets, now mostly parked in Zurich and the Cayman Islands.

Willard sips Johnny Walker from a silver flask, burps loudly, and finally asks, "What's the date?"

"August 28. That gives us just enough time to finish preparations."

"What happens on D-Day?" asks Casper.

Brody, is irritated. "We have discussed this before. We have specific targets that are operationally and symbolically important. The attacks will be simultaneous."

"I'm ready," says Willard, lifting his flask in a toast.

"To the new America," Casper responds.

Brody lifts a water bottle.

"God speed, gentlemen," and he leaves.

This planning huddle, like all previous ones over the past five years, has lasted precisely one hour.

Back in the Duck Springs Café, Clover brings a cup of hot, fresh coffee to Grant Terwilliger, the town's fire chief and the day's first customer.

"Morning Clover."

"Morning Grant. Same as usual?" He usually orders French toast and bacon.

"I'm going big and I'm really hungry today! Spent all day yesterday working on the pumper. Waffles, scrambled eggs, and a small steak!"

PART I

1

DANNY WAS A HABITUAL SCRIBBLER AND KEPT A RUNNING JOURNAL, DAILY IF HE COULD, WEEKLY OR MONTHLY WHEN EVENTS OVERTOOK HIM. It was a long habit that started in the Marine Corps. Lately, when he woke up, he jotted notes about his dreams before they dissipated. Later, he might clean up the notes, extract the to-dos and grocery lists, and sometimes try to make them into something readable.

Even though he and Kirsten had come to detest each other, he tried not to wake her. Enough battles. Danny dressed, padded downstairs to the kitchen, flipped on the light, and assembled his sandwich for the long ride. Everything was preplanned, including lunch in the car.

He cut two thick slices of sourdough bread, slathered one with mayonnaise, smeared spicy horseradish on the other, then laid on a helping of roast beef and Swiss cheese. He added a slab of sweet Vidalia onion, a slice of tomato, some crisp lettuce, put the sandwich in a Ziploc bag, stuck two kosher dill pickles in another, grabbed a bottle of water, and looked down.

Elvira was staring up at him. Elvira was Kirsten's dog, a mostly black-and-white cocker spaniel with a few patches of brown. If it was up to him, he would have called her Elvis. Dog looked up with big eyes, polished the floor with her wagging stump, and cocked her head to the side to divine his intent. This was Cocker Spaniel Standard Look Number Two, second only to when she wanted to pee.

Danny followed the map in his brain: 195th Street out of Richmond Beach to the I-5, then south through the city. His departure was through the early morning fog. Lights on, low beams, ten miles per hour. Despite the emancipation, he slipped out of town like a rat chased by cats.

Traffic thickened. Early commuters streamed onto the freeway from the city's arteries. Past downtown, past the stadiums and the fingers of water cutting in from Puget Sound and the cranes and railroads of the industrial district, traffic thinned.

On the edge of a watery horizon, a weak sun was rising, just the rim of an arc, gauzy, vaguely orange as it began to emerge. He left the freeway at Auburn and turned east, following his memorized map and enjoying his revery about unshackled liberation. Still, somewhere in the back of his brain, deep in the folds where family memes lie buried, there was that Yiddish proverb passed down the Goodman line: *Mann Tracht, Un Gott Lacht.*

He had first heard this phrase from his great-grandfather, whose old-world name was Oskar Gutterman and who immigrated to the United States from the porous border between Poland and Germany, acquiring the new Goodman name at Ellis Island.

Oskar left home in the wake of a pogrom after armed Christians on massive horses rampaged through his little town. Land, money, donkeys, cows, chickens, turkeys, and what little farming equipment people had, were stolen. Dozens of people were indiscriminately killed, including Oskar's older brother, the rabbi.

In America, Oskar and his young wife, Rachel, made new lives and produced a thin line of heirs. Many of the old shtetl ways fell away, but memories of inflicted violence never fully leave. Historical injustices are traumas that lie dormant, only to come back at some later moment when inner and outer geographies converge.

Oskar sent a message down the Goodman line. "Don't forget," he would say, *"Mann Tracht, Un Gott Lacht."* Man plans and God laughs.

2

THE ANCIENT AM CAR RADIO WORKED INTERMITTENTLY BUT BLARED AN ANNOUNCEMENT. A large riot had broken out in Chicago. Student demonstrators marching north on Michigan Avenue were being attacked by a crowd of opponents wearing berets and red scarves. There were reports of deaths and injuries.

Just before Berwick along Washington 983, Danny stopped at a Chevron station to get coffee and gas. On the TV above the cashier, a blond newsman was speaking. He looked like he had just graduated from high school and was wearing a suit for the first time. His newsreader voice was steady, even as events shrieked at the viewers. A few customers near Danny were wide-eyed, their ears hearing what their minds couldn't quite absorb. Danny joined them and was riveted to the broadcast.

Beginning at 2:17 p.m. bombs had gone off three minutes apart at the Lincoln, Jefferson, and FDR Memorials. Someone had sent assassins to take out President Norma Chavez's motorcade and tried to kill Vice President Marcus Longborn in his home at the Naval Observatory.

Norma Chavez's armored limousine withstood a bomb blast. In Bethesda, assassins made it over the fence and partway to

Longborn's house before they were killed. A reporter at the scene said the dead assassins wore black berets, camo pants, and red scarves.

The picture on the screen showed a partially demolished Lincoln Memorial with Honest Abe's marble chair and body split in half and his bearded head on the ground. Several columns were shattered, and bodies were covered with plastic sheets. Paramedics were ministering to others.

The crawler at the bottom of the screen said that at least thirty-four deaths had been confirmed and scores more injured by attack drones and explosions of ball bearings, screws, and nails. The body count was rising.

Then, a third report broke in. Details were sketchy, but more bombs and drone attacks had hit the federal courthouses in New York, Chicago, San Francisco, Portland, Atlanta, and St. Louis; at FBI headquarters, the Supreme Court, the J. Edgar Hoover Building in DC; and at the Federal Reserve Bank in Dallas. The baby-faced newscaster said that machine-gun assaults were also underway at the King and Jefferson Memorials and at park headquarters at the Grand Canyon.

There were no accurate numbers yet, but the newsreader suggested that hundreds had died. A picture from the Jefferson Memorial next to the Tidal Basin flashed on the screen. It was in shambles. Everyone was told to standby. Danny stared at the monitor as talking heads jumped in to comment on the images of destruction and close-ups of the dead and wounded.

Hastily assembled pundits talked about wingnuts and crackpots. An unctuous Republican senator from Iowa in a three-piece suit with a flag pin in his lapel, said it could be a peak moment in the long cyberwar with the Russians. He called for reflection and prayer.

His equally smug Democratic counterpart reported that it was a murky right-wing group called Pharaoh. The announcer asked who was behind Pharaoh. The senators shrugged off his question. Danny had heard vague snippets about Pharaoh as a source of shadowy rumors that President Chavez and Vice President Longborn were sex-traffickers, pedophiles, and the spawn of demons from outer space.

Danny could envision a frenzy of social media messages suddenly lighting up millions of handhelds as storylines accelerated. There would be electronic locker-room brawls of verbal nose pulling and towel snapping and thousands of anonymous poison darts and sharpened electronic sticks flying through the ether from a million unnamed keyboard cowards. The toxicity would churn around the world in seconds.

Years before, the Department of Homeland Security had warned that lone offenders and small groups driven by ideological grievances posed lethal threats to the country. After domestic terrorists smashed into the Capitol in January 2021 looking for public officials to assassinate, most people thought the arrest of the insurrectionists was the end of it. It wasn't. It was the beginning.

Even after that, national polls repeatedly showed a rising majority of people bracing for violent change. Homeland Security had a report calling virulent white supremacists "the most persistent threat in America." Seventy-five percent of all Americans thought armed insurrection was inevitable. Smart historians, philosophers, and respected former government officials agreed.

"It's 1859 again, and just like the civil war," one of them argued. "Everyone is angry, everyone is tribal, and everyone has a gun." He laid odds at 95 percent on a second civil war.

Back in Danny's high school science class, Mr. Meyers taught everyone that water boils at exactly 212 degrees Fahrenheit. What nobody could accurately predict, Meyers said, was which molecule would agitate first and start the simmer. When it came to combustible national politics, no one could tell what would kickstart a boil.

Actually, it didn't matter. He listened to the news with curiosity but deep down, Danny didn't care. The car was gassed up but he himself was running on fumes. He could have headed to Bora Bora or set off for a fishing port in Canada. Instead, his inglorious retreat was 140 miles eastward over the mountains and into a remote forest. He just wanted to fall off the edge of the map, find a place to leave it all behind, and hide from everything.

He drank more coffee and took another look at the map to check his route. First to Berwick, then through the small logging towns of Silver River and Snooker Falls, then over 6,000 feet high Wild Wind Pass, beyond where the Western Crest Trail crossed the highway, then finally down the grade to the cabin at the 5,200-foot level called Indian Creek on the Little Green River.

"It's not much," Gracie and Michael had said, "but it's right on the river and you can use it as long as you want. You may want to get out and hunker down someplace lower and warmer when it snows. It's an old inholding in the national forest. The cabin has a propane range and running water in the sink. The potbelly stove is creaky and makes a lot of noise but puts out plenty of heat once it's stoked. The field mice will make you nuts."

Danny got back in the Karmann Ghia, which was holding its own even though it was overloaded. There were boxes and duffels in the backseat and gear stuffed onto an oversized roof rack covered with a tarp.

The Ghia was an ancient toy from a kit, a 1970s hobby model that his brother Josh played around with for years. He kept this mechanical creature in his garage in Seattle and fussed with it on weekends when he and his wife Sharon weren't at work or volunteering on trail crews and fire tower restorations.

The Ghia had a forest-green paint job, good winter tires, and a well-tuned engine that could make it up mountains. He drove it slowly. It had an AM radio that didn't work all the time, but no clock, which was fine since, other than flashlights, he wanted to leave anything with connectivity, voice recognition, and on-off buttons behind.

No computer, email, video meetings, or webinars. No weather forecasts, fresh headlines, or stories that started with, "And this just in . . ." He didn't even bring a watch and wanted to fully check out. The world and its constant clamoring for attention had become nonstop noise, not just from the media-chattering classes, but also from colleagues, friends, and family who had given him unsolicited and discordant advice on the state of the nation generally, and his personal decline and fall in particular.

Through it all, he had finally seen matters clearly. His life and the world's trajectory were disconnected and progressively more and more out of sync. Like other lawyers he knew, he had become a domesticated rodent searching in a maze that had no route to the prize. He understood. There is no cheese.

In the unlikely and remote event that anyone needed him, they would have to drive to Indian Creek, find Mike and Gracie's primordial one-room cabin with the leaky roof and, if he was out, wait until he returned from somewhere. Or didn't.

Mike and Gracie's cabin was built in the late 1920s and was slowly slipping into oblivion. *In the end*, he thought, *we are all carbon.*

Danny just wanted to escape. He didn't care much about America's gloom. His own small cosmos was unmoored, and it had nothing to do with the country's unrest. They just happened to coincide.

3

DANNY WAS HAPPY TO LEAVE SEATTLE WHICH WAS OVERBUILT, EXPENSIVE, AND CROWDED. Still, even with cold rains, there were days when the gloom melted and Mount Rainier poked its head above the clouds. Sunlight would flood down and the world suddenly acquired more possibility. Near as he could tell, and beyond the pure biology of being alive, the presence of "possibility" was the only enduring meaning of life. When you run out of possibility, he believed, you are dead, either physically, emotionally, or intellectually.

Rainier was out now showing its sweet side, and the farther he got from the city, the more he allowed himself the vague notion that it isn't just a big mountain in the Cascades, but a sentinel.

A warm wind was blowing on his arm cocked out of the driver's window. He caught the occasional loamy smells of pastures and saw cows standing in fields, jaws swinging side to side as they chewed on sweet, green grass. He saw water birds by a pond and a red fox ran across the road.

As he drove out of the city and east on Washington 983, some of the world's weight lifted and his shoulders relaxed.

4

ALL HIS LIFE WHEN EVENTS HEMMED HIM IN AND HUMAN AFFAIRS FELT OVERWHELMING, BACKCOUNTRIES BECKONED. Forests, mountains, flowing rivers, deep valleys, high meadows, and other wild spaces were perfect places to refresh—whether running away from the daily grind, or in Daniel Goodman's case, from a shattered legal career, a bad marriage, and occasional PTSD.

Sometimes, his coping went in one direction and he was drawn to things brighter and more vibrant than his own bad mood: a bit of peace, a moment of joy, a small respite. Sometimes, it went the other way and his mood got dark. These had always been his South and North Poles, lost causes and fresh possibilities.

In Kashmir, following a short but furious firefight in the Vale, Kenny Stokes and Danny wrangled time off from Lieutenant Fuentes and headed up to a lake at fifteen thousand feet in the Himalayas. Those were meager foothills in the eyes of the locals. The real mountains, the massifs, were in Tibet, Nepal, and China.

Still, at that height, away from the apple orchards and saffron fields below, the lake was high enough. It was oblong, cradled under the lip of a glacier and ringed by a snow-covered saw-toothed ridge line. Tired of mess food at the fortified base outside Kishtwar, they went off to catch and eat rainbows. Big ones. This particular lake had been stocked years before. Because it was remote, it went largely unfished. Rainbows ran to twenty pounds and more.

After considerable haggling with bluffs and false walkaways, they hired a guide named Baktoo and his son Amal who owned some small Himalayan horses. Baktoo's ponies were sturdy enough. Kenny and his horse fell in love with each other and got along fine; Danny's horse held some kind of grudge against Americans, Jews, white boys, or all three. Like every other horse he'd ridden before, this one tried to bite and kick him.

He understood. Horses were one of life's many smaller feuds, unlike the big ones that really mattered. He put his gear on the horse and walked up the mountain thinking, *More proof that horses whisper to each other about certain humans.*

At the lake, they fished off big rocks on the water's edge laid down by glaciers centuries ago and then gorged on the fish they caught. Baktoo and his boy salted baskets of them to sell in Kishtwar. Drinking the cold, clean water made Danny's teeth chatter, and breathing the thin air was like sucking ice cream through a straw.

Stokes and Goodman slept in a lean-to under huge pine trees. At midnight, the horses bolted when a bear sniffed around. Baktoo rounded them up the next morning.

Time out from explosive gun fights, a break from the running instinct to protect yourself, and a pause from the exhaustion of constantly looking for courage in the face of serious danger, that piece of nature in Kashmir was more than he hoped for. It was a momentary refuge.

But maybe remote mountains and lakes were the real world, and Danny Goodman just didn't know it yet.

5

FORTY-FIVE MINUTES BEYOND BERWICK, A BEEFY, UNIFORMED STATE TROOPER STOPPED HIM. His globe light was flashing, but he hadn't used his siren. He stepped up to Danny's window cautiously.

"What's your name?" he asked.

"Daniel Goodman," he answered, handing him his license and keeping his hands on the steering wheel where the cop could see them, a lesson he learned from a Black man in the Marines who said he did that so he wouldn't get shot right off.

He asked Danny where he was from. "Portland, but coming from Seattle right now," he said. Then he asked where he was headed, and Danny told him—Indian Creek, not far from a town called Duck Springs.

"Nice up there," the trooper said affably. "Used to fish and hunt with my dad there when I was a kid. Hand me your registration certificate."

Danny passed it over and said, "It's my brother's car, Joshua Goodman. I'm borrowing it."

Then the cop noticed the long guns in the back seat, asked what kind they were, and if they were registered. Danny told him. A Marlin .22, a Remington 30.06, and a .40 caliber Sig Sauer pistol in a canvas duffel. Said he would be pleased to show him the guns and his papers but would need to dig them out from the boxes and duffel bags in the back seat.

"You ex-military?" the cop asked.

He looked ex-military himself. A lot of cops are former soldiers. Men and women who have served seem to have a sixth sense about others who were military.

"Yes, sir. First Marines."

"Thought so," he said. "So was I. Afghanistan. No need for the gun licenses, Mr. Goodman. I believe you. Where'd you do your tour?"

"Srinagar in Kashmir."

"I heard those were hard fights."

Danny nodded. Then the cop said, "You hear about the bombings and killings in DC?"

Danny nodded again.

"United States is going to the dogs. No matter what your politics are, you may need to stay up there. I just heard some paramilitaries called the Western Badgers tried to kidnap Idaho's attorney general. They failed, but the mayor of San Francisco was killed in a knife attack." Then he looked at the car more carefully. "Nice Karmann Ghia, Mr. Goodman. Don't see many of those. Tell me about it."

"It's actually a replica, mostly fiberglass, an oversized version on a bigger frame with strong springs and shocks and a Ford engine, so it has some juice. It's a kit car, a hobby my brother Josh put together in Seattle."

"Mr. Goodman, tell your brother his safety sticker is out of date. Get that fixed."

Danny thanked him and said he would, even though he knew he wouldn't. He drove on.

At Wild Wind Pass, the top of the Cascades, a cluster of men and women with black berets and dozens of rifles were building some kind of checkpoint structure. He rolled through and headed downhill on 983.

6

HEADING ANOTHER TWENTY MILES TOWARD THE OLD LOGGING COMMUNITY OF SILVER RIVER, DANNY'S MIND WANDERED. He thought about Evan Fisher, another undergraduate at Portland State University who Danny had roomed with off campus. Fisher was a trim, sandy-haired evangelical Christian from Idaho who kept trying to convert him. He was a lifelong member of Church of The Truth, which had branches across the West.

Evan was convinced that non-believers, especially Danny's people, were headed for eternal damnation unless they converted. Jews were going to fry. The more he talked about that, the more Danny ignored him. Jews had been hearing it for two thousand years. But one evening a more convivial classmate named Jimmy Boylan asked Danny, "How come everyone hates you people so much?"

Jimmy and Danny had become drinking friends as a result of a late afternoon class taught by a professor they both loathed. After class, they would adjourn to a local saloon to drink beer and discuss the sorry state of their class. Somehow, that moved from grumbling about the professor to dissecting ethnic voting differences between American Irish and American Jews. Danny knew he wasn't much of a Jew other than bloodlines and a deep love for corned beef sandwiches and dill pickles. But Jimmy's question was a good one.

"It's an ancient hatred, a virus that keeps being spread by Nazi and radical Christian and Muslim types," he told Jimmy, "but it goes way back. Underneath all our own hocus pocus, we really are different, stubborn, and clannish. Plus, we are waiting for the real Messiah to show up. And now that I think about it, this would be a good time for him or her to appear."

Jimmy himself was a grinning, red-haired, well-freckled Scot-Irish mix. He said his people had Danny's completely beat. He said a Scot or Mick will walk fifty miles out of his way to receive an insult, then brood on it for the next five years before he walks back and returns his own.

Meanwhile Evan Fisher, pleasant but relentless, kept at it. Danny listened to all his evangelical gobbledygook but followed Jimmy Boylan's sage advice: "A shut mouth gathers no foot." Danny said nothing to Evan but slowly became curious about Evan's big question.

Back in his high school science lab, Mr. Meyers said the sound of real learning at work was never "Aha!" It was "Huh?"—the arousal of curiosity. What happens after we are done with life became a fair question.

Danny pondered the idea of a possible heaven while he was daydreaming during the more boring classes that were required if he was ever to be released from his undergraduate chains. What he finally concluded, reaffirmed by his marriage and career meltdowns, is there is no afterlife. No eternal paradise. No Valhalla, Elysian Fields, and no shining City on a Hill.

The notion of hell was the same. He read about Dante's ladder that descended into eternal fires and all the collateral notions of purgatory, perdition, and eternal damnation full of demons with snake tails tossing unrepentant sinners into blazing pits.

The next time Evan obliquely raised the question and asked what Danny thought, he finally said, "Evan, I don't think there is anything up there. What we have here, what we do now, that's what counts."

Danny needed to coexist with Evan, so he didn't criticize or tell him heaven is just higher-vibrational schmaltz. In the end, he said it was about how people behave in the face of tough choices that have consequences from the stones they toss in the waters of life. It's what we actually do that counts.

When you are young, he thought, people can be forgiven for most of their poorly launched rocks. But Danny had also met people who acted with relentless deep-seated malice, as if there was a malevolent wound in their chest that never healed and leaked pus forever. Most of us, he thought, harm others through blunders and errors of judgment we only come to regret with hindsight.

Somewhere in his college ruminations, Albert Camus emerged and said that after a certain age, everyone is accountable for the face they wear.

If life were really fair, Danny thought, the penalties we incur would reverberate back in a precise, knowable quantum. Sometimes they do. More often they don't. Intentionally or unintentionally, we inflict hurts on others, and occasionally on innocent bystanders. In the military and the courtroom, he had been a part of damage to innocent victims.

Maybe that is what I am too. Collateral damage.

Danny was in that netherworld now. Any bliss he once had was gone. America seemed the same. The country might be descending into more than its usual daily diet of stabbings, robberies, and muggings, but he wanted none of it.

He remembered a saying how in dark times, you begin to see things clearly. You meet your shadow in the shade and find yourself behind it.

7

DANNY PASSED THROUGH HIS CLASSES AT PSU LIKE A GHOST, AVOIDING SERIOUS PERSONAL, POLITICAL, AND SOCIAL ENTANGLEMENTS. He cruised, half-listening for anything that might seem important but nothing much did until his third year when, by sheer luck, he took a bonehead philosophy course because he needed what was supposed to be an easy A.

The survey course was taught by an oddly cheerful professor named Stanley Sager. Sager was lean, fit, and tan, and wore wire-rimmed glasses. Danny read the textbook, listened to the lectures, and took notes for a future exam. Then, that strange sense of "Huh?" popped up.

It started with Plato's allegorical cave where he suggested we are all prisoners chained to a wall peering at flickering shadows. Beyond their individual experiences of being alive, Sager said, the shadows were the only things the prisoners knew and they assumed them to be real. But they weren't.

Sager summarized Plato's metaphoric cave like this: we are captive to kaleidoscopic perceptions, but once freed from transitory images, we come to understand the world we perceive may feel tangible. But it isn't, nor is it the one that counts. There are bigger truths that everyone has to discover themself.

This was interesting. Weeks later, when Sager worked his way to Kierkegaard, Nietzsche, and the existentialists, Danny read with much greater interest. Even though he was still in college, the existentialists somehow seemed pertinent to both himself and America's strange demons and discontents.

He summarized Simone de Beauvoir, Maurice Merleau-Ponty, and others. Albert Camus in particular grabbed his attention, and he found himself prowling used bookstores and buying dog-eared copies of *The Stranger, The Plague, The Rebel,* and his other intellectual dramas.

Philosophers were in a bad mood back then and so was Camus. Existentialism emerged in Europe at the close of the First World War and the dawn of the second. Danny thought their outlook explained a few things. And even if it didn't, it seemed like a good set of clothes to wear when confronted by the Evan Fishers. Albert argued that life has no intrinsic meaning. We are born, we die, and in between, we just exist.

It became Danny's armor for a time but that belief soon faded. Behind the chain mail and weaponized debating points, life seemed ambiguous and neither all good nor all bad. Then he discovered what felt like a larger truth in a poem called "Directions to the Armorer" written by a man named Elder Olson back in the 1950s.

> All right, armorer,
>
> make me a sword—
>
> not too sharp,
>
> a bit hard to draw,
>
> and of cardboard, preferably,
>
> on second thought, stick

an eraser on the handle.
Somehow, I always
clobber the wrong guy.

Make me a shield with
easy-to-change insignia. I'm often
a little vague as to which side I'm on,
what battle I'm in.
And listen, make it
a trifle flimsy,
not too hard to pierce.
I'm not absolutely sure
I want to win.

Make the armor itself
as tough as possible,
but on a reverse
principle: Don't
worry about its
saving my hide;
just fit it to give me
some sort of protection—
any sort of protection—
from a possible enemy
inside.

Danny thought about his old law firm mentor, Sam Johnson who would have detested this and called him an idiot. He would have said, "Winning is the only thing that matters. Clobber the other guy and sort your feelings out later."

8

FARTHER EAST ON 983, AT SNOOKER FALLS, ANOTHER SMALL TOWN FADING FROM THE LOGGING TRADE, HE STOPPED AT BILLY'S BAR AND GRILL. It looked like a lively joint in the middle of nowhere. A dozen cars and pickups were parked in front and country music throbbed from a jukebox. Danny needed to use the bathroom.

The counterman came over. "Beer?" he asked.

"No thanks. I'll have a coffee. This place busy like this all the time?"

"Mostly lunch, weekends, and holidays for the locals and a few people like you driving through."

"You must be Billy."

"Yep, owner, cook, barkeep, and bouncer."

He looked the part. Tall, full red beard, long hair, tattoos on thick arms, and a small baseball bat under the mirror. Danny and Billy talked. He had two cups of excellent coffee, used the bathroom, then went out to the parking lot.

Handbills had been tucked under every windshield wiper. He pulled his out and looked it over. The title in bold print said, READY FOR ACTION? JOIN THE WASHINGTON WOLVES! Underneath it showed a man in fatigues with the head of a smiling wolf. The man cradled an AR-15.

Danny read the recruiting message.

> Had enough of other races taking over? Tired of Left Wing women from California who want to give your wives and daughters abortions? Ready to get rid of Chavez and Longborn? The next war won't be at Shiloh or Bull Run. It will be right here, where you are. Get ready, get armed, get trained!

He crushed the handbill in a ball, tossed it on the Ghia's floor, and headed to Indian Creek.

9

IN THE EARLY AFTERNOON LIGHT, DANNY UNLOADED HIS CAR AND ORGANIZED THE CABIN. He put the perishables in coolers with tight lids to fend off Mickey and Minnie, laid out blankets, put his sleeping bag on the bed, and set the two rifles, the pistol, and the boxes of ammunition on a bookshelf. He put the flashlights and Coleman lanterns where he could get to them when it turned dark and split a few chunks of wood to try out the stove later. Then he took a walk.

The nearest cabin was upstream a quarter mile away and set back from the spring flood line of sticks, pebbles, and bits of plastic trash. He kept walking and scouting the spot where he would be living. The Little Green River bubbled and splattered onto rocks. It was a shallow, narrow river most of the year. Low as it was, it rolled over drift logs and bottom snags and washed tiny waves onto the bank.

His mind turned back to Albert. There was a small note in one of Camus's journals, the *Carnets*, that said, "An overwhelming impulse to cast ourselves away, to become like nothing at all, utterly destroying what we are, offering the present only solitude and nothingness . . ."

What caused him to write that note? It seemed fitting to Danny's life.

10

THE LITTLE GREEN RIVER THAT RAN IN FRONT OF MIKE AND GRACIE'S CABIN WAS A FINE PLACE TO TRY AND UNLOAD ALL THE BAGGAGE DANNY WAS CARRYING. It was a small tributary to the Big Green, which flowed down from one of Mount Rainier's glaciers into the Douglas Elway Wilderness, then into the Schema and Crockett Rivers, both of which are part of the larger Columbia River watershed.

These were the traditional summer hunting grounds for the now Yakama Nation. The nearest place of any size was Crockett City with a quarter million people.

East of the Cascade crest there was still an abundance of forest habitats. If you liked trees, there were plenty: oaks, firs, cedars, larches, and alders. Underneath thick overstories there were shrubs and edibles: manzanita, huckleberries, elderberries, and blueberries. And flowers: asters, lupine, yarrow, Nootka rose, Indian paintbrush, and sprigs of sage. There also was poison oak and devil's club, both of which could hurt.

And there were critters. Common ones like deer, elk, coyotes, bears, and rarer ones like cougars, lynx, wolves, fishers, and reputedly, a few last wolverines. Smaller ones, lower on the food chain, included raccoons, mice, shrews, skunks, rabbits, marmots, martens, minks, moles, squirrels, and chipmunks. And birds: eagles, swallows, swifts, ospreys, hawks, woodpeckers, nuthatches, hummingbirds, ducks, and more.

Gracie and Mike had told Danny the Elway Wilderness was a fine area to get lost in, especially in the late fall and winter when the fishermen, hunters, bird watchers, mushroom pickers, tree huggers, and leaf lookers left, and the only people around were the full-timers in the nearby unincorporated town of Duck Springs, along with loners like himself, living on the outskirts.

Duck Springs was a quirky name for a town. It was, and still is, off the beaten path from every major thoroughfare going east, west, north, or south. It has some natural springs and ponds with freshwater bubbling up, hence the name. But remote was precisely why Danny was there. He wanted to be lost.

If someone looked hard, they could find Duck Springs on Old County Road 18, more or less eight miles off Washington 983, the highway leading from Seattle via Berwick to Wild Wind Pass at the Cascade crest, then downslope to Crockett City and beyond. The town is at the base of an 800-foot escarpment with a plateau at the top. A small perennial stream drops over the lip of the cliff above and trickles down into a little freshwater spring.

The stream flowing out of the pond rolled through the middle of what the local Ducklings called "town" and emptied into the Big Green, which is deeper and wider than the Little Green where Danny settled at Indian Creek. Most of the year, other than spring snowmelt, it was about a thousand feet across and five or six feet deep in the middle.

Beyond Duck Springs, County 18 is paved for another three miles, then turns to gravel. Some families had built houses in the puckerbrush and lived off the grid, but C-18 dead-ended another ten miles south at an abandoned military base.

The town center of Duck Springs had Slim's Grocery, Mo's Bakery (which wasn't open all the time), and an infirmary with a few cots and an on-call nurse. It had a three-room schoolhouse, a laundromat, a postal station, and a community center with a gym and a small swimming pool. Just outside town off Ogden Road and past the cemetery, American Cement Company had offices and a truck wash which serviced their quarry ten miles away.

There was a district forest ranger office on Fern Street and an oversized Quonset for the volunteer fire department with an adjoining shed that housed a 1984 Ford fire truck the town bought for $6,500 and fixed up. Duck Springs also had the Duck Springs Café at the corner of Duck Boulevard and Ponderosa Street, which Danny visited when he was sick of his own cooking. Slowly, the café became his North Star.

It was owned and run by "Pops" Thornton and his wife Thelma. Pops's real name was Elmer, but he hated it and loved Pops. Pops and Thelma made fine, meaty burgers, crisp, salty french fries, and wonderous onion rings. They were known for desserts. Apple, pecan, lemon meringue, and strawberry rhubarb pies. And homemade ice creams in different seasonal flavors.

They also had a waitress and co-owner named Clover Fiffe, Pops's niece. Beautiful to look at and wonderful to talk with. Weeks might go by without a piece of pie or a Clover sighting, but every once in a while, Danny drove into Duck Springs to get gas, propane, batteries, toilet paper, flour, eggs, or something else he needed to make his increasingly meager existence work. He would always stop at the café.

If a bigger shopping trip was required, he could head east past Secah to Crockett City, but those trips were rare. He didn't want to be in big towns or small cities. He actually didn't want to go anywhere.

Retreating to Gracie and Mike's cabin on the eastern slope of the Cascades, hiding away from civilization's incessant distractions, and living alone gave him time to read. He had always been a reader and packed some favorite books, along with a few that he ransacked from Kirsten.

He'd brought paperbacks by Nikos Kazantzakis which he had read at Portland State. He had stuff from Mark Twain, Ernest Hemingway, Henry David Thoreau, Norman Maclean, a copy of the United States Constitution that Professor Shapiro made him buy in law school, and a recent history of the Middle East wars, what veterans called "The Sandbox."

Settled into his hidey-hole on the Little Green, it somehow seemed obligatory to start with Thoreau's *Walden, or Life in the Woods*. He had read it in a freshman class at Portland State, but now with more years and accumulated barnacles, it read differently.

The story took place in the 1850s. Prima facie, Thoreau, son of a pencil maker and a convert to transcendentalism, retreated to Walden Pond to ponder life. There, by the pond, he meticulously detailed his two years, two months, and forty-eight hours in a cabin not far from today's Boston.

He famously said, "I went to the woods, because I wished to live deliberately, to front only the essential facts of life, and see if I could not learn what it had to teach, and not, when I came to die, discover that I had not lived." That was the essence of Henry's big quest. But that wasn't Danny's story. Goodman was a forty-one-year-old ex-soldier and defrocked lawyer wanting to withdraw from life.

In *Walden*, he could see a few similarities, but mostly differences. Henry was a thinker who had not really lived. Danny had lived but wanted to stop thinking. Both of them, he thought, were sad creatures running from their different realities and looking for exits from failure.

Danny had come to Indian Creek out of weariness, shame, fear, and a desire to jump off the edge of the planet. Henry, on the other hand, was seeking insight and truth. Danny wanted deliverance or death, whichever came first. Death would be fine if it wasn't lingering and excruciating.

11

IMMEDIATELY AFTER BEGINNING HIS EXISTENCE AT INDIAN CREEK, DANNY STARTED CIRCLING FARTHER FROM THE CABIN, OFTEN RANDOMLY WITH NO BIG PLAN. Midmornings after coffee and some oatmeal or eggs if he hadn't run out, he set off and walked up or down his side of the Little Green. Soon enough, he waded across, walked the other side, and clambered up the bank. He followed side creeks, scrambled up hills, and explored animal trails and water-carved gulches up to the ridge where the forest thickened.

Afternoons he would come back, chop wood, fire up lanterns and, when the afternoon cooled, fuel the stove, and keep a small, low fire running. Some days he would fish and catch trout. One day, he took his .22 and went hunting. He shot a couple of fat grouse even though he was not really looking for them. Basically, they were chicken dinners.

At night he read some of the books he had brought and, later, new ones he picked up at the book exchange in the Anthony C. Holbrooke Community Center when he drove into Duck Springs. Mostly he gravitated back to a few old ones he rescued from Seattle and Kirsten's clutches.

Some spoke to him about his earlier life: *The Old Man and the Sea* and Hemingway's macho-man hunting and bullfighting stories. Nature books by Peter Matthiessen, Barry Lopez, and Annie Dillard. And yet, he kept wandering back into Camus's *Carnets*, which felt like footprints on some long, slow-winding path of philosophical self-discovery.

Since he kept his own, he had also come to like reading other people's journals. They revealed the grist out of which more sophisticated writings evolved. Søren Kierkegaard, the first existentialist, had a diary. The comparative mythology teacher, Joseph Campbell, kept intellectual logs of his Asian forays. Dag Hammarskjöld, the UN Secretary-General whose plane was likely shot down on a mediation mission in Africa, maintained journals that revealed the deep Catholicism that infused his politics.

Danny had books by others too. Some essays and poems had magic in them, words that sparkled and jumped off the page and had spaces between certain words that amplified the author's intentions and captured some truth about the world. Some writings sang to him.

He also had practical stuff. Gazetteers for Washington, Oregon, and California, and a portfolio of detailed topographic maps of the Eastern Cascades. Books on Northwest Indian tribes, a fresh interpretation of Sun Tzu called *The Way* that applied the old warlord's tactics to negotiation and conflict resolution, and *Simms's Weapons*, a catalog of small arms, which had all anyone ever wanted to know about interchangeable ammunitions.

Most nights he read or wrote by lantern until he got sleepy or let the stove go cold. But sleep wasn't always a place to hide. Night often bred garbled dreams full of odd symbols and ancient fears. Snippets of disturbing memories rose up. The ghosts of dead platoon mates. The fat court reporter at his disbarment hearing. Glimpses of that amazing Clover at the café, the smell of hot apple pie, roasting grouse, the sound of wind blowing outside the cabin, and the strange water dippers called ouzels that he watched from a comfortable boulder as they hunted their food at the bottom of the stream.

What he hated most were the dreams from Kashmir. Too many phantoms, too much hate. After he returned from Kashmir, he met other vets who couldn't shake their horrors. Before he killed himself, one of them told Danny there was nothing in the world as tangible and visceral as war. You were down to basics and, in some odd way, at your most alive.

In the midst of ferocious cruelty, even when everyone was frenzied and filled with bloodlust, there was duty. You did your job, took care of your brothers in arms, remained as attached as you could to your beliefs, and tried hard to stay alive.

Pieces of one dream were especially garish.

Danny's squad, part of a larger platoon based outside Srinagar, was camped uphill from the river in the long valley known as the Vale of Kashmir. It was a recon mission. Observe, stay hidden, don't engage unless fired upon. They were concealed behind boulders close to the seven-thousand-foot level, the Pir Panjal Range to the left, the Himalayas upslope. Nine of them also knew they were being hunted by the Pakistanis.

A large patrol had spotted them earlier and was searching for them. They could see the Paks below but, so far, there had been no gunfire. Suddenly, an attack chopper, a retrofitted Cobra, came in low over the bluff above them. They heard it just as it cleared the mountain, guns chattering.

Three of his team were killed; two more were wounded. One died an hour later, bleeding out from the mutilations of the chopper's canons. In his dreams, their faces stayed with Danny. He could still see Buster, Ray, Kirk, and the others.

Churchill knew that combat was a defining moment in the lives of people who had been there. But that was for the living. The dead didn't care.

12

ONE DAY AFTER COFFEE, JAWBONING WITH POPS, AND RECIPROCAL FLIRTATIONS WITH CLOVER AT THE CAFÉ, DANNY HEADED OUT OF TOWN, PARKED HIS GHIA AT GREEN LAKE, AND TOOK OFF ON A SIDE TRAIL. Walking through thick stands of lodgepole pines and Douglas firs, a few deer looked up from their browse, then bolted. Two miles in he came to a tree branch hanging over the trail with a large capped, empty jar suspended on it. It originally held Extra Fancy Spanish Queen Olives.

He saw a handwritten note inside, untied the bottle, sat down on a log, opened the jar, and read the paper:

> Here is a gift. When your memories are working too hard, you lose your focus. How can your vision be anything but fuzzy? Stop your jitterbugging and nostalgias and the rising and falling tides inside you, and all will be unblemished. There is a perfectly incandescent center if you can find it. Look for it in the mirror.

> Your Most Humble Servants,
> Shane, Masaji, Alyssaranda, and the Parliament of Owls

He thought, *What the fuck is this?* No ocean within a long, slow day of driving but a message in an olive jar as if it had washed up on a beach? *How strange*, he thought.

Danny read it a few times, copied it into his notepad, put it back in the jar, and retied it on the branch. Then he headed farther up the trail, gaining elevation. A mile and a half later, he found another jar tied to a branch, this one formerly in the service of Dora's Strawberry Preserves. Inside, another note:

> Here is another gift. The river doesn't go around listening to TV and podcasts, looking for heroes, imitating others, or hoping to see one of society's beautiful people. It is here alone, water moving contentedly, always in solitude, perfect in peace. You and I should be like water. Maybe we will.
>
> Your Most Humble Servants,
> Shane, Masaji, Alyssaranda, and the Parliament of Owls

Strange and quirky as they were, there was something charming about them. They seemed like horoscopes or fortune cookies, small bits of wisdom that were completely out of place in the woods and didn't make much sense being in jars.

He copied the second one also, added it to his random notes about weather, directions, groceries, and repairs, and then headed back to the car at Green Lake.

The Karmann Ghia was where he left it under a large pine tree but was covered in crow shit. He thought, *Same as horses . . . crows conspire against people like me.*

Back at the cabin, he ate dinner and worked through a few more chapters of Peter Matthiessen's *Far Tortuga,* a story written in a remarkable Caribbean pidgin.

That night, the Kashmiri channel in his head was off. He dreamed of singing turtles living in jars hanging from ropes on coconut trees on sandy beaches.

13

A LARGE, STURDY-LOOKING BLUE JAY STARTED TAPPING ON HIS WINDOW. It came around most mornings and some afternoons. Danny took to leaving table scraps on the sill. He pecked at stuff, ate some, but didn't like cooked vegetables.

Before The Troubles, Kirsten, who wasn't very good with food, sometimes made mushy greens that he would slip under the table for Dog. Dog wasn't the sharpest canine he had ever known, but like all mutts, attentive to food.

The words from his last conversation with Kirsten were still in his head.

"I'm glad you are leaving," she said.

"I am too."

"Good luck and good riddance."

"We weren't meant to be, Kirsten."

"Where are you going?"

"East."

"Is there anything here you still care about?"

The pieces of their life together had burned out.

"I'll miss the pickled herring and smoked salmon from that little store at Fishermen's Terminal."

"You're such an asshole, Danny."

There were no real goodbyes. She winced and turned away.

Danny looked up the blue jay in a book called *Cascade Wildlife* that Mike and Gracie had in their cabin. It was a Steller's jay. This one had a limp. Danny guessed he once had a broken leg that came from fending off a raccoon or fox. He called him Stumpy.

Late afternoons and evenings, he cooked simple meals or ate leftovers, heated water for a bucket shower, wrote in his notebook, and read until he fell asleep. Stumpy might come around once or twice a day. Danny would tap back at him on the window, which startled him at first before he got habituated and expectant. Smart bird, that jay.

14

ANOTHER NOTE WAS HANGING FROM A BRANCH IN AN ORANGE JUICE BOTTLE HALF A MILE DOWNSTREAM FROM THE CABIN. This one said:

> People ask the way to Superstition Pass. There is no road that goes there. Even in summer the ice won't melt. When the sun comes out or the fog is blinding, how can you hope to get there by imitating me? Your heart and mine are not alike. If they were, we would see each other perfectly.
>
> Your Most Humble Servants,
> Shane, Masaji, Alyssaranda, and the Parliament of Owls

Danny had thought the previous notes were random. Now he wondered if this Parliament of Owls was stalking him with their little notes of celestial baloney. He loaded the two rifles and parked the Sig Sauer next to his bed.

15

AT SLIM'S, DANNY PAID USURIOUS PRICES FOR GAS, CEREAL, AND MILK. Slim McGee, owner, clerk, and grocery bagger, was a bony, angular man who looked like he might weigh a hundred pounds soaking wet. He had a hatchet-shaped head, a crooked nose, sallow skin, and beady eyes, but warmly introduced himself.

"You're that feller lives up by Indian Creek," he said. They shook hands, and when Danny winced at the bill, he said, "I know, I know, everyone does that. Truth is, every grocery runs on thin margins. Transportation to little joints like mine costs more. Usually, grocers make their money on volume. This place barely breaks even. Want to buy it?" he said with a grin.

Danny asked, "What's your best-selling item?"

"Besides powdered donuts? Salt."

Danny told him no thanks but appreciated the offer. Then Slim said, "You hear about Topeka and Cheyenne?"

"I haven't heard anything. What's up?"

"Lot of people killed, but no one quite knows what's going on. That fat senator from Oklahoma said it was justified, that a reckoning was coming for America."

Danny nodded. "Thanks for the heads-up, Slim. I'll let you know if I change my mind about buying your store."

Then he stopped at the café and settled onto a stool at the counter. The day's special was meat loaf, mashed potatoes, and lima beans. Meat loaf sounded good but he wished Dog was available for the beans. Mostly he hoped to rest his eyes on Clover, who was the single most splendid-looking woman he had ever met.

Pops emerged from the kitchen, poured two coffees, and came over to talk. He repeated Slim's news and told Danny about explosions in Kansas, Michigan, and Wyoming's capitals. Then he added: "There have been church bombings in Michigan, Pennsylvania, and Wisconsin. A Black Baptist congregation, a Jewish temple. Unitarian-Universalists, some United Church of Christ people."

Pops shook his head, but later, when Danny asked him about the town, he went into a long narrative that he clearly loved reciting, having inflicted it on hundreds of people over the years. Danny enjoyed it.

The café was a tightly constructed log building with rough timber uprights and a knotty pine interior. It was clean and well lit. Pops had a kind face and wore a nice smile that comported with being a patient and good-natured restaurateur and fine storyteller.

Turned out, Duck Springs was founded in 1881 by a man named William Pfeiffer, who was prospecting nearby creeks and streams. He camped out for a few days and took a shine to what was basically a grassy alluvial clearing on the Big Green. Supposedly, Pfeiffer saw a couple of mallards drop down on the little spring at the base of the escarpment.

The ducks left, Pfeiffer stayed, built a cabin, and when others came, he started a general store. The West was growing and an assortment of gold seekers, entrepreneurs, and riffraff wandered through. Lumberjacks, cowboys, and peddlers came by. So did immigrants from Sweden, Ireland, China, and Poland. Freighters, whiskey salesmen, and preachers. Klickitat and Walla Walla Indians all found their way there. Drifters, grifters, fugitives, con men, and a few honest opportunists came by looking to start or restart lives.

Some stayed, most didn't.

For a short while, Duck Springs was part of a stage route. Land speculators from Seattle thought it might grow into a sizable city and be an east–west transport hub over the Cascades. Pfeiffer himself was the self-appointed mayor and a powerful entrepreneur. He owned the store, a saloon, a laundry that employed three Chinese families, and a whorehouse.

He also staged an election, had his friend Frankie Sniffen elected sheriff and himself appointed justice of the peace. In that capacity, he reputedly tried to fine a man who got drunk and was threatening some local ladies. In the ensuing cloud of threats, Pfeiffer shot the man off his horse.

Pfeiffer married a buxom young woman who bore him three daughters and two sons. After his passing, the Pfeiffer clan grew but many moved away. Not, however, before sowing seeds that would sprout into a small but complicated genealogy of uncles, aunts, and cousins.

During WWII, a few Japanese couples from Seattle showed up. Most of their people had been shipped to the camps at Manzanar and Tule Lake. Later, a few hippies and retirees trickled in, and eventually summer tourists, campers, and second-home buyers.

Pops stopped his narration for a minute, sipped his cold coffee, and crested his rising tide of history to tell Danny about some of the locals.

Danny could hardly keep the names straight, but Pops rolled them off like a sportscaster. There was a county cop named Bucky Fontaine; a Catholic priest named Diego Owens; and Roy Voss, a Congregational minister. There was a big stocky guy named

Horace Gruber—once a high school football hero—who now drove D9 Cats and haul trucks at the quarry.

More coffee. Pops continued.

"There's Moses Ersbeck who owns the bakery. He leaves a screened nightstand full of bread on his porch after hours or when he's taking a nap. Asks people to take what they want and put what's fair in a little box." He also mentioned Slim McGee who had tried to sell Danny his grocery store.

"There's Ian Jeffers, the forest ranger. Straight shooter. I think you'd like him. Some kind of ex-military. Then there's Ted Cingcade who is boss at the American Cement Company. There are my good friends Kenny and Yoko Miyamoto who have a big orchard and berry patch and make jams and jellies that they sell to visitors. We feature them here. Damned tasty!"

He mentioned Bob Williams, an engineer and soil scientist who traveled the Northwest doing technical consulting work but holed up in Duck Springs. And Vernon Craft, a retired Air Force mechanic who had a little business called VGAA that stood for Vern's Guns, Ammo, and Archery, and which he ran out of the front of his house. Bob and Vern co-owned an old two-seat Cessna 152, which they parked on a grassy field with a windsock near Ogden Road. Sometimes the plane ran, sometimes it didn't.

"Any famous people ever visit here?" Danny asked him.

"Matter of fact, yes. Some years back, a movie star, I think it was Brad Pitt, came by with a couple of nice-looking young ladies. Pitt looked older and had gotten flabby, but he was all eyes for Clover and kept sneaking looks at her legs. He and his people wolfed down pancakes, bacon, and eggs, and left. Our own native son here is Marcus Longborn. Name ring a bell?"

"He's the vice president, at least he was when I was leaving Seattle. I hear there have been assassinations."

"I'm hoping he is OK. Longborn brought President Chavez by here a few years ago when they were campaigning. Marcus wanted her to see where he was from and harvest votes." Pops pointed toward the front door and said, "There's a picture of the two of them right over there."

"How did he get to be VP?"

"He was trained as a lawyer, but I don't think he did anything except a few wills and land transfers. Got appointed representative to the State House when Stinky's dad passed away, then got elected to the United States Senate and eventually became a wheel in the Democratic Party."

Pops leaned in and whispered, "Between you and me, I always thought Longborn was a moron. When we were growing up, nobody called him Marcus. His nickname was Mucus, Mucus Dickbrain."

Thelma, his handsome wife in her late sixties, called Pops back to the kitchen, Clover came over. She served Danny more hot coffee and a jumbo piece of pie with a massive scoop of homemade vanilla ice cream. Only one other customer was at a corner table, so Clover came around the counter and sat on the stool next to him.

Clover was about five feet, five inches. She had beautiful blonde hair, sort of a wheat color with soft streaks of darker yellow and red. Danny didn't know what color to call it. He'd never been good with colors. Or hair. Or, for that matter, women.

Added to that, she had a perfectly clear complexion, soft hazel eyes that changed colors depending on the light, and long eyelashes set in a slight slant, as if she may have had a Native American or Asian ancestor tucked into some corner of her gene pool. She carried wide shoulders like a swimmer with muscular arms, shapely legs, and a perfectly beautiful ass.

He took a bite of her pie and went into a rapture. "My God, that is amazing. I'm not big on sweets but this is something else. What is in it?"

"Good! You didn't die. It's a peanut butter pie, an experiment that Thelma and I have been fiddling with. You're a guinea pig. Beyond a graham cracker crust, it's got plenty of peanut butter, cream cheese, dark chocolate, powdered sugar, butter, sea salt, sour cream, and a few chili-powder flakes just to cut into the sweetness."

"It's amazing but I can't eat all this. Grab a fork and help me."

Which she did.

A truly amazing woman. But mainly it was the warmth and smile that animated her face. Danny reckoned her to be under forty, but it was hard to tell.

She asked him what he was doing and he explained. Gracie and Michael's cabin at Indian Creek, brother Josh in Seattle, hiking, retreating, reading books, wanting to get lost for a while.

"You look sad," she said, "like you're running away from something."

"From everything."

"That's too bad, but you've come to the right place. Duck Springs is near the end of the road that disappears into the back of beyond. All we get here are tourists in the summer. Winter, fall, or spring, it's an occasional cross-country skier and us locals. Not much else."

She talked, he listened, they flirted. Her eyes flashed with intelligence and humor and her voice—sweet, soft, resonant—was hypnotic.

Then Danny asked her, "What's a Parliament of Owls? I keep finding odd notes in jars and bottles hanging on trees."

"They're harmless. They come in once in a while for meals. Nice enough. I think they are waiting for all the planets to align. They leave notes here too. I don't know why but I save them. I kind of like them."

She headed over to a shelf behind the cash register, pulled some out, and showed him one that said:

> You are the ocean. In a clear sky, moonlight reflects off you as if you were snow. Maybe you

> think you are a realm without a trace of the holy or anything special. At the opening of your diamond eye, the flowers of vanity will fall away. The universe will vanish into the realm of extinction. But it doesn't matter. Love endures.

"What does all that stuff mean?" he asked her.

"I don't really understand it," she told him, "but I like the words and images. We have other strange groups around here too. A bunch of survivalists by name of the New American Defense Force run by a skinny little twerp named Herman Matthews who calls himself Commander and is preparing for a revolution which, according to the TV and radio, may be coming soon. They all come in for meals now and then."

Her eyes were soft, deep, inviting. No makeup. Country girl manners over a keen sense of humor and a sharp intelligence.

"You have a lot of crazies up here," he said. "I should fit right in."

"You will," she responded with a sly smile.

When Danny came in a few weeks later, he told her he needed to make a trip to Crockett City to find a dentist, get a haircut, and buy some stuff a little cheaper than Slim's. He asked if she might want to go.

"Yep, but I can give you a haircut right here if you want," she said with a sly smile. "Comes with a shoulder massage." He grinned and stared into her face, alive with some sweet nature he didn't much remember among the people he had been interacting with in the military and the courts.

He said, "If the Chinese communists, Mexican cartels, or Middle East terrorists ever capture me, they won't need to bring out the water board. Give me a back rub, I'll tell them everything."

She laughed and said, "Good to know. I may try that on you sometime!"

16

SOME NIGHTS, HIS BRAIN WAS FULL OF DREAMS THAT TANGLED EVENTS INTO A MIDNIGHT STIR FRY.

Boot camp and long runs with full packs. A fever and chest cold. Josh and Danny climbing the big tree in their front yard and peeing down on a kid they hated. Armed militants in Srinagar and a Kashmiri translator who kept trying to tell him something he couldn't understand. Bodies with cut throats hanging from utility poles. Then back in law school with Professor Myron Shapiro asking some Socratic question he couldn't answer.

Shapiro taught evidence and trial practice when Danny studied law at Willamette University, and had him for contracts and negotiable instruments. He was a brilliant legal thinker but fond of dropping odd stories and quotes into his lectures in the forlorn hope that something might inspire students to higher ground. With his bow tie and starched white shirts, he would quote famous litigators who had won big suits and made case law, and renowned judges who had issued clever rulings citing what is vaguely referred to as "Natural Justice."

Danny never understood what Natural Justice was. The world he knew was more like a swamp full of water snakes and alligators than a farm with orderly rows of cabbages. Shapiro's students never quite knew what might pop out of his head. He would quote some biblical, Hindu, or Koranic parable, or read a poem by Langston Hughes to the effect that justice is a blind goddess who Black people are especially wary of. Hughes thought the bandage around her eyes hid empty sockets.

Personally, Goodman was less interested in missing eyeballs and far more focused on battle plans. He loved the courthouse and the litigation process: the assessment, reconnaissance, preparation, trickery and maneuvering. He got a visceral charge out of the decision-making that went into every lawsuit of any complexity and he liked achievement and loved making money. It was a game and winning was everything.

In the Malcolm Crowley Smith firm, behind Sam Johnson and other senior partners, he second chaired a few cases, then took on his own. It was thrilling—much better than the real combat at which he had been reasonably competent. He was on a fast track to becoming a partner specializing in high-stakes corporate litigation.

Thanks to Johnson, his slave driver, and MCS's wealthy client list, Danny excelled at business law as it was practiced in Washington, Oregon, and California. He became ever more proficient at researching opposing counsel and their clients and adept at calculating the risks of trial. And even when he knew he didn't have much of a case, he could still position clients for reasonable negotiated settlements.

Ambrose Bierce called a litigant "A person about to give up his skin for the hope of retaining his bones." And there was the much-traveled story about some guy in a small Midwest town who had a sign out front that said, HOMER SMITH, VETERINARIAN AND TAXIDERMIST and underneath in smaller letters, EITHER WAY YOU GET YOUR DOG BACK.

Litigation was exactly that. Danny lived for winning verdicts or bargaining clever settlements that favored his side. Where the

Marines had taught him how to fight with guns, Johnson taught him to battle with filings and appearances. Law was war without blood.

The firm also sent him to training courses at elite schools: advanced trial practice at Stanford. Foundation building and evidence presentation at the University of Chicago. Opening and closing arguments at Georgetown. And several especially useful negotiation courses at Harvard and Pepperdine.

If litigation became his religion, closing arguments and opening windows for productive negotiation was his catechism. Very few lawsuits actually go to trial and most armed conflicts eventually come to a close through negotiation, but only after both sides have inflicted noticeable wounds on each other.

In the Harvard and Pepperdine courses he took on negotiation, he got a solid education on the tactical planning of concession patterns; the politics of anchoring, bluffing, and deadlines; brinksmanship and last-minute standoffs; and the use of reputable third parties to avoid the instinctive tendency to devalue offers or demands from the other side.

But not everything was in harmony. What accompanied Danny during his pole-vaulting legal career was addiction. He wasn't especially interested in a cure even though he knew he was seriously hooked. It was all rationalization and delusion. Everyone had some sort of addiction he told himself, and smart people always found ways to function.

When Churchill was prime minister, there was never a time when he didn't have alcohol in his bloodstream. Ulysses S. Grant won the civil war while he was pretty well hammered. While he was in the White House, John F. Kennedy lived on a diet of anti-anxiety agents, sleeping pills, and pain killers. And Vincent van Gogh did his best painting while he was high as a kite on absinthe.

Danny Goodman's compulsion wasn't booze or needles. It was gambling. Games of chance and sparring with fate. He loved the thrill of the bet, the exhilaration of winning, and the ease of rationalizing losses. He remembered someone saying there was nothing like winning at poker to restore your faith in the greater goodness of the universe.

He loved fighting the odds that came with betting and loved taking risks. He studied and played poker, Keno, Roulette, the probabilities in horse races, dog races, rotisserie and fantasy football, local and national elections, and even once betting on roosters with some Filipino chicken fighters who were laying down big money in a Sacramento vacant lot.

Blackjack, Texas Hold 'Em, and Pai Gow were especially kind to him. He once turned $6,000 into $55,000 in a seven-hour binge at a casino owned by the Apaches. When he was in the groove, it never felt electric. It was more like a low-octave thrumming, some kind of fugue state. Hitting his mojo in cards and numbers, he was scoring goal after goal and touchdown after touchdown. In those moments, he was in the sweetest of sweet spots where nothing ever goes wrong.

When he lost it all in downturns, he might borrow a fresh $5,000, and promptly lose that, and then borrow ten thousand more. But even the downturns didn't dampen his appetite for the tables. Casinos became his natural habitat. A good run might mean days of coffee, junk food, comfort from local hookers, and endless evening nightcaps. Bad runs were the same.

None of this affected his work. In fact, gaming seemed to sharpen it. But only for a while. Robert Louis Stevenson said it this way: "Sooner or later, everyone sits down to a banquet of consequences." Danny's banquet table got longer and deeper. He piled up debts, then borrowed big money from a large client trust account, sure he would pay it back with his next set of winnings which, even if he did, was still a legal no-no. Fifty thousand no-nos, to be exact.

The money came from an especially nasty divorce case between John and Lilly Frizell, a rich husband and wife who had started a successful company trading exclusive properties in different high-end real estate markets around the world. They had grown their customer base in New York, Hong Kong, London, and the Emirates into a fabulous business with snazzy clientele and were now extremely wealthy. Danny's kind of clients.

The case had been referred to Judge Arakawa's civil calendar from divorce court and it was stacking up to be the Battle of Gettysburg. There were little-whispered and supposedly humorous sayings around the courthouse that explained what was really going on. One divorce attorney said, "They will fight over the house, then they sell it to pay our fees after all the carnage is sorted out."

But Danny's favorite came from Johnson, his mentor. Sam was a true shapeshifter. In trial he could be a sweet and courtly gentleman, then abruptly turn into a bare-knuckled brawler. At the firm, and as a senior partner, he might be regal and gently advisory to younger lawyers, then turn brutally blunt.

"Remember Danny," he once said, "justice delayed is profit! Always follow the money. No matter what they say or how much they whine and plead, no matter what web of big principles they spin, it's always about the money."

Danny liked that. He liked money and he liked people who had plenty of it. And he would earn it whether the Frizells went to trial or not. With his marriage souring, Danny's purpose in life was now winning money. Representing Lilly, he followed all the Frizell financial trails which produced lots of billable hours. He also knew it would eventually come down to how many zeros were in a settlement package.

Meanwhile, Danny borrowed $50,000 from Lilly's client trust account to settle with certain heavies who were harassing him for owed money. His losing streak had amplified and he was into everyone with interest on loans piling up fast.

The thing about betting is this. Bets are always monetized guesses, but you never have all the data you need and you're vulnerable to unconscious biases and sap-headed thinking. Everyone rationalizes "I'm on a roll" or "It's not my day." Even the pros, people who make millions, know the best of them will lose 40 percent of the time over eight hours of play.

Danny was increasingly vulnerable. He knew the loan sharks who swam in casino waters would eventually be sent out to break his bones. Goodman was completely overdrawn and couldn't pay back the $50,000 to Lilly's trust account, which actually held a retainer of $100,000. He had harbored every loser's fatal fantasy: *use that, then repay it with winnings from the next trip to Reno.*

Then came the last scene in the final act of Daniel Goodman Esq.'s case of "The Troubles" and his denouement.

Man plans (and plans and plans), and God just laughs . . .

First came admonishment and public shaming. Then the loss of his law license. Next, Sam Johnson gave him the big lecture of parental disappointment and fired him from Malcolm Crowley Smith. He didn't mince words.

"Danny, you screwed the pooch. You're out. Now. Go pack your stuff and turn in your keys."

He understood. He would have done the same thing.

Then, it was over to another judge who ordered restitution to Lilly and added some extra penalties to warn other lawyers. After that came the divorce from Kirsten who had been looking for a reason anyway. He hired his friend Lenny Jones who did him a favor and just charged out-of-pockets, but Kirsten got the house and the bank accounts. It was a relief for them both to be done. Then, personal bankruptcy.

Danny went through all of Kübler-Ross's grief stages, spiced up with constant self-pity. Denial. Anger. Bargaining. Depression. Acceptance. Most of all, he had to confront the full terror of losing everything in midlife just as he was starting to succeed. He desperately sought some mouse hole he could chew his way into and escape but finally, he accepted it.

In *Carnets,* Camus said we are all, every one of us, some version of the myth of Sisyphus pushing our personal boulders uphill and losing the daily battle with gravity. The only antidote, he concluded, was to be brave, do your job, stop whining, and wear a happier face. Danny knew the story but still didn't quite know what his best face might be.

He had some rainy-day money squirreled away that Kirsten, the courts, and the loan sharks couldn't get to. That's when he lit out for Indian Creek, his new foxhole in the middle of nowhere.

17

ANNOUNCED MONTHS AHEAD, THE PATRIOTS RISING RALLY WAS BILLED AS A GRAND, TWO-DAY EVENT GUARANTEED TO MOVE THE NEEDLE FOR AMERICA'S BIG REFORMATION. Registration instructions went out by newspaper, radio, and on underground channels spoking out from Pharaoh. When rally day arrived, 40,000 people came to Busch Stadium in St. Louis.

Nearly packed, a surprising number of seats were occupied by women, some older with blue hair, many more of them younger holding babies or towing kids. Men mostly wore farm overalls. Thousands were dressed in hunting versions of camo with sidearms in holsters. A few wore sport coats.

The rally was spectacular, an amplified cultural and political counterpoint to the hippies who gathered in the mud at Woodstock back in 1969. The event was headlined by famous speakers, singers, and film stars working from a giant platform in center field. Offstage, there were cheerleaders, rodeo girls on fast horses, and a huge jumbotron high up that flashed messages, announcements, and close-ups of speakers and entertainers.

A giant yellow Gadsden flag flew over the stadium. Under the words "Patriots Rising" was the famous "Don't Tread on Me" coiled rattlesnake.

At the top of the steps in the outer corridors were hundreds of booths manned by food sellers, gun dealers, and militia recruiters. The Louisiana Lions and the Ancient Order of Christian Knights had tables and one booth of anti-vaxxers displayed a banner about vaccines that simply said LIARS! Another sold hundreds of books and pamphlets on rally themes: the right to bear arms, abortion, the sins of Mexicans, Asian, and Muslim hordes taking over, and the "Big Lies" of Socialists and Democrats.

The Hammond brothers and a few other billionaires called "The Freedom Club" looked on from tinted glass luxury suites. On the stage, singer Calvin Thomas was joined by the ever-popular Debbie Calhoun. They sang "If We're Gonna Do It, Let's Do It All Over Them." They were followed by the Ten-Girl High School Band from Tulsa Oklahoma, a warm-up group for Remus Willard.

Willard's prerecorded speech on the jumbotron was greeted by thunderous applause and a standing ovation.

"My fellow countrymen," he drawled, "you wonderful patriots, today is not entertainment. It is the beginning of a new day and our call to action. Our United States of America is neck deep in jeopardy from people who despise us and control the corridors of power. We are going to change that." Willard went on for forty minutes and ended with a raised fist and "Jesus is with us!"

When he finished, movie actor Jimmy Sixkiller, fresh from Hollywood where he was working on a western called *The Scalpers*, sang Kate Smith's old "God Bless America" and was joined by Calvin Thomas, Debbie Calhoun, and the Ten-Girl High School Band, all dressed in red, white, and blue. Forty thousand people stood, sang, and cheered.

At a luxury booth away from the others, one man looked through binoculars. Now and then he added reminders on a small pad. Eugene Brody watched and listened, preoccupied with battle plans.

18

MORE LITTLE PAPERS IN BOTTLES SHOWED UP ON THE TRAILS. One day, he found a Claussen pickle jar with a note inside on the second step of his front porch.

> You find a flower half-buried in leaves, and in your eye, fate resides there. It is a loving beauty. You caress the bloom and soon enough, you sweep petals from the floor. It is terrible to love the lovely, to count your years, to find a flower half-buried in leaves, and come at last face-to-face with what you really are: nobody. Rejoice!
>
> Your humble servants,
> Shane, Masaji, Alyssaranda, and the Parliament of Owls

He saved the note and replaced it with his own. "Gracias, whoever you are."

A few days later, it was gone.

19

CLOVER BEGGED OFF THE TRIP TO CROCKETT AT THE LAST MINUTE BECAUSE SHE NEEDED TO ATTEND AN AUNT'S FUNERAL IN BERWICK. That vaporized Danny's fantasy of spending a few days and nights exploring mutual social, physical, and intellectual attractions with the most beautiful and interesting woman he had ever met. Still, off he went to the "big city." He fired up the Karmann Ghia and drove east.

A few static-filled radio reports on the AM told of spreading violence across the country: killings in North Carolina, bombings in Texas, and the fall of county governments in California. Then reception died.

Just outside Crockett City he stopped at a Chinese restaurant called Happy Valley Snow Garden where he was thinking about having some noodles and tea. He sat down. Suddenly, a young woman came out from behind the register to run him off.

"We no serve you," she barked. When he asked why not, she said, "You a dirty man."

He headed into the men's room and looked in the mirror. Even though his eyes could use reading glasses, they were still hazel peepers sitting atop a reasonably fit body. His external parts were intact, including the old broken nose which slightly canted to the left from a high school fist fight he lost.

Looking closer though, he understood.

His hair was long and greasy. Spiny, unkempt whiskers with an increasing number of grays poked out of a grimy face. His blue jeans were frayed at the bottom and had holes in the knees. His old tennis shoes were caked with mud and his shirt was half out of his pants. He was wearing a beat-up Vietnam-era army jacket he bought in a secondhand store in Tacoma, and he had the general look of a drunk who had just crawled out of a culvert.

An older Chinese man, probably her father, came in and said, "Get out." Danny started to explain, but he cut him off and barked. "Get out."

Danny lost his temper. "Fuck you. All I wanted was some hot tea."

He got to Crockett City in the afternoon, found a motel, paid cash in advance, showered, and shaved. His cultivated system of making to-do lists and writing notes that he would later rewrite into his journal sometimes failed him, like when he scribbled items on random scraps of paper, stuffed them into a pocket, then lost those treasures in the washing machine. This time, he had a list.

First and foremost, he needed to get a filling replaced, find a barber, and call his brother. He also needed razor blades, warmer clothes, coffee, condensed milk, nuts or sunflower seeds for Stumpy, mouse traps for Mickey and Minnie, and a pile of canned items. He wanted soups, beans, stewed tomatoes, sardines, canned meat, ramen, spaghetti sauces, and other things he could buy cheaper here than at Slim's.

Danny asked the clerk at the front desk to find him a dentist he could see the next day. Then, he headed out on his shopping expedition, and that is when he got sidetracked, committing an unforced error on what should have been a fast, easy trip in and out of Crockett. The blunder took him off his path of righteous renunciation and self-flagellation. Extracting himself from the world had been his major agenda. Now he was seduced back to the dark side in a single instant.

He entered a pleasant-looking Crockett City coffee shop called The Ars. It was aromatic with roasting coffee beans and a display case full of crusty scones and buttery croissants. Even though he had scrubbed up, a girl named Julie asked what he wanted and gave him the same suspicious look he had gotten at Happy Valley Snow Garden.

Julie was clad in all black, a purple-and-orange chicken-feather Mohawk haircut, a bunch of painful-looking metal studs in her ears, nose, cheeks, and tongue, and she had tats on her right arm.

"What are you having?" she asked.

He ordered a jumbo cappuccino and a cinnamon roll. While he was waiting, he asked Julie, "How come you wear all black?"

She cracked a small smile and said, "Why would anyone wear anything else? And how come you're so dressed up yourself?"

Girl with an attitude. He admired that, even though she looked a little freaky.

He found an old wall phone and called Josh in Seattle while goth girl brewed his coffee. As he was talking with Josh, he noticed newspapers and magazines on a stand. He finished his call and started shuffling through them. Julie brought his coffee and roll. He scooped up sections of the latest *New York Times* and settled at a corner table to read and get caffeinated. His bad tooth throbbed when the hot coffee hit it.

Very quickly, he realized the papers and magazines were an airplane crash on his glidepath to peaceful oblivion. Retrospectively, it was also the precise turning point when he couldn't put his personal genie back in the bottle.

In the weeks he had been gone, the world was far worse than when Lincoln's head was rolling on the floor of the monument. In addition to the political turmoil, which he had caught snippets of, the economy was shredding. Twenty-two percent of the country was either unemployed or woefully underemployed. Militias, paramilitary units, survivalists, and white patriot groups were popping out of the woods and infiltrating cities and towns everywhere.

A *New York Times* piece said the groups sparking the new American civil disturbances were a gumbo of extreme right-wingers that normally quarreled with each other but had enough in common to coagulate. All of them were anti-government and conspiratorial, and hated people who weren't white and Christian. They wanted to turn the clock back to 1860. And all of them were rallied behind Senator Willard.

Danny drank his coffee slowly, ate the pastry, and devoured the news and commentaries the way thirsty people suddenly find water. Then he fingered through other papers and magazines and scanned pieces from *Forbes*, *The International Economist*, and *The New Yorker*. He ordered a second coffee.

He was hungrier than he knew for news, political speculation, and social gossip. Thinking he had relinquished all that when he left Seattle, he really hadn't. He was now in the deep end of the pool. Once an addict, always an addict, even if you are on the wagon.

He felt old compulsions and when he synthesized the particulars, it was this: the country was seriously fucked up and falling apart. The United States had become a combustible front of violent storms and squall lines congealing into a massive cyclone spawning political floods and economic tornadoes as it made landfall.

After three successive, deeply conservative presidencies, America had finally elected a moderate center-left Hispanic: Norma Chavez, a junior senator from Arizona. Like Barack Obama in the old days, Chavez was instantly saddled with a right-wing, do-nothing, poke-your-opponent-in-the-eye-whenever-you-can Congress. Chavez and her small band of progressives were paying the stiffest price for trying to bring reform.

One *Forbes* writer said, "The United States is in a death spiral, dismembering itself limb by limb on the way to a complete paralysis and, most tragically, destroying the rule of law which is our backbone."

Was all this really happening? Were things that bad, or was this just hyperbolic media bullshit?

Taking advantage of all the bedlam was Senator Remus Willard from Oklahoma. Danny had seen pictures of him, a jowly, overweight gasbag who hailed from a flea-bitten town outside of Tulsa. One commentator called him "the stupidest man alive." Feigned or real, his idiocy masked reptilian thinking.

Willard rose professionally in the ranks of DC's interlocking and superheated worlds of political elites. He had a powerful congressional majority in his hands, outspoken support from high-ranking military leaders, the support of corporate tycoons, and a growing following of poorly educated, populist knuckleheads who were convinced only Willard could save the country. These were the people he would eventually call on to overthrow the legitimate government.

The International Economist had a photo of Willard and General Brody in a two-page spread. Willard was in his mid-eighties, moving from paunch to obesity but with a still-strong voice. He was pasty-looking, wearing a rumpled brown suit and a sweat-stained white shirt. Another close-up showed rolls of double chins, thinning hair, and porky hands with a high school ring permanently embedded in a fat finger.

In public, Willard came across as a folksy, extroverted elder on a family outing—full of entertaining stories, jokes, and proverbs. He had a strong public persona but suspicions were that he might just be a front man for the brooding and reputedly smarter, General Brody. Brody was rumored to be the mastermind behind the internet snake pit of Pharaoh.

That made sense. As a ranking military man, he would have access to the most sophisticated cybersecurity experts in the world. Brody's image was slightly blurry. He had black hair and wore a tailored dark suit. His head was turned toward Willard, who was the center of attention. Brody seemed mysterious, obscure, as if he didn't want to be photographed.

Willard was the opposite. He bathed in the camera's attention. If he was slowing down, you wouldn't know it from public appearances where he puffed up and exuded interminable stem-winder orations, a mishmash extolling Christian white culture, eviscerating unions, stripping out regulations that were bad for business, giving massive low-interest loans to corporations; and scapegoating Jews, Blacks, gays, lesbians, Muslims, and Mexicans.

Willard was as slippery as a sea snake. He was doing everything possible to stir old hatreds, keep himself at the center of things, engage in pandering and sloganeering, but always avoiding responsibility. One article quoted him from a recent speech to the New John Birch Society: "We know for a fact that the wealthiest 10 percent of the United States population are the real breadwinners. They pay the bills. The rest are parasites, tax dodgers, and freeloaders. Time for us to get rid of all the vermin."

And, in an off-camera hot mic slip he was heard saying, "Money doesn't trickle downhill unless there is a goddamn hole in your pocket. We'll fix that too!"

In retrospect, Willard's movement appeared to have been built on time-honored forms of repression, plus some new ones. The older ones were suppression of minority votes, squelching public dissent, and the dystopian tactics of *1984* and *Animal Farm*. The new deceits were the older ones amplified and sharpened by sophisticated social media technologies.

What Danny gathered from his progressively deeper descent into the magazines and newspapers at The Ars was this: first, there was a trickle of media messages from people like Willard and the Hammonds. Those became a faster-moving stream of craftily mixed true and fake news. Next came gushing rivers full of trolls, hackers, gas lighters, and covert communication farms sending contagions out from Russia, China, and North Korea through subcontractors in Africa, Syria, and inside the United States.

Around the world companies big and small feverishly developed business models powered by artificial intelligence, biometrics, neural interfaces, and proprietary algorithms. They figured out how to connect everything at home to everything in corporate and government databases. Basically, the new tech companies learned how to grab your full attention and monetize it.

Finding worthy signals in all the white noise got harder. The new media was the incubator and purveyor for driverless vehicles, wearable technology, and surgically implanted body parts. Internet purchasing powered everything. It enabled the knowing of every possible thing about everyone, no matter how public or private. In real time, a few corporations were studying every person on the planet. That specific sequence was the midwife that birthed Pharaoh.

Over a few decades of using AI, a handful of global companies learned exactly how to capture preferences and hold them. Companies merged. Facebook was bought by China Pinnacle and Clockwork Five became the metaverse for all of them. Behind the new corporate giants, software experts and internet engineers learned how to manipulate media by sprinkling a few real facts into a story, then layering them with counterfeit news until no one could precisely tell what was real and what was malarky.

Big companies, including many owned by the Hammonds and their friends, created a new economy out of this. They acquired the science of precision forecasting, and they set in motion empirically robust techniques for modifying behaviors without anyone knowing they were being modified.

Danny understood the central through line. Devices got smarter, databases grew bigger, knowledge centers interlaced, communication became a hall of mirrors, and people got dumber. The more personal proclivities could be identified, the more people were bombarded with messages that cultivated their wants and fears. It was the perfect petri dish for breeding Willard, Brody, and the Hammonds.

This same confluence also enabled hundreds of domestic hate groups to connect into a network. According to the *New World Bulletin*, Pharaoh was the catalytic converter. It catered to anti-vaxxers, flat-earthers, survivalists, and unhappy military and intelligence officers.

Pharaoh stoked small embers into bigger fires. It created daily stories about the president and vice president, accusing Chavez and Longborn of stealing millions from taxpayers to organizing drug rings. The business model of Pharaoh was clever: pricey membership fees, carefully coded lists of members that were secretly shielded, and subscriptions and dues for a growing spiderweb of groups.

There were escalating repercussions. Small banks were crashing. Soup kitchens, homeless camps, and shantytowns were springing up and arming themselves. Pipe bombs were shoved into the mailboxes of certain leaders, and local public officials with liberal views were being kidnapped.

In his first season of retreat at Indian Creek, Danny had missed a lot of bombings, shootings, and assassinations. The governors of Illinois and Kansas had been killed. Armed confrontations with police had broken out at sprawling jobless demonstrations around big cities. Roads and bridges, which had been in decline for years anyway, were becoming impassable because state and federal road crews weren't being paid. Half of the active United States military was on furlough or partial pay.

Danny lingered for several hours at The Ars, drinking another cup of coffee as his sensitive tooth, kidneys, and bladder could attest. He took a break and relieved himself, then tapped his mug for another caffeine fill-up from Julie.

Even though the financial stuff he was reading was above his freshman economics, it was clear that the new populism and old neocons had chipped away at every cornerstone entitlement: Medicaid, Medicare, Social Security, food stamps. Stitch by stitch, piece by piece, the American safety net had frayed, and vast numbers of Americans had fallen through. Trust in the compact of laws and norms that connect the governed to government is a fragile thread and confidence had evaporated. It had become a Sicilian proverb that said, roughly translated, "Live in hope, die in the mud."

Danny left The Ars after three hours, when Julie suggested he move on.

20

THE NEXT DAY, DANNY WENT BACK TO THE ARS FOR AN HOUR, INDULGING IN MORE OF JULIE'S GOOD COFFEE AND A PIÑA COLADA SCONE WITH LEMON FROSTING. She was a wee bit friendlier, but just as cocky.

"You're back," she said.

"We meet again," he responded. "I missed you and your coffee."

"I'm still wearing all black."

"If I had the money," he said, "so would I."

He chewed his pastry and had a restorative second coffee.

"Who makes this stuff?" he asked, pointing at the remnants of the scone he had just scarfed down.

"Me, and once in a while Willy in the back. But he's a lazy bastard and doesn't come in all the time."

Danny inhaled a bagel, slurped coffee, avoided the newspapers and magazines, brushed his teeth in the restroom, and headed off for a haircut.

"Chop it off," he told Ralph the barber. Which Ralph did. He didn't have any other customers so Ralph buzzed the top and sides, then worked off stray bits with a scissors. When he was done, Danny's scalp showed through.

"Good enough?" asked Ralph.

Danny looked like his first days in boot camp but it was definitely a full-value haircut. It would last a while.

After that, he walked around town and slowly made his way to the dentist. The city seemed emptier than he expected and there were drones hovering over certain streets. A lot of military-looking people in black berets and camo pants were hanging out on street corners. One of them checked him out, but Danny walked on and arrived at the office of Dr. Eric Abbott. The sign on the door said: DENTISTRY, IMPLANTS, AND ORAL SURGERY.

They instantly hit it off.

Abbott was a tall, muscular Black man about Danny's age. He'd moved to Crockett City from Gary, Indiana several years earlier because he liked the outdoors and Crockett had clean air. He had a wife and young kids and a now diminishing practice because folks could no longer afford professional dentistry. He said some people were pulling out their own teeth.

"Call me Eric," he said.

Eric was a former football and hockey player with a tall frame and strong arms, but small hands that could work their way inside and around a person's mouth. He asked what was going on and Danny told him a filling fell out and the tooth was sensitive to heat and cold. Eric agreed to help him but said he needed to pay cash up front.

After numbing his mouth and doing some poking and drilling, Eric stopped for a minute, squinted, and dug around with a dental pick. Then he put in a temporary filling but said the tooth was rotten, and Danny would need a root canal and an implant.

Danny told him he would come back to Crockett when things started to hurt, which Eric said would be soon. Then Danny asked, "So what's going on here?"

Eric didn't hesitate. "Crockett is going to hell," he said. "In fact, I think the whole country is."

Danny loved the candor.

"What do you mean?"

"Look, I don't know what your politics are, but you seem like a decent guy. There's a group here called the New American Defense Force that has taken over the city council. They may be part of something bigger or just local gangbangers. I can't say for sure. But what I do know is they rigged our local election. A lot of them look like high school losers trying to be badasses, like the ghetto gangs back in Gary. The NADF gives them status. They dress up with hats and scarves, pack guns, and strut a lot. They think this guy Remus Willard is a genius. They got in a fight and killed several people near Hayes Park. They have their own 'Don't Tread on Me' flag."

"A friend of mine in Duck Springs mentioned them. She said some of them are living in the woods near where I'm staying."

"They're paramilitary and want a completely white America. You won't see any of my people with them. I heard they have little camps all over Washington, Oregon, and Idaho. Maybe other parts of the country too."

He stopped and had Danny rinse his mouth.

"Just watch out for them," he warned. "They're zombies. Brainless and nasty, but they seem organized."

Danny liked this man—sensible, practical, direct. Reminded him of Kenny Stokes, who hailed from Alabama and managed to survive their squad's disasters in Kashmir, losing only his right eye. Kenny was one of the few people in the platoon Danny got close to in Kashmir.

He and Abbott talked more and then Danny asked him what lay ahead for the country.

"Pardon my French," he said. "but I think we're fucked."

"That's just what I've been thinking after catching up on some news, which I never should have done."

They shook hands and Danny left to do his shopping. At Costless, most of the shelves were empty, but he stocked up on a few supplies. He headed into a nondescript clothing store and bought flannel-lined pants, then gassed up the Ghia. It was good to head back to the mountains.

He was also disappointed in himself. He had fallen off yet another wagon, succumbed to the tractor beam of current events, and accidentally opened himself up to the universe. Current events were just another compulsion, like poker or racetracks. When he opened the shutters of his seclusion, the netherworld whooshed in on a hot, oily wind.

Good thing I don't see a casino, he thought.

Once again, he figured his hidey-hole at Indian Creek was a good place to wait out what might be a massive maelstrom. People like Willard might be taking over the country, but he felt confident he could tuck himself away and sit out the bad weather that was building.

Sometimes when the sun was out, Danny would sit by the stream and watch water ouzels swim through a pool, dive down, and walk on the bottom. One of the oddest birds he had ever seen. About the size of a robin. Thick body and short tail. Ate little fish, bugs, and crustaceans. An appropriate metaphor: *I'm a human ouzel hiding underwater.*

21

TWO DAYS LATER, THE CROCKETT CITY TRIP AND HIS CONVERSATION WITH ABBOTT WERE STILL ON HIS MIND. That night he cooked a pot of spaghetti that would last awhile and tucked back into *Walden*. Thoreau and a giant tangle of noodles with garlic, onions, basil-flavored tomato sauce, and chopped cubes of Spam somehow went together. Simple fare that didn't really look like a good meal but had an acceptable taste.

In his theorizing, Einstein called separate objects sharing a completely similar condition "spooky." Spooky al dente.

Danny figured Thoreau might help inform the realities he was seeing. In his own time, America was also on the cusp of civil war. So he read Henry David slowly, dog-earing pages, underlining certain passages, mulling what he wrote, and exploring the inevitable comparison with his own world at Indian Creek.

Like Henry, Danny had gone off the grid to flee personal troubles. Monkish immersion in nature, refreshing as it might seem, didn't feel like a real cure to Danny's quandaries, but it had possibilities. It was a way to discover what was missing—or bring it all to some private close.

His plan was far less intentional than Thoreau's. Henry was running toward some source of transcending luminescence. Danny was just running away. He simply wanted to skedaddle and do simple day-to-day tasks until he found the right conclusion. In light of finding something better, if it existed, he had his pistol.

Danny had vaguely admired Henry from an undergraduate perspective, but the closer he got to him, the more he encountered contradictions and irritations. For example, Danny had gone through periodic and sometimes near debilitating bouts of boredom in Mike and Gracie's cabin. For a man who wanted to front up life, how come Henry never talked about tedium? Or losing his notes and to-do lists? Or, for that matter, fantasizing about wild sex?

Thoreau grew up around Concord and went to Harvard, where he hung out with Emerson, Channing, and others who believed that any understanding of reality must be derived from intuitive sources rather than analysis and fact-finding. The military and the law drilled those tendencies out of Danny and his Indo-Pak and MCS experiences didn't invite intuitions about that thin, dotted line that sits between visions and hallucinations.

On the other hand, there were similarities. Thoreau was fidgety. Even in hermit-hood, he sallied back and forth into town once a week, just like Goodman went to Duck Springs. Like Goodman, Thoreau needed a supply chain. The trait he liked least was Henry the Self-Righteous, the pious killjoy treating everyone else like moral inferiors as if his big mission in life was to correct them.

When the logs in the stove burned down and the cabin cooled, Danny crawled into bed still pondering. Danny's universe was completely different and Thoreau's version of the world didn't seem replicable. Henry didn't need a permit to camp at Walden or a Notice of Intent to take water from an ouzel's habitat. Nor, so far as Danny knew, did he have nearby encampments of paramilitary dipshits who had designs on conquering Walden Pond.

22

NORMALLY NOBODY IN TOWN HELD BIG CITY-TYPE COCKTAIL PARTIES, BUT TWICE A YEAR POPS AND THELMA SPONSORED SOMETHING AKIN TO AN OLD-FASHIONED ICE CREAM SOCIAL AT THE DUCK SPRINGS CAFÉ. The first one was usually in September or October, just as the snows started. The second was in spring, when the ice was melting; there was a hint of warmth in the air, and the out-of-town tourists, fishermen, and hunters hadn't yet shown up.

Clover had invited him the last time he drove to Duck Springs for groceries and to drop books at the exchange shelf. He had stopped at the café for coffee; then tried hard to wriggle out of the invitation, but she twined her long fingers around his, gave them a squeeze, and looked him straight in the eye. Hers were innocent, bright, and curious and never wavered. Nor did his. When their fingers braided, her touch was atomic.

"Just come by and stop being stuck up. You'll enjoy it. And oh, by the way," she said as she was going back to the kitchen and glancing over her shoulder, "nice haircut. You look like you just got out of prison."

For this year's fall event, they had invited about forty people—friends, reliable patrons, and a few people who had done them favors. They tended to exclude people who pissed them off, but they always welcomed a few strays like Danny. The local Duckbergers who weren't invited sat on their hands, fumed, and claimed they didn't really want to go anyway.

The café was decorated with Japanese paper lanterns, streamers, doilies, and party goods. There were eye-catching, Georgia O'Keeffe–looking paintings of flowers and pine cones on the walls, and plastic flowers in vases and battery-operated candles on each table. A boom box was playing a weird mix of taped music with tunes for everyone: Elvis Presley, Ferrante and Teicher, Mariah Carey, and the Royal Canadian Mounted Police Band.

When Danny walked in, Thelma greeted him. She was replenishing a bowl of fruit punch and smiled warmly. "I'm so glad you could come, Daniel."

A few older gents were waiting patiently with outstretched paper cups. One of them carried a small flask and was "freshening up" the punch bowl.

"Help yourself, Daniel," Thelma told him. "We want everyone to have a good time, and we want you to meet people."

Some little kids, the five-to-ten-year-olds with ants in their pants, were jitterbugging around and looking for trouble until their parents corralled them. Others were talking in little knots or loading up on scoops of vanilla, chocolate, strawberry, or coffee ice cream and then adding stuff that morphed them into banana splits and chocolate sundaes.

Thelma, Clover, Clover's third cousin Anastasia, who had driven from Secah, Thelma's best friend Yoko Miyamoto, and Yoko's shy younger sister Daisy Yoshimoto, were all wearing old-time pink waitress outfits with white aprons and collars. They were making their way around, ensuring that everyone had plenty to eat and drink. But Danny thought this was a party where people just jabbered.

For a while, he sat in the corner spooning down a small cup of strawberry ice cream, then he started talking with a lanky beanpole with springy blond hair and black-framed glasses with lenses like the bottom of Coke bottles. Izzy Watts was maybe in his mid-twenties. He had moved to Duck Springs three years before, was from San Francisco, seemed to be a technology geek, and liked to call people "dude." Danny got the impression he maybe had some kind of trust fund.

"What do you do?" Danny asked.

"Well, some accounting and odd jobs, but mostly I just help Uncle Maynard put out the *Duck Springs Chronicle* once a month. He's getting old so I round up a few stories for him and run off copies on his press. He really should computerize all this shit, but he's old school."

He pointed to his Uncle Maynard, a slight man with snow-white hair and a red nose who was spicing up his punch with a flask. He looked happy but seemed frail, as if he needed more connective tissue. Izzy said he was slowly dying of congestive heart failure.

"Dude," Izzy said to put a point on it, "he's outlived all the predictions the quacks have given him. Bad heart, great vibes, and a totally cool personality!"

Danny was curious about the *Chronicle.* He'd had a friend in the Marines who was a printer. Once in a while when he was running behind, Danny helped him put out the base newsletter, which was mostly military gossip read by lower ranks. The officers used it to line their bird cages.

Izzy told him about printing presses and newspaper production. "It's the only really honest trade," the baby sage pronounced. "Every fuck-up is there for the world to see. You can't hide your mistakes like doctors and lawyers."

Danny was interested in details. "Tell me about the writing and the paper"

"Used to be a weekly. Now it's a monthly, but irregular at that. I write a few pieces, but I like doing other stuff: essays, short stories, a few poems, that sort of thing. I know I'm a dweeb but it feels good."

"What about numbers?"

"Usually a thousand copies. I deliver them around town and as far away as Secah. We have about eight-hundred people in Duck Springs, sometimes more, sometimes less, but people near town also like to know what's going on here. Not that there's much happening. I collect the money from subscribers and advertisers. Uncle Maynard should really close the whole thing down. He loses money, but he's a stubborn old goat and loves the *Chronicle*."

Izzy was a talker, but Danny enjoyed the chatter and liked hearing about the town paper.

"Most runs are four pages," continued Izzy. "It's all local stuff: births, deaths, school sports, garden club meetings, the Girl Scouts' twirling contest, yard sales, school fundraisers, ads for pickup trucks and babysitting services, a photo of the big bull trout Jankowski caught, and a couple of women who offer Pilates and aromatherapy classes. And yeah, once in a while Bucky Fontaine over there gives us an item or two for the police beat—a break-in or some kids busted for dope—but those are rare."

Bucky was standing at the ice cream counter, eyeballing Clover.

"Sounds like pretty regular stuff for a small town."

"Before she croaked," Izzy told him, "Myra Whittier used to write an advice column for people with problems. She once set off an awesome debate about having your morning toast with butter versus margarine and working it from the outside in or the center out. Once in a while someone will write a letter to the editor, which Uncle shortens up. When Maynard gets pissed, he writes long screeds lambasting the mayor, the council, the governor, the legislature, the Congress, the Supreme Court, the UN, or all of them all at once. For old guys like you and him, he has some excellent rants inside him."

Danny mentally estimated Maynard Porter to be at least forty-five years older.

"You like it here?" Danny asked.

"I do. It's the right size, off the map, and even though most of these people are your age, it's a pretty friendly place."

A second ding. Danny didn't really think of himself as old. Then he asked about the mechanics of the *Chronicle*'s production system.

"We use a multilith sheet-fed offset with a stapler gizmo. He also has an old platen press and a 1962 hand-cranked mimeograph. He collects antique presses and typewriters and a lot of other old crap. He hardly ever uses the mimeograph except for an occasional handbill someone asks him to do."

"You work hard for him," said Danny, "and you seem to like it."

"I do. Well, I have to. He's a first cousin on my father's side. But I really do like putting out the paper and I like this town. It's a nice little place."

After a while, Izzy headed off to talk with the Nazzara twins, Gloria and Penelope, who were more his age. Both, with tomato-red hair, had just rolled in on skateboards with another guy. Before he took off, Izzy told Danny about the twins, who were brunettes but liked to dye their dos. Penelope and Izzy obviously had eyes for each other.

Danny enjoyed hearing people's histories. Stories took him out of his own head. That's why he'd brought storytellers like Camus and Thoreau with him to Indian Creek.

He chatted with Cynthia McDonald, the town's nurse, then met Bob Williams, an engineer and soil expert. They shook hands. Bob was in his mid-fifties and had gotten serious about designing buildings after a construction stint in Sierra Leone with the Peace Corps. After that, it was Rensselaer Polytechnic studying engineering, followed by a job with a prestigious West Coast architectural firm.

Turned out Bob helped invent sophisticated ground pilings for skyscrapers in Saudi Arabia and did forensic analyses on buildings that had collapsed in Buenos Aires. He gave Bob an abbreviated version of his own history. When the talk turned to airplanes, Bob told Danny about the Cessna 152 he co-owned with Vernon Craft that was parked near Ogden Road.

"It's a hobby," he said. "Vern and I and a couple other guys fly it around once in a while just for fun. Good little plane even though it needs some work right now. Interested in going up sometime and getting a view?"

"I'd like to once it flies. I hate planes that crash."

"That's why I always sit in the back on commercial flights. I mean, you've never seen a plane back into a mountain, have you?"

Danny liked the humor. Dark, like his.

"You'll want to get to know Vern Craft," said Bob. "He and his buddy Thomas Quinn are veterans. Cantankerous, thick as thieves, and can fix anything or stock you up with rifles, knives, or any other gear you need for hunting."

Later he met Harlan Morgan, who seemed to be in his seventies, maybe older, and had a hawk nose and a full head of white hair cropped close to his skull. He was wearing khaki pants, a blue work shirt, and a black quilted vest. Danny knew right away he was military.

Morgan was originally from Port Townsend in Jefferson County and had retired to Duck Springs after teaching at the Naval War College and The Citadel. He'd been a Marine—they exchanged some 'Semper Fis' but they were from different eras. Plus, he was an officer and Danny had been a grunt.

Morgan had made his bones in the Gulf War in 1990 and 1991 and was eventually promoted to major general. Turned out he was in a command position at the Battle of Khafji, which was initially viewed as a minor attack on an abandoned Saudi border town. In fact, it turned out to be a defining moment in Operation Desert Storm, when the First Marines formed the nucleus of the massive force sent to Iraq. Morgan distinguished himself there.

Danny's war was later as subsequent administrations kept putting Americans back into one or another fight in The Sandbox. After he retired from the Marines Corps, Harlan became a professor of military science, wrote several books, and helped ghostwrite a counterinsurgency manual.

Danny liked him. Harlan seemed low key and not full of himself, unlike so many of the West Point and Annapolis officers Danny had encountered.

The ice cream social turned out to be better than Danny anticipated. He mixed around and met others he had seen around town, plus some new folks. He talked with a tall Black man named Amos Arnold, his beautiful wife Susan, and their two handsome boys. He never quite caught what Amos did for a living.

Then Grant Terwilliger, the garrulous chief of the volunteer fire department, introduced himself and regaled him with a story about when Yoko's kitchen stove burst into flames. Nobody was hurt, he said, but the jam Yoko was cooking exploded and was all over the kitchen and in her hair."

"She was mortified. You like jokes?" he asked.

"Sometimes . . ." Danny didn't know what to expect.

"Pops's ice cream counter brought this one back. An old guy shuffles into a diner and painfully pulls himself onto a stool. After catching his breath, he orders a banana split. The waitress asks him, 'Crushed nuts?' 'No,' he says, 'arthritis.'"

As Terwilliger laughed with a toothy grin, Danny looked down and studied his shoelaces.

After that, he chatted with Ted Cingcade about the cement company. Ted moved a lot of rock and turned it into gravel for road repairs on a state contract, though he said it was harder and harder to get paid. Then he met Alberto Hernandez, who was the mayor of Duck Springs, another more or less volunteer job like Terwilliger's.

Hernandez was in his sixties, a small, reasonably fit man with olive skin, thinning black hair, and a genial smile. Danny asked him what his biggest challenge was.

"The city council," he said with a laugh.

"How come?"

"Everyone here gets taxed on their property, but we also collect organizational dues. It's not a lot, but those who officially join the township get to elect a three-member council, attend annual town meetings, and help decide priorities. That's one of the city councillors over there," he said, pointing with his little finger. "Sammy Hart. Sammy runs garbage pickup and the landfill. His nickname is Stinky but not many people call him that to his face unless they've known him for a long time.

"The one who's not here," he continued, "is Peter Ashkin. Peter is a lawyer, a former Navy Judge Advocate. Served part of his time on some big aircraft carrier in the South China Sea and then taught new JAGs at the Navy's Officer Development School. He keeps to himself except for the council. Smart, detailed, and watchful, but a formal sort of feller. Wears a sports coat and tie to our meetings. He's pretty good with numbers and contracts, though, and keeps us out of trouble."

Hernandez had a big smile and seemed like an affable man who took life with several grains of salt.

"My main job," he continued, "is to arm wrestle with the three councillors. You know, small town, big needs, a tiny budget. Whether we should put speed bumps up at Ogden Road, save money for a new snowplow, fix the grader, or try to attract new businesses this way."

Hernandez was a man who kept smiling even when he was being harassed by some of the Duckbergers who were slowly nibbling off his fingers and toes with grievances. He was philosophical even when he mentioned the names of a few especially persistent whiners. His humor was subtle, intelligent, and self-effacing.

Hernandez said he recalled someone saying that when humans emerged out of the Pleistocene, our ancestors initially developed language out of a profound need to complain.

Danny talked with Kenny Miyamoto and his wife. Kenny had the narrowest eyes he had ever seen on an Asian person and he acknowledged that right after they shook hands.

"My name is Ken, but all my friends call me Squints."

Squints explained some of the intricacies of strawberries, plums, and peaches—how to grow them, sort them, save them, mash them, and cook them into first class jams.

Mabel Wolff came over and introduced herself. She ran Duck Springs's contract postal station that was open three days a week but had an official United States Post Office flagpole in front. She introduced Danny to a five-foot tall man who pumped his hand a minute longer than he was accustomed to. He seemed to be her cousin—a chatty little guy, good-natured but slightly scatterbrained.

"Name's Tiny Porter," he said. "Tiny Porter," he repeated. "My real name is Thor but childhood nicknames tend to stick around here. I actually don't mind. I drive the school bus and you can see why they call me Tiny! Even the kids call me Tiny. I also have a yellow VW microbus and it's a taxi when people need a ride. My wife, she's eight inches taller than me and calls me Tiny, but so what?" He winked. "I'm not tiny everywhere."

Then, Danny talked at length with Brian Jankowski, an independent freighter who owned two long-haul tractor-trailer rigs. Mabel was his girlfriend. Jankowski was wearing a black western shirt with blue embroidery and white snap buttons. He had baggy jeans riding low under an immense belly and sported a bright-red baseball hat. When he took it off, he was bald as an eight ball. He said he had regular runs between certain cities and had just come back from a delivery of electric generators to San Diego, and more in another warehouse that would go to Salt Lake City soon.

"What's it like in the cities and on the road?" Danny asked.

"The truth?" He shrugged. "It's bad. We've started organizing convoys. There are more and more robberies and hijackings. Some militia guys wearing NADF colors pulled a friend of mine out of his vehicle at a rest stop just south of Eugene. He was carrying electronics and going to a big box in Sacramento with radios, computers, that kind of stuff. They wanted his truck. Shot him right there at the rest stop when he pushed back."

"Jesus . . ."

"It's worse than that. There's unrest all over the Northwest. Word is the NADF is assembling into armies."

"Any pushback?" Danny asked.

"Not that I've heard of, but I bet it will happen once the shock wears off."

They talked for a while, then he started looking for Clover. He wanted to say goodbye and slip back to Indian Creek.

"You having a good time?" she asked when he caught up with her.

"Nice people and a fine soiree, but talking with Brian I'm getting more news than I should. I swore off that stuff when I came here but I slip once in a while. I need to avoid current events."

"That shouldn't worry you. You're a hermit anyway."

She was stunning in her pink waitress dress.

"I know, but somehow the world keeps busting in without asking first. You want to have dinner with me in Crockett one evening?" he asked her. "I have to go back down and get a root canal."

"I'd like that," she said.

Her blonde hair was in a braid that fell across the left side of her neck and over her breast. Her face was radiant as she smiled with pearly teeth and eyes twinkling and changing colors. Her gaze liquefied him.

Then the Duck Springs electricity flickered off and stayed off for a week. When it came back on, it was progressively more intermittent and unpredictable. Everyone hauled out their lanterns and Slim sold out of candles.

23

DANNY WAS SITTING ON THE WOODEN BENCH IN FRONT OF HIS CABIN AT INDIAN CREEK, AVOIDING THE NAIL STICKING UP ON THE LEFT SIDE AND SMOKING A PLEASANT AFTERNOON CIGAR, WHEN HIS BROTHER DROVE UP IN HIS SUBARU. Josh got out with packages, which turned out to be a box of mail, two six-packs of beer, some bags of good coffee, a vacuum-sealed package of smoked salmon, a large bottle of herring in wine and vinegar from Fishermen's Terminal, sandwiches for lunch, a fishing rod, and two loaves of bread that Sharon had baked.

"How's it hanging Danny?"

"All good. What are you doing here?"

"Came up to make sure you hadn't driven my Karmann Ghia into the river. It's a collector's item, you know. Much more valuable than you. Also, brought your mail. A few things look important."

"Come in and let's drink a beer."

"Good idea. Long drive with a lot of detours. And some NADF guys on the road with black berets playing soldier stopping cars at Wild Wind Pass. A bunch of them were carrying submachine guns. Wanted to see my ID and know where I was going. Told them I was going fishing. Ugly-looking bunch."

Josh was about Danny's height but had blond hair and blue eyes. When he would get dressed up for a date or prom, their mom used to say some Viking or Nazi had snuck into their bloodline.

"It's nice up here. Good place for a loner like you to hide away, though that stogie is stinking up the place."

"Keeps the bears away. Also unwanted humans. Want one?"

Josh nodded and Danny handed him a cigar. He snipped the end with a pocketknife and lit it with a kitchen match.

Josh and Danny were close. He was six years younger than Danny but had managed to calm their mom and dad when they initially freaked out over the news that Danny had been wounded in Kashmir and had hot IED shrapnel extracted from his side. The Marine Corps was slow to tell them that it wasn't fatal, but good enough to get him home.

They talked and drank, walked up the Little Green to look for rainbows, and started casting into a few pools.

"What's it like in Seattle?"

"Bad. Sharon and I are still working, but our hours have been cut. Even the cops and firefighters are having a hard time getting paid. The mayor and city council members mostly argue with each other behind closed doors, then issue joint statements saying it will all be better soon. Nobody believes them."

Josh told him there had been a run on certain banks and that a homeless camp at Lake Washington had grown to 2,000 restless, angry people living under tarps without much sanitation. There was a lot of looting and mugging, food shortages, and the streets weren't safe. People were hungry. Someone from a nearby camp went to a local mall with a lot of Japanese stores and grabbed all the colorful koi to boil for fish soup.

According to Josh, the NADF was becoming a serious enterprise and coming out of the shadows to create a martial law government. Their patrols were everywhere.

"You and Sharon armed?"

"I have that old over-and-under shotgun and my own .38 Special," he said. "I refurbished both and they shoot reasonably straight, though that .38 is not very good beyond a few feet."

Danny shook his head. "You were never a very good shot. You better let Sharon shoot and you stand behind her. She's more of a warrior than you anyway."

Josh laughed. "She hates guns. Won't touch 'em."

Josh said the NADF had brought a lot of small paramilitary units together in the Northwest. They were adding members fast and equipping themselves with military-grade weapons. Most carried pistols, shotguns, and combat knives. They were also issuing daily proclamations calling for order. They said that they were now the real government and the transition to the new America. They were issuing identity papers, commandeering homes, and demanding to be fed.

"That's illegal."

"Doesn't make any difference," Josh said. "They suspend laws and make their own rules. I'm sure they've tampered with elections and are sending out teams to knock out anyone who looks like serious political opposition.

There had been executions, he explained, some done randomly by NADF squads, others when local leaders suddenly disappeared. At night, they went into the homeless camps, giving speeches, handing out food and clothing, and signing up new members who had to take loyalty oaths. They were constantly recruiting and shaking down people for money and goods.

"You and Sharon leaving?"

"We've talked about it. We may go to a place near Tillamook. We've got friends who have a farm over there. They have cows and make cheese and yogurt."

"You could come up here," said Danny. "Duck Springs is a nice little place, good people, out of the way and probably in nobody's binoculars. There are places you could rent in town, or we can gin up some kind of arrangement here at Indian Creek. Maybe turn the cabin into a central kitchen and living room and work up tents, tarps, and sheds. Get some heat and turn this joint into Camp Goodman."

"It's possible, I suppose. Have to talk more with Sharon. We haven't really figured out a plan."

They cleaned and iced a few trout for Josh to take back, drank a beer, and then drove over to the Duck Springs Café so Danny could introduce him around. He prattled on a bit about Clover, who was away on an errand, but Pops and Thelma were there. He introduced them, bought coffees and two pieces of peanut butter pie.

"This pie is fantastic," Josh said through a mouthful.

"Too bad Clover isn't here."

"You're smitten, Danny, I can tell!"

He changed the subject but Danny bought a pie for him to take home. Then they jawboned with others who wandered in—Stinky Hart, Izzy Watts, and Penelope Nazzara, who now had blue hair.

Before Josh headed back, Danny asked him to call Lenny Jones to offer his personal thank you. It was fine seeing Josh, and he felt better than before he showed up. Kin and community are wired into us, he knew. People like him who flee and choose to live on the margins, they're the mutants. It was his personal problem, the choice between living with others and being alone. One of his many Goodman paradoxes.

Back at the cabin, he read through the mail Josh brought. Aside from a letter from Lenny closing one of his cases, most of it was unimportant. Catalogs. A few threatening past due invoices. One note from the firm saying Sam Johnson had suddenly died from a massive heart attack, and several solicitations from ambulance chasers in case he needed more legal defense.

He thought about Sam, his mentor before The Troubles. He owed most of what he had learned about the law and fighting passionately for clients to him. He silently assumed Sam was filing objections and interlocutory appeals right up to the second he keeled over. In fact, he was probably sitting on a cloud, sending down interrogatories. Danny thought about his tough, hard manner and behind that, the many kind considerations he had showed him before he flamed out.

Then he fed everything into the stove for heat.

24

ON A WARM DAY, HE SAT ON A STUMP CLOSE TO THE RIVER, WATCHING THE WIND MOVE PINES AND COTTONWOODS, AND BUBBLES OF FOAM FLOAT BY. He was whittling a piece of wood that could become a bird. It was a peaceful Thoreauvian moment. A small trout was finning in the lee of a large rock. Yellow butterflies fluttered down, as did a large iridescent green dragonfly hunting gnats. A Douglas squirrel chattered away nearby.

Suddenly, one of the new generation of fast-moving reconnaissance drones swooped down and hovered over the cabin. The squirrel raced off. Danny heard it before he saw it, propellers whistling. He remembered small hand-launched units like these in Kashmir, along with guided Short Range Armed Drones, small weaponized SRADs that could focus on individuals and kill them. And, at the other end, massive Reaper drones that launched guided missiles.

This one dropped down and hovered above the front of the cabin. It had multiple propellers and a camera underneath snapping pictures.

He went inside, grabbed his 30.06, raced back out, and clicked off the safety. As the drone drifted higher, heading north, he got off three quick shots, but his drone-hunting skills had lapsed.

25

DAYLIGHT HOURS SHORTENED, LEAVES TURNED YELLOW, AND THE WEATHER CHANGED. While he ranged out one day for firewood, the wind came up and turned fierce. Insects stopped buzzing and birds paused their chirpings. Leftover flower petals flew off stems, grasses bent, trees groaned, bursts of rain intensified, and small branches and twigs snapped through the air. Snow flurries mixed with rain blew in. Then hail hit.

Half a mile from the cabin without rain gear, he was soaked and chilled.

When heavier snows came later, Danny spent more time inside cleaning equipment and watching Stumpy, who was a relentless mooch. He turned back to *Walden*. Thoreau tended toward long moralisms but occasionally, out would come some green eyeshade observation about how much he spent for a couple of casks of lime. Even his catalog of plants and animals had a bookkeeper quality, as Danny's often did in his own journal, though Henry's commentaries on what he was seeing and his speculations on how to live in perfect harmony with them burned through the audits.

Always there was nature, which he seemed to think of as if it were a faraway continent that he had just discovered. Here, for example, was Henry at noon, wrapped in a reverie, about water. "Time is the stream I go fishing in. I drink at it; but while I drink, I see the sandy bottom and detect how shallow it is. Its thin current slides away but eternity remains."

At Indian Creek by the Little Green, with slivers of snowmelt trickling down, Henry would have seen evidence of the everlasting that Danny completely missed. Still, if Henry were around now, what would he do with spy drones overhead or when the NADF or some other group of idiots showed up at the front door and asked for his papers so they could be sure he wasn't Mexican?

He still liked Henry. Thoreau was an original, a dropout, and an excellent fly in the American ointment but Danny preferred the solace he got from Camus.

On his next trip to town, he put *Walden* on the giveaway shelf.

26

AT THE CAFÉ, HE SAT DOWN AT THE COUNTER AND ORDERED A COFFEE. Grant Terwilliger wandered over. They had met briefly at the ice cream social, but he reintroduced himself. He was a compact man, friendly, maybe slightly older than Danny. He had a crew cut and a wrinkled, wind-blasted face but looked fit.

"I sell propane and kerosene from my backyard," he said, shaking Danny's hand. "I'm also chief of the Duck Springs All Volunteer Fire Department. We're actually trained and certified. Most people who don't know anything about fires think we are a bunch of bozos playing firemen, but we're pretty fucking good. A fire starts, we jump into our gear and get on the truck, which is locked and loaded at all times. At least that's how it was before the electricity went off."

Then he asked Danny if he'd heard about the volunteer fire department in the nearby town of Woodburn. He said their group, like Duck Springs, was all volunteers. Seems a fire broke out in a farmer's barn outside of town. Grant said the farm, a hay and horse operation, was owned by a Mr. Barnaby Smith.

"As soon as Smith saw smoke, he called my friend Ernie Sweet, Woodburn's fire chief, who assembled his team. They leaped on their old pumper and roared over to Barnaby's place."

Terwilliger was a good storyteller. Still, Danny couldn't tell whether this was real stuff or small-town cracker-barrel bullshit. His stories were told with exquisite timing and a dog-friendly manner. He always ended with his own infectious laugh.

"They came to the top of a rise and saw Smith's barn smoldering a quarter mile ahead, so they raced down the hill and drove straight into the burning barn and started spraying water. When they finally got the burn out, old man Barnaby praised the bravery of Ernie's crew and instantly wrote out a check to the Woodburn Volunteer Fire Department for a thousand bucks. A reporter from the *Crockett City Herald* saw Barnaby pass the check over and asked Chief Sweet, 'What are you gonna do with the money?'

"'Well, sir, we sure can use some new hoses,' he said, 'but first thing we're gonna do is fix the brakes on that goddamned truck.'"

27

ON ANOTHER TRIP TO DUCK SPRINGS TO BUY SOME FLOUR FOR TORTILLAS HE WANTED TO MAKE, DANNY RAN INTO VERN CRAFT, THOMAS QUINN, AND QUINN'S TWO DOGS AT SLIM'S. They stopped inside at the corner of canned goods and ice cream.

Vern said he had driven to a suburb of Seattle to get some new hunting rifles and the store owner said he couldn't sell him any. They had all been confiscated by NADF goons commanded by someone named Ned O'Reilly.

"I bought some other supplies but couldn't wait to get out of town. I hate those guys."

28

THEN, ON A COLD DAY, CLOVER DROPPED BY IN A LARGE, WHITE JEEP STATION WAGON WITH CAFÉ DECALS ON BOTH FRONT DOORS. The decals were bright-blue circles with curved script wrapping around the outside. Inside the circles were two cartoon ducks laughing as they frolicked in a pond under a small waterfall.

Clover was wearing snug-fitting jeans, a flannel shirt, a maroon sweater, and a baby-blue down vest. Her thick blonde hair looked different, the streaks of yellow and red replaced with silver and ash. She was stunning. Danny tried not to stare, but it was impossible.

"How you doing, caveman?"

"Your hair looks different."

"Yep," she said, fumbling with it. "I changed a few colors. Yours is growing out, too, but you still look like a convict."

"Your hair is way nicer than mine. What's up?"

"Thanks. I wanted to see what kind of place you live in. No one in town quite gets you, me included. Plus, I figure even hermits have to eat, so I brought dinner and some wine so I could check out if you really are a troglodyte."

It was picnic food: cold roast beef on focaccia bread with lettuce, tomato, and Dijon mustard; potato salad; apples; and a small bottle of Merlot. She also brought along a peanut butter pie. She saw him eyeballing it.

"For dessert later," she said, then asked, "What do you eat around here?"

"I have a pot of beans and wieners if you want some."

She walked over to the range, lifted the lid, bent over, and peered down. "No thanks. I think there's something alive in there."

"Could be a mouse. Lots of them here, even though I've been chasing them around ever since I got here. It's war. They started it."

"No thanks. I don't do mice even if they are cooked extra fancy like this one."

They talked for a while, then she said, "You ever jumped into that river? Let's go do that!"

"Really? Are you crazy? It's snowing out there and the river is just a few degrees above freezing."

"Don't you do anything on impulse?"

"Not usually."

"You're a solitary guy, aren't you? Is it you don't like people?"

"Actually, I don't trust people. Most make me uncomfortable and wary. Not you though."

"Why?"

"Because a lot of people are morons, some are risky, and a few will always betray you and break your heart. Eight out of ten times I'm right."

"Scratch a cynic and eight out of ten times he's a wounded optimist. Is that you?"

Danny said, "I have to think about that. You seriously want to jump in the river?"

"Of course. We used to do that when we were kids. The Duck Springs Polar Bear Club. Plenty of double dares and pinky promises. You'll see. It'll be fun. Everyone needs a little craziness in their lives, even you. Just fire up the stove so it's warm in here when we get back. Look tough guy, I'll bet dollars to donuts I can take it longer than you. You may have been a Marine, but I don't think you can handle it, Goodman."

She jumped out of her clothes, grabbed a towel, and watched Danny undress. Then she came over and ran her hand over the scars on his left side where the docs had extracted IED shrapnel, pumped in plasma and antibiotics, and stitched him back together. A lot of tissue damage, but it had missed important organs.

Her hand slipped around his waist and up his back, and then she kissed him. A sweet, gentle kiss with a slow electric current. He kissed her back harder and then she pushed him away with a laugh and said, "Not now, buddy. Into the water."

They walked down to the water's edge and left their shoes and towels on a boulder. She stepped in, found a pool, and jumped in while he tiptoed out. Then she grabbed his hand and pulled him into the water. Everything shriveled.

They dried off, defrosted, had dinner, and made their way to bed. It was a slow, soft, quiet courtship, exploratory and careful. He was nervous and out of practice. It had been a long time since he had been with a woman, since he'd even wanted to. But bodies tend to remember what minds forget.

Later, before she left, they fell back into bed again, this time deep in heat. Two animals voraciously in need of each other. They felt each other everywhere, kissed all over, gently, slowly, feeling the joy and warmth of the cell-to-cell contact of legs, arms, crevices, torsos, faces, and chins. They explored the hollows behind necks, knees, and arms. Caressing each other's hair and fingertips, mouths touching lightly and then fiercely, hands together, palm to palm, fingers braided, tasting the salt of sweat, long and slow and hungry. Then the rising urgency as passions merged and they both exploded.

Over coffee, they talked. He asked her to tell him about herself, and she wanted to know about him. Beyond things seen and sensed, and contrary to Mr. Plato's idea of flickering shadows, Danny believed the world was made of stories. Law is a story. Malcolm Crowley and Kashmir were stories. Science is a story. Towns like Duck Springs are a story. Fire departments and cafés are stories.

Clover was a story and he was hungry for it.

She grew up in Duck Springs and was distantly descended from town founder, William Pfeiffer. As WWI broke out, her great-grandfather changed his name to Fiffe and enlisted in the Marines. He wanted to be part of the War to End All Wars against the Kaiser and was killed at Belleau Wood in 1918, not far from the Marne River.

Clover and her older sisters, Zephyr and Meadow, all went away to college. Clover studied business and management in Seattle, but there wasn't much need for those qualifications in Duck Springs, other than a short-lived competition from some summer people who wanted to start another café in town.

"How did you and your sisters get all these unusual names?" he asked. "Most women here seem like Brendas and Jennifers."

"Our parents were late-blooming hippies. My mom read *Rolling Stone*. Stuff like that."

After their parents were killed in a car crash, Meadow married a lawyer from Vancouver and Zephyr became a bank auditor in New York. Clover went to work for Pops and Thelma and became part owner of the café.

When Danny asked her about Duck Springs, she talked about some of the people he had briefly met. He heard more about the café and about Pops and Thelma, who had been so kind to her, and about their friends, Kenny and Yoko Miyamoto. Clover told him about Donny Benton, a thirty-year-old boy-child with Down syndrome, and Crazy Mary who sometimes got it in her head to walk around naked, babbling about radio transmissions from another planet coming through her teeth.

Clover mentioned other women she was close with, including Cynthia McDonald, Mabel Wolff, and Alberto Hernandez's wife, Heather. Beyond work and friends, Clover's great passion was painting. All those Georgia O'Keeffe–looking pictures of flowers and trees at the café were hers. Unlike O'Keeffe, only a few of Clover's paintings were in pastels. Most had vibrant reds and yellows, cobalt, and turquoise blues and soft shades of gray and amber for shadows.

"Painting soothes me," she said. "I paint mosses and trees and close-ups of leaves, lichens, and mushrooms on logs, but what I love to paint most are flowers. Flowers are soul food."

He loved that description. The same solitary entertainment he found in his feeble writings, she found in her brushes and canvasses, trying to bring a spruce tree or alpine flower to life with dabs and strokes of color.

As her life story rolled out, he listened and asked a few questions. Obliquely, she described some lovers and boyfriends, a few of them serious, none of them permanent. Unlike him, she knew exactly who she was. She had deep anchors in Duck Springs.

"How come you never married?" he finally asked.

"Slim pickings in Duck Springs," she said, her hair curving down and covering the sides of her face. "Never met a guy I wanted to settle down with. Lots of nice men, but the ones who interested me most were either under ten or over seventy. Now, tell me about you, and tell me everything. I want to hear the whole story and full truth. No bullshit, Danny. We're too old for that."

He said, "You won't like what you hear."

"Everything."

His story spilled out, truncated at first, then in longer pieces, and in ways he had never quite shared, even with his family or with Kirsten in their best moments.

He told her about growing up in Portland in a lower-middle-class, blue-collar Jewish family of plumbers, carpenters, and shopkeepers; of his younger brother Josh, who was a builder for the City of Seattle's construction department; about his dad's alcoholism, and his feeling completely inadequate during high school except for his English teacher, Mrs. Annan, who urged him to read more and write. He told her about being a mediocre college student on his best day, of having a few intriguing courses in philosophy and literature, and about studying political science because it was easy, kind of like why jocks took sociology.

If he retained any residual value from his early education, he said, it was that he liked reading and admired good writing. The more he tried it, the more he found jiggling ideas into experimental paragraphs was a way to connect the different dots sweeping through his life. It was a pastime and it brought him pleasure. His goal in writing was to think like chess and write like ballet, though it never really worked like that.

With an instinct for emotional acupuncture, she probed into sensitive spots while he waxed on.

"Tell me about your time in the Marines. I really want to understand that."

More spilled out. He described how he joined the military after listening to an older recruiter at the Portland State career fair who had fought in Vietnam and spent a long time asking questions and telling Danny stories about how military life gave him purpose and promise.

He talked about enlisting in the Marines and about boot camp and acquiring a discipline that had never been asked of him, about rising from private to corporal and then culminating in the rank of E-6 as a staff sergeant. He recounted how he became an accidental leader when his sergeant was killed and described running a reconnaissance squad.

He described being deployed to Pakistani-occupied Srinagar, which was full of warlords and gangsters who had killed and mutilated their own civilians for political reasons. He talked about Operation Takeback and street-by-street, house-by-house fighting. He told her about shoot-outs with men who were just as lost as he had been, just as hungry for belonging, and who had been seduced by notions of a flower-draped paradise blessed with endless food, drink, and the fawning attentions of young girls.

Then he returned to how it felt to wend through the narrow streets in Srinagar, the rabbit warrens of souks and alleys with front doors opening into courtyards and stairs leading up to murky-looking apartments. Slowly, he talked of finding the bodies of executed civilians and of going street by street and killing the enemy without compunction in explosive firefights.

He shared the loss of comrades, and of being wounded by a roadside bomb buried in the dust as his vehicle passed over it. He described his slow recovery through medicines and talking sessions long after the physical wounds had healed. He admitted to bouts of PTSD, of his personal post-war shadowland when life suddenly went blank, and an inexplicable soul-deadening darkness descended and his mind was filled with the toxins of past terrors. And how, for a time, he would cry or rage for no obvious reason.

He called up the faces of others he had met in the hospital and later in outpatient meetings with an insightful therapist, herself a wounded veteran. He mentioned men who had gone to Iraq and Afghanistan who had chronic pains, or were perpetually depressed or enraged, or both. He described men who could still feel the toes on their missing feet, and the gravitational pull of suicide. And then he told her about one perpetually smiling infantry man named Sammy whom he met in the outpatient meetings and who seemed perfectly fine until he stepped in front of a bus.

Looking into Clover's eyes, he spoke of his recovery and going to law school and then joining the Malcolm Crowley firm. And all about Sam Johnson, his mentor and tormentor. And getting married to Kirsten Briley, a stern and unforgiving college teacher in what was from the start an arrangement of convenience.

He confessed his deep hunger for money and power that had driven him into the maelstrom of gambling and the unwavering delusion that he could beat the odds in everything he did. Finally, he told her of his collapse, his exit from MCS, and his current escape to Indian Creek.

Having talked nonstop he could sense a shift. Behind all his spoken words, he was beguiled by Clover. She was a candle that met his darkness with light, warmth, and acceptance.

Later, Clover asked what kept bringing him back to Albert Camus. He said Camus wasn't a philosopher. He was a storyteller who discovered his philosophy. He believed that every person had the job of finding their own touchstone in a meaningless world, and that was the dilemma—The Camus Paradox—similar to some of his own paradoxes. Nothingness into somethingness, and then back again to death and nothingness. Our first breath an inhale, our last one an exhale, and in between, the search for something bigger than either of those chests full of air.

After Clover left, he lay awake thinking he was finding something different and important. Camus talked about how falling in love with someone who loves you back unconditionally is a redemption.

"Beauty is unbearable," Camus wrote. It "drives us to despair, offering us for a minute the glimpse of an eternity that we should like to stretch out over the whole of time."

But with all that he revealed, he couldn't tell Clover everything. Some monsters block the sun and drag you back into the abyss you thought, for just a moment, you had escaped.

PART II

29

CLOVER AND DANNY DROVE TO CROCKETT CITY. On the way she caught him up on town news. Brian Jankowski was pulled off the freeway by the NADF, robbed, roughed up, but not seriously hurt. Electric power remained unstable. It flickered on for an hour or two and then blinked off for days. Some Duck Springs residents had left.

Sadly, Maynard Porter, owner and editor of the *Duck Springs Chronicle,* had finally succumbed to his heart condition. The entire town turned out for a candlelight service. Izzy read a remembrance and said he would try to keep Maynard's paper alive. Privately, he was doubtful the paper could survive.

Meanwhile, mail, food, and fuel deliveries to Duck Springs had stopped, and radio and TV announcements were intermittent and unreliable. The occasional broadcasts that came through spoke of bank robberies, vigilantes, and right-wing takeovers around the country. There were reports of assassinations, declarations of martial law, imprisonment of dissenters, civilian curfews, public executions of local officials, confiscations of homes and businesses, and reeducation camps. How much was true was unclear.

One report discussed training sites in remote parts of the Utah desert, the Maine woods, and the Louisiana bayous. NADF opponents were rumored to have been poisoned with weaponized viruses stolen from the National Institutes of Health. Rumors were thick, but it was always unclear what had real facts behind them.

The answer began to reveal itself in Crockett City when Danny and Clover became what litigators call "percipient witnesses." Which meant, they saw it firsthand. They checked into a small motel, and the next morning Danny took Clover to The Ars for coffee and breakfast. Julie with the chicken-feather hairdo and nose rings served, but the place was empty.

"Where is everyone?" Danny asked her. She remembered him.

"It's like this everywhere. Half the people have left town. Some have joined the Defense Force. They killed the mayor and several objectors on the city council and took over local government. We're under some kind of martial law. Jed, the owner, is closing tomorrow."

"What are you going to do?"

"Try to hitch my way home to Pennsylvania."

"Better get rid of all that hardware on your face and maybe grow out your hair," said Danny.

When Julie looked hurt, Clover said, "Honey, what Danny is trying to say is it's dangerous out there and there are a lot of unsavory people. A pretty girl like you will attract nasty men."

After coffee, Danny reconnected with Eric Abbott for his root canal. Abbott had more stories about the NADF but waxed philosophical as he worked on the tooth. Danny had suction and water tubes hanging off his mouth, plus half of Eric's toolbox of picks and scrapers working the inside of his yapper.

Like his first visit, Eric was talkative and candid.

"I just finished a book that mirrors what is happening right now in the United States. It's a history of Rome."

Danny rasped, "Howww thoooo?"

"Even before the barbarians charged in, the Roman Empire was in decline. Internal rot. The middle class had withered and oligarchs controlled the government. Rich people thought they were paying too much and the lower classes weren't doing enough. Sound familiar?"

"I should read that book," he garbled.

"Ordinary people saw their lands confiscated, men and boys conscripted, and slaves fed to lions and crocodiles for entertainment. After centuries of relative stability, Rome just collapsed."

"You think that's what's going on now?"

"That's exactly what I think."

As Eric worked on the bad tooth, Danny asked, "What are you going to do?"

"We need to leave. You may see me and my family in your neck of the woods."

"Thanks, Eric. Hope you're wrong about Rome, but consider moving our way just in case. We could use a dentist and you'd like the people up there. It's an island frozen in time. The best of old-time, small-town stuff from another era."

When he was finished, Clover and Danny went shopping. As the anesthetic wore off, Danny announced, "I have a hankering for bacon—a bacon, lettuce, and tomato sandwich in particular. In fact, I've always thought that women who really want to attract men should wear bacon perfume. Or eau de beer. Or chocolate chip cookie toilet water. Better yet, a cologne distilled from peanut butter pie."

She said, "You're truly weird, Goodman."

Most stores were boarded up and the few that were open had a lot of empty shelves. No cheese, butter, beef, pork, milk, or fresh veggies. And no bacon. Mostly potatoes, white bread, apples, and some very expensive chicken. Prices had quintupled. Clover paid for the groceries since most of them were for the café.

Danny shared Abbott's ideas about history with Clover. The political and social rot now showing its ugly face had been evolving over decades as the United States had become like Germany in the 1930s: volatile, susceptible to an authoritarian like Hitler, and especially dangerous for Goodman's people. The Goodmans who didn't escape wound up in the ovens or as lampshades.

He liked talking with Clover about all this as they walked around Crockett City. They tended to think alike, though Clover wasn't especially sympathetic to his Camus ravings.

Meanwhile, patrols of NADF soldiers were walking up and down the streets. Most were young studs, but a surprising number were middle-aged women. All of them were wearing black shirts and berets, red scarves, camo pants, and laced-up army boots. All of them were armed with pistols, knives, long guns, truncheons, hand grenades, or shotguns. All of them had patches on their shirts that said "NADF."

As they walked back to Clover's Jeep with their boxes and bags, a patrol confronted them. Two men and a woman blocked their way. The youngest, a pimply-faced man with slicked-back hair and a red ribbon pinned to the front of his beret was waving a pistol around.

Danny knew the type. These were swagger and strut bullies, with a few that were genuinely tough, which was how he came by his crooked nose.

"Who are you? Where are you going?" the guy demanded.

Danny tensed up, ready to beef if he had to. His instinct from the military and even from litigation was to stay calm but be ready to punch.

Clover stepped in front of him, flashed a smile, batted her eyelashes, and sweetly said, "Sir, we came to town to buy some food and see the dentist."

She was looking innocent for both of them.

Her manner was disquieting, the sweet cheerleader everyone looks at while they are ostensibly paying attention to the game.

"Papers," the pimple demanded.

"Papers? What papers?" Danny said, as politely as he could.

"Crockett City is under martial law by the New American Defense Force. So are most other cities. We are issuing identity papers for everyone here."

"But we aren't from here," said Clover with a flutter. "We're from a tiny town west of here."

"Where do you live?" said the older man. He was hard-looking, in his mid-fifties, tall with muscled arms, ratty hair, and fading tattoos. He kept brushing one hand over a truncheon.

"Duck Springs, west, this side of Wild Wind Pass," said Danny.

"Show us some identification," the meathead said.

Which they did. Driver's licenses.

"We'll get to your town soon enough, but next time you come to Crockett, go to city hall, take the oath, and register. You'd better have NADF papers."

"Thank you so much," said Clover, wearing a completely contrived smile. Danny smiled too. Later she said he looked like a jack-o'-lantern.

30

ONE VERY COLD AND DRY AFTERNOON A FEW DAYS LATER, TWO OF THE AUTHORS OF THE MESSAGES IN THE BOTTLES SHOWED UP. Stumpy was on the windowsill cracking sunflower seeds when he squawked and flew off. Danny heard voices and footsteps crunching in the snow, grabbed his Sig, cocked it, shoved it into the back of his pants, and stepped to the rear of the cabin. There was a knock on the door.

"Come in," he called out.

An Asian man and a younger Caucasian woman stepped in. The man was limping, his arm was in a makeshift sling, and he'd been beaten in the face. The woman had wounds on her arms and legs and a black eye that was turning radish red.

"What can I do for you?" Danny asked.

The woman gasped, "We need help . . ."

"What's going on?"

"I'm sorry to bother you," said the woman, "but we were attacked. Can you help us?"

"Come in and sit down. I don't have a phone but you both look banged up. I'll drive you to Duck Springs and see if we can find Cynthia McDonald, the nurse there."

"That would be kind, sir," she said.

He heated water to wash their injuries. "What happened?"

The man spoke up. He said his name was Masaji Hiraoka and the two of them were part of the Parliament of Owls. "And this is Alyssaranda Gibson. We're the ones who leave poems in bottles." He choked back a wave of pain. "We left some for you, gifts."

"Thank you for those," Danny said. "I don't always understand them, but I like them."

Masaji looked to be in his fifties—tall, dark-complexioned, and strong, like he was used to hard work.

Alyssaranda said, "Out of the blue, we were attacked by people with guns. They burned down several houses and I think they beat Shane, our leader, senseless. He had a terrible wound on the side of his head. I think they might have killed him and his partner, Cloud Watcher."

"They kept firing into our homes and beating people, even kids," said Hiraoka.

Alyssaranda was crying.

"Ms. Gibson and Mr. Hiraoka," Danny said, "grab some blankets off the bed and let's get into my car. It's about ten miles from Indian Creek to Duck Springs. My heater isn't working but let's see if we can find nurse McDonald."

On the drive to Duck Springs, he asked about the Owls. The Parliament was made up of about thirty people who lived in a clearing at a place called Superstition Pass. Owls, real ones they said, are solitary birds, but they sometimes gather in groups that biologists call parliaments.

This parliament carved out a little village with cabins, yurts, and domes. They had clean water and sanitation and were off the grid. Most of them were older, but there were a few small children and some teenagers. They were vegetarians and practiced what they called "Crazy Wisdom."

Danny asked about that and Alyssaranda explained it this way: "We try to live by truths that are eternal, old and new wisdom that leads to calmness inside ourselves and in the world. We think real wisdom sits inside paradoxical injunctions. You know, things like 'Laugh when you are in sorrow.' 'Less is more.' 'Start with the end in mind.' 'Speak without words.' Or 'Practice what you preach.'"

"Why are those crazy?"

"Because nobody follows them. Some of our best crazy knowledge comes to us from Lao Tzu, Buddha, Jesus, and Mohammed. Other bits come from poets and dreamers like Kabir, Rumi, and Thoreau."

He didn't know who Kabir or Rumi were, but Thoreau caught his attention.

"Henry David Thoreau?" he asked. "I just finished rereading *Walden*."

"Yes. We study him too. He once said it's 'not until we are completely lost that we begin to understand.' That's a paradox right there."

Danny drove, they talked, he listened and admired how larger spirits seemed to call to them.

In town, he found Cynthia McDonald, and knocked on her door. She was patching the elbow of a thirteen-year-old kid who had fallen off his moped, picking out pieces of gravel with a forceps.

"Cynthia, I brought you some customers. These folks could use your help."

Wearing her usual wine-red scrubs, she looked up from the elbow and peered over her half-frame glasses, looking like a big, burgundy owl herself.

"Bring them in."

To Danny's eye, Cynthia was endlessly interesting and likable. She reminded him of most of the military medics and doctors he had known. They all possessed optimism about healing bodies coupled with a profound skepticism about the human condition. Despite an endless line of sickness and injury, she was unflappably pragmatic.

He left Alyssaranda and Masaji with her and headed over to the café to see what was going on. When he walked in, Clover surprised him by rushing over with a frightened look.

"You haven't heard, have you?" she asked.

"Heard what? I've been hanging out with Stumpy and just brought some beat-up people to Cynthia. What's going on?"

Electricity, water, radio, television, and broadband are down all over the country but Izzy heard it on a shortwave radio. Norma Chavez was assassinated, shot point-blank in the face. In addition to the president, 275 congressional leaders have disappeared. Maybe more. Rumor has it they were executed but no one knows for sure."

"What about Longborn?" he asked.

"The vice president is in Canada with Prime Minister Michael Maclean. He and a few cabinet members and legislators, the ones who weren't killed or stuck in prison camps, escaped DC by plane and were given asylum in Ottawa. They sent out a few messages that they are the United States government in exile and managed to cancel the nuclear launch codes since the president's football disappeared. Now even those broadcasts have stopped."

Huddled near Pops and Thelma's radio were Mayor Hernandez and Fire Chief Terwilliger, stone-faced. The Miyamotos, Peter Ashkin, and others were there too. The radio, powered by a generator, had drawn people in like a campfire on a wet night. Izzy was holding Penelope Nazzara's hand.

What he had read at The Ars, the reports from Josh, Abbott's fears, Jankowski's encounters, and others, made sense. A successful coup d'état was in full motion.

Danny thought, *What happens to this little place?*

He hadn't been around that long, but he guessed that if you gave Duck Springs a collective political MRI, you would find most people held a core fidelity to America's social compact even if they whined and complained. In the café's men's room, there was a fading sticker that someone had put up years ago. I MAY NOT AGREE WITH YOUR BUMPER STICKER, BUT I WILL DEFEND TO THE DEATH YOUR RIGHT TO STICK IT.

"How do we know all this is happening?" he asked Clover. She was trying to stay calm, but he could tell her alarm bells were going off. He felt the old shivers and fears himself, forebodings from Kashmir or from lawsuits during moments of high drama in litigation.

Clover said, "Izzy loaned us his shortwave radio. And Brian has a ham and CB set up. We've been getting some broadcasts from CBC in Canada, BBC in London, and some offshore pirate radio stations, but even those are slowing down."

I never thought it could actually come to this, Danny thought.

Pops looked up, his normal easy-going face replaced by a fierce look Danny hadn't seen before. "From what we've heard, the NADF is led by Remus Willard and a group of senators and businessmen. They've pulled off a takeover with hundreds of hate groups, paramilitaries, and domestic terrorists. I just assumed they were screwballs and would fade away if we ignored them. I was dead wrong."

Amos added, "BBC named a bunch of them: The Five Percenters, the Oath Holders, the Ancient Order of Christian Knights, the United Minutemen, and the Louisiana Lions."

Danny assumed a lot of those people were flat-earthers and crackpot followers of Pharaoh.

Ted Cingcade added, "Willard and his people say it's all fake news, but BBC and CBC have done interviews with independent reporters who said Willard was behind the plot to kill Chavez and declare martial law."

"That would require major organization," said Ian Jeffers, his voice flat, almost clinical. "I wonder where Remus got all the money and military expertise?"

Everyone was pouring out opinions, purported facts, and speculations. None of it was reliable.

Alberto Hernandez: "Willard said the long-awaited day for American liberation has arrived. Law and order will soon be restored."

Vern Craft said, "I heard pitched battles were underway between generals led by Eugene Brody and those who are still loyal to the existing United States. What the NADF hasn't captured, loyal armed forces are either securing or destroying so those coup fuckers can't get them."

Thelma whispered to him, "Vernon, please don't use that language. There are kids in here."

Vern blushed.

While he was on the road delivering freight, Brian said he heard that newspaper reporters had disappeared into prisons or death camps.

Mo Ersbeck came in from the bakery. So did Vern's buddy Thomas Quinn in a wheelchair with his two Labrador service dogs, one black, the other white, respectively named Rosa Parks and Ladybird Johnson. More little kids ran loose while their moms and dads clustered by the radio. Peter Ashkin, the buttoned-down lawyer who was on the town council, came in. He was wearing jeans and a hooded sweatshirt. With his hood up, he looked like he was off to rob a liquor store.

The town was congregating, the mood somber.

Then, Harlan Morgan walked in. He joined the back of the scrum around the radio.

"Clover, I'm going to check on the people I brought to Cynthia's. They were pretty banged up. After that, I'm going back to Indian Creek."

"Come back quick. You may not be able to stay at Indian Creek much longer if the NADF is really taking over."

"Why would they bother with Indian Creek or Duck Springs?"

"Because that's what people like them do," she said, her steadiness restored.

When he got to the clinic, Cynthia had wrapped Masaji's arm, which was badly bruised but not broken, and she had put disinfectant, ointment, and bandages on their other injuries. Danny told her he was going back to his cabin.

"I'll find places for them," she assured him. "They're odd people, but gentle and polite."

Then Alyssaranda looked at Danny. She choked up. "Mr. Goodman, thank you for helping us but can I ask you for another favor if you are able? Would you or someone go up to Superstition Pass and see if anyone from the Parliament is left and try to help them?"

"No promises, but I'll see what I can do."

On the way back to Indian Creek, he thought about the implications of a takeover, but his monkey mind was jumping around making lists of ideas. He thought of Clover. He thought about supplies and ammunition. He thought about coffee and peanut butter pie, Josh and Sharon in Seattle, and the idiots that stopped them in Crockett City.

And he remembered something he once read, maybe from one of the existentialists. The world never leaves you alone. It sends out feelers to find you and bring troubles, usually, just when you were feeling a little sunshine on your face.

31

BACK AT HIS CABIN, HE BRUSHED SNOW OFF THE PORCH, LIT THE STOVE, AND PUT SOME SEEDS OUT FOR STUMPY. The temperature was dropping. He fried some little sausages, put them into ramen, sprinkled some chili flakes, and pulled out his topo maps to find Superstition Pass.

After a quick boil, the food was ready. Then, his thoughts careened off in another direction. He recalled Joseph Campbell, an erudite man who searched the world's cultures for patterns similar in their legends and wrote about one he called a monomyth.

According to Campbell, somewhere, deep in our common humanity, sits "The Hero's Journey" in which ordinary people are suddenly called to adventure and away from their normal existence. They descend into strange realms, confront monsters, and either die or are transformed. "Where you stumble," said Campbell, "there sits your treasure."

Danny didn't think he was on that kind of odyssey, but something was different now. It had to do with Clover. *Maybe she is my treasure.*

The next morning, he packed some gear, stuffed food into a cooler, loaded his three weapons, and headed to town. On Duck

Road, he found Ian Jeffers, the United States Forest Service ranger. Ian was well-built with sandy hair, nondescript except for a thick handlebar mustache and an evolving pot belly which Danny reckoned came from excessive deskwork.

Ian was ex-military too. Before the Forest Service, he was with NATO in Europe. He didn't say much about it and Danny didn't pry.

Danny had heard that Ian and his wife had a daughter in college on the East Coast and that another child died very young. Some kind of heart defect. If local gossip was true, Ian's wife had never gotten over their child's death. She became a recluse. Ian did all the shopping and housework when he wasn't chasing raccoons out of government garbage cans.

Danny told Ian what he was about to do, and Ian gave Danny better directions, a more up-to-date topo map, and pointers to where he thought Superstition Pass might be, though he had never been there. He thought the road had been bladed but said it might still be rutted, potholed, or snow packed.

Danny asked him where he could borrow a four-wheel drive and get more ammunition.

"Take mine," Ian said. "I don't think the Forest Service will give a shit, assuming they still exist."

"Can I borrow a watch too? I left mine in Seattle."

Ian pulled his off and handed Danny the keys to his Nissan Pathfinder. Danny gave him the keys to the Ghia and drove off. He liked Jeffers.

Then he went looking for Alyssaranda and Masaji. Cynthia said they had a place to stay but were currently at the café. When he got there, it seemed as if all of Duck Springs were still glued to the CB radio even though there was no additional news.

Masaji was talking with Squints and Yoko but gave him better details on what had happened. He said there were about twenty-five NADF people who roared in on jeeps and ATVs.

They demanded the Owls turn over their weapons and sign loyalty pledges.

Shane, their leader, explained that they didn't have weapons and didn't need new identity cards since they knew who they were. That's when beatings started. When other Parliamentarians rushed in to help Shane, the NADF beat them too, and then proceeded to burn the huts.

Masaji said, "Want me to come with you?"

He thought, *I don't need a poet for this.* Danny told him to stay and heal up.

When he told Clover where he was going and asked for a thermos of coffee, she wanted to come too. He didn't give her a reason but told her no. She asked him to step outside for a minute.

"I know this could be dangerous, but I can help. I'm not a little girl and I can make my way through these mountains with the best of them, maybe better than you, and shoot more accurately than most of the men and boys around here."

Danny stared at her. She was an enigma, strong as ironwood, soft as a puppy growing into its feet, and even more endearing. He couldn't stand the thought of her in harm's way.

"Clover, I want to get in and get out fast. It's a scouting mission, which goes better alone. Trust me on this."

"When you get back, I want you to move to Duck Springs," she said.

"Where would I stay?"

"My place, with me. I love you."

Danny's heart did a somersault. She saw it. He loved her and wanted to tell her that and a thousand other things, but words wouldn't come.

32

DANNY COULD FEEL A GROWING UNDERTOW, A RIPTIDE PULLING HIMSELF AND EVERYONE ELSE AWAY FROM THE SAFETY OF SHORE AND INTO A CONFRONTATION WITH THE WORLD OUTSIDE. The NADF had taken a page from Germany's WWII strategy of Blitzkrieg. The Nazi attack was built on three tactics: a focus on your enemy's weakest point; the use of modern technologies like dive bombers and fast tanks; and overwhelming speed and force.

Fanatic troops moved like lightning, took Poland in a month, blew through Holland in four days, promised to leave Czechoslovakia alone, and then conquered it in days.

Maybe Duck Springs was headed into something like that. The NADF takeover seemed to be succeeding because of a weak and dysfunctional government, public indifference, and the mesmeric influence of social media. America was a vacuum: a sprawling emptiness that the crazies were filling with paramilitaries. The beguiling ideas of Willard and the attention-demanding technologies of Pharaoh were hypnotic.

A writer, Camus said, should at least be an outspoken witness if not an actual foot soldier reaching for liberation. Maybe that was the job for Izzy the printer and scribblers like himself. Danny knew he was not the thinker or storyteller Camus was. But he was armed with lessons from soldiering, court brawls, and his study of Camus's inner turmoil in Algeria and Paris.

33

HE FOLLOWED IAN'S GENERAL DIRECTIONS TO WHERE HE THOUGHT SUPERSTITION PASS WOULD BE AND ENJOYED DRIVING THE PATHFINDER. Black ice had melted in the midday sun. As the Nissan's tires hummed on the pavement, Danny started thinking about moving to town with Clover. It scared him.

In law school, he had a classmate named Stanley Krebbs who graduated and decided he wanted nothing to do with the law. He wanted nothing to do with most people, cities, and organizations. He met a nice lady in San Francisco named Ivy who wore long gypsy skirts, sported a buckskin jacket with fringes, and worshipped the moon.

They got married, eschewed careers, and decided to live off the grid where they would have a greener, cleaner life. They moved out to the woods and became vegans, built a yurt next to a stream, practiced tantric yoga for hours, then tended their gardens and beehives. They both did odd jobs in a nearby town to earn what little money they needed, but their goal was to get as close to "zero" as possible: zero money; zero energy; zero pollution; zero footprint; and zero conflicts with others.

They were happy enough their first two years. Then Ivy got pregnant, which they both celebrated, but everything changed when Luna was born. Soon enough, Ivy got tired of not having formula and baby food handy, and Stanley wearied of washing diapers in a bucket.

One day, Krebbs bought a used washing machine, parked it in the open under the nearest electric pole half a mile away, shinnied up, and poached electricity from the local utility. That was the start. Soon enough, they wanted a refrigerator, a pickup truck, toys, a preschool for Luna, and a chance to take in a movie and eat out.

Finally, they just moved to town and settled into what Zorba the Greek called "The Full Catastrophe"—paying jobs, a house, mortgage, kids, pets. Danny was afraid that might be his destiny and wasn't 100 percent sure it fit.

He liked relying on himself at Indian Creek without massive obligations and entanglements. He was into cooking what he wanted to eat, taking hikes and naps, catching a few fish, and reading and writing a lot. He also liked going to town on his own terms, mostly to see Clover even though he didn't really know where that was leading.

When he hit gravel, he slowed the Nissan and drove as quietly as he could. He pulled off the fire road about a mile from where he thought the Owls' camp was and studied the topo map Ian had given him. Then he set off with a water bottle, knife, binoculars, his pistol, the 30.06, and some extra clips.

He bushwhacked off the road, stopping often to listen. Finally he emerged at the top of what he was sure was the east side of Superstition Pass. He scanned the area with his binoculars. Below him he could see the rubble of handmade buildings.

He crept down slowly, pausing, watching, and scrutinizing. When he was sure no one was around, he walked in.

A yurt and small cabin had been partially burned. Inside a dome he found a dead woman and a teenager. They were both shot in the back of the head. Just outside the dome, he found two more men who had been savagely beaten to death. He assumed they were Shane and Cloud Watcher but wasn't sure. Some parts of their faces and bodies were missing where animals had been eating them.

He looked around and stirred through the debris. Clothes and cooking pots had been dragged out of the Parliament's structures. Broken picture frames, tools, bottles, and pieces of books littered the ground. He found a note that an Owl must have intended to hang on a tree or leave on someone's porch. It was especially ironic:

> This is the place I will rest. I know the best place to retreat because breezes blow through the pines and the sound is more beautiful the closer you come to the source. All the while, you are reading old texts to forget the way you came or where you are going. Me? All I know is now. I've given up everything. If you do the same, luck and blessings will find you.

He put the note in his pocket.

Next, he found NADF debris: discarded food pouches; plastic water bottles; a red scarf and a beret with NADF stenciled on it. He didn't have a camera but he wrote in a pocket notebook. With a shovel he found, he did his best to bury the bodies in the hard ground. Then he made his way to the Nissan, and drove back to Duck Springs, by way of a short side trip to his Indian Creek cabin to wash and pack some belongings to take to Clover's house.

On 983 he picked up a faint skunk smell. He turned on the Nissan's radio and buttoned his way across the dial but all he got was static. Submerged memories of Srinagar came back, along with bits and pieces of his recurring nightmare.

34

IN DUCK SPRINGS, HE RETURNED IAN'S PATHFINDER AND RETRIEVED HIS GHIA.

"How was the road?" Ian asked.

"Passable."

"Did you find those people?"

Danny told him the encampment was abandoned and people had been killed.

"Jesus . . ."

"I owe you," he told Ian.

"These are mean days. I think we're in for worse."

"Same here," said Danny. "We may be in for a serious storm. I know you are ex-military like me. Combat?"

"I saw more than enough. That's why I prefer squirrels and woodpeckers."

They talked about their war experiences, neither of them bragging, just exchanging data. Danny sensed Ian's strength, skill, and leadership. He was smart, and tough.

Next, he found Cynthia, who told him Masaji and Alyssa-randa had found a place to stay on Fern Street. He drove over and told them what he had seen and gave them the note he had picked up. Masaji was stone-faced. Alyssaranda cried and asked where he thought the others were.

"There are a couple possibilities," he said. "They may have fled and are hiding out. The weather is turning cold, so maybe they found shelter and food. It could also be they were taken away by the NADF and conscripted. Or they may be dead."

Alyssaranda gasped.

"I'm sorry for all this. I will say though, I think things may get worse, so you need to heal and be brave."

"I know you were a military man once," said Masaji, "but the Parliament of Owls was made of writers and artists and people looking for new ways to live peacefully. I suppose that's an old dream. I'm not entirely ready to abandon it. The world is a hard place. Good people suffer and bad people seem to prosper, which makes it hard to find any kind of serenity, but that's the quest."

Danny shook his hand and looked him in the eye. There was more to him than first impressions.

"I wish the rest of the world felt the way you do, and I hope you and your friends hold onto your vision. Rest and heal."

Next, he drove over to the Hernandez house. He needed to let the mayor know what he had found.

Alberto was inside building bookshelves. There were boards and sawdust on the floor. He welcomed Danny and Heather, his wife, greeted him warmly and asked if he would like hot tea. He gratefully accepted.

"What can I do for you Danny?"

Alberto's smile evaporated when Danny reported his journey. Then Alberto said, "Can you be available later today? I want to get some people in here to hear this."

Danny said he would be staying at Clover's house and would come back in an hour.

"You're a lucky man," said Alberto. "She's special."

35

LIKE THE HERNANDEZES, CLOVER HAD A COMFORTABLE THREE-BEDROOM HOUSE ON AN ACRE OF LAND. There was a massive Douglas fir in front, maybe a hundred feet tall and six feet thick at the base. There was a small shed made of weathered wood attached to the house holding rakes, shovels, and tools.

Like Alberto's, it had thick-cut beams, a stone fireplace, skylights, and a spacious kitchen. There were dozens of special Cloveresque features: paintings, sculptures, colorful rugs, and tasteful wall hangings. Outside the front door there was a spacious porch with rocking chairs, a low table, and a gonging wind chime hanging from a chain.

He left his things stacked in a corner. He needed to make one more trip to Indian Creek to retrieve other items but first he headed to the café.

Pops, Thelma, and Clover were there, but not many customers. Grant Terwilliger was having coffee and a slice of pie at a corner table. Grant saw Danny and waved him over. First, he let Clover know he was back.

"I left my stuff at your place. You sure you want me moving in? It's OK if you changed your mind."

"Of course I haven't," she said, but she wanted to know about his reconnaissance. He mouthed "Later." He actually wanted to hug her and tell her what he found, but he didn't want to set off more alarms. Bad news in small communities moves fast.

Instead, he grabbed a coffee and joined Terwilliger. "What's up Daniel? Hernandez asked me to come to his place at four and said you'd be there too."

"Let's talk about it then. What I will say is it's important."

Grant looked pensive. Danny asked him how the volunteers were doing and if he had enough equipment to fight serious fires. He smiled but the question troubled him.

36

HOWEVER GOOD OR BAD HE WAS AS A FIREFIGHTER, GRANT TERWILLIGER HAD ONE ENDEARING TRAIT THAT COULD HELP EVEN THE GRUMPIEST SOURPUSS IN HARD TIMES: HE MADE PEOPLE GRIN. In fact, Danny thought he would probably laugh in the teeth of a typhoon while his ship was sinking. His last words would be, "Have you heard this one?"

While they were chatting, Thomas Quinn rolled up. Terwilliger said, "Thomas my man, I have a special story for you. You too, Danny, you'd better listen up. You look like you could use a smile."

Quinn's white and black Labradors, Rosa and Ladybird, sat on their haunches, looking at Thomas in his wheelchair. Thomas didn't have much of a sense of humor, but he knew what to expect and braced for it. Grant looked down at the dogs, who stared back and wagged their tails. "This is for you guys too."

Rosa cocked one ear up.

"A guy is driving around Seattle," said Terwilliger, "and he sees a sign in front of a house that says, TALKING DOG FOR SALE - TEN DOLLARS. He rings the bell, and the owner appears and asks if the guy is interested in the dog. The man says yes and goes out to the back porch and sees a small, ordinary-looking mutt sitting there staring straight up at him.

'You talk?' he asks.

'Sure do,' says the mutt.

"After the guy recovers from shock, he says, 'So, what's your story?'

"The pooch looks up and tells him, 'Well, when I was young, I discovered that I had this special gift and could think and talk like humans. I watched a lot of old movies on television and decided I wanted to help the government, so I told the CIA about it, and in no time at all, they had me jetting from country to country, sitting in rooms with world leaders because no one figured a dog was eavesdropping.

"'Turns out, I was their most valuable asset for eight years running, but the jetting around really tired me out so I settled down. I signed up for a part-time job at the airport. I uncovered some smugglers and was awarded a batch of medals. I got married to a fine-looking terrier, had a mess of puppies, and now I'm just retired.'

"The guy is stunned. He goes back in and asks the owner what he wants for the dog.

"'Ten bucks,' the guy says.

"'Ten dollars? Why on Earth are you selling that dog so cheap?'

"'Because he's a liar. He didn't do any of that shit and he's never been out of the yard.'"

Grant grinned. Rosa and Ladybird wagged their tails and Thomas cracked the edge of a smile.

"I have more," said Terwilliger.

Thomas said, "I have clocks to repair."

37

WHEN HE ARRIVED AT ALBERTO'S AT FOUR, HARLAN, PETER, GRANT, BRIAN, TED, CYNTHIA, AND IAN WERE THERE. Heather put out refreshments. Up to then, Danny had only seen Alberto's amiable face. A different Hernandez was in front of him now.

"Thanks for coming. I want to talk in confidence. Danny can report on what he found at Superstition Pass and then we can discuss the implications. Hard as it is, let's not scare the bejesus out of everyone prematurely. People here are a jumpy bunch. Danny, give your report."

Danny replayed the trip starting with Masaji and Alyssaranda, taking them to Cynthia and making his way to Superstition Pass courtesy of Ian's Nissan. He told them exactly what he saw.

There was a long silence, then the questions flowed.

Brian asked, "What do you know about these Owls? Are they crazies or druggies? Is there some reason people would hate them?"

"I don't think so," said Danny. "They seem like peaceful people who just want to be left alone to be with nature."

"Danny is right," said Cynthia. "They're eccentric but they don't mean anyone harm. The two I treated took serious beatings."

Ted Cingcade spoke next. "We know from the sporadic reports we are getting that the country is ripping apart and that asshole Remus Willard and his asshole sidekicks seem to be running things. What do we know about the local NADF?"

Heather winced each time Ted swore.

"Clover and I had an encounter with one of their street patrols in Crockett City not long ago. They're paramilitary." He mentioned their leader's warning that they would get to Duck Springs at some point.

"Why would anyone want this place?" Grant mused out loud. "Nothing much here of big value: no airports, rail lines, or government buildings. We don't have much of anything here beyond a quarry that makes gravel and a few small shops."

"What about locally?" Cingcade asked. "What do we know about the NADF around here?"

Brian Jankowski piped in. "Somewhere I recall hearing about a guy in this area called Matthews."

"I know him," said Cynthia. "He's from Seattle. He and his family used to come here to hunt and fish. I know because he once got a fishhook stuck in his hand which I had to cut out and disinfect. Sniveling guy with a big mouth. Whined a lot."

"You think they are watching us?" Terwilliger asked.

"I would guess yes," said Jankowski, "but we don't know where they are or how many people Matthews might have."

Danny mentioned the drone that hovered over his cabin. Others had also seen a few drones. Alberto said he wanted a little time to think and asked everyone to come back the following day with their best ideas for responding. As people were leaving, he asked Harlan, Peter, Ian, and Danny to stay.

When the others left, he said, "Gentlemen, the four of you were military. I wasn't. I'd like to have your thoughts before we meet tomorrow. Tell me what you think and give me the unvarnished version."

The others looked at Harlan Morgan. Everyone knew he had been a general. "Harlan," Ashkin asked, "what's your thinking?"

Morgan had been silent but now he spoke.

"We don't have reliable information to go on, but let's assume the following: first, the country is disintegrating, so whatever happens, we are probably on our own. Nobody will rescue us. Second, we don't understand why anyone would bother with a place like ours. We are out of the way, all civilians, and wouldn't appear to have any strategic value."

"Third, you will need to make a choice, Mr. Mayor. You probably need to alert people so they can make whatever personal choices they want, which could include staying here or heading out. We also need to avoid creating fear and panic."

Hernandez then said, "Peter, Ian, and Danny, what do you think?"

"I don't have a view yet," said Danny. "I'm too new to Duck Springs." He had heard you had to be at least a third-generation resident to be considered a "local."

"I'd still like to hear what you think."

"My only comment is what the NADF did at Superstition Pass was unnecessarily vicious. These were innocent people—blameless and inoffensive. I suspect none of the raiders were professionals. Or if they were, they've gone rogue."

"Thanks. Peter?"

Ashkin had been a captain in the Navy's Judge Advocate General's Corps, a legal beagle, but he had also been deployed on a carrier in the South China Sea that came under fire. He had a little experience operating in combat conditions.

He stroked his neatly trimmed beard then said, "General Morgan is right, but I disagree on one point, and that's our possible strategic value. Down the road there's an old training center that was used by the Army and National Guard years ago. It's the Bradford Thaddeus Roman United States Army Military Training Facility, called Bradford for short. I think it's abandoned."

Alberto asked, "What's there?"

Ashkin paused. He had a lawyerly way about him, competent but a bit scholastic. "Bradford, south of here, was used to train for high-desert warfare. The facility was downsized and I'm guessing abandoned, but if the NADF thinks it has weapons and equipment, they might want them. To get there, they have to come through Duck Springs, which wouldn't be hard. And depending on how many people Herman Matthews has and how well armed they are, I can see them doing just that."

"You're right," said Morgan. "We should go have a peek."

Alberto looked at Harlan. "I'll get us back together soon, but meanwhile, would you huddle and give me any further recommendations?"

"I'll do that, Alberto," said Harlan. "Danny, would you, Ian, and Peter meet with me tomorrow morning to think this through?"

They all agreed.

38

IAN, PETER, AND DANNY GATHERED WITH HARLAN THE NEXT MORNING TO PREPARE A MISSION TO THE OLD TRAINING FACILITY. Harlan said, "To get to Bradford, they need to come through here, but I'd like to get there first and see whatever supplies and weapons they have, if any."

Ian chimed in, "Precisely what I was thinking, sir."

"I keep trying to tell all of you. Stop with the 'sir' stuff. I no longer have a commission."

Harlan paused.

"OK, here's my thinking. In Afghanistan," he continued, "when we were winning skirmishes but losing battles, one of my colleagues reminded everyone that amateurs talk strategy but professionals talk tactics. So as quick as we can, let's take a bunch of us down the road, get through the gate, and see what's there. Ian, would you organize that? We need our team dressed in fatigues or camo hunting garb in case someone is still there. We also need pickups, panel vans, and maybe a flatbed."

Ian said, "We need Clover or Pops to come along to check out if they have food, and Cynthia to pick through medical supplies."

"All good ideas," said Harlan. "I also suggest we go find Meghan Turnbull. We'll want her."

"Who is Meghan Turnbull?" asked Ian, looking at Danny.

Danny shrugged. "Never heard of her."

Harlan explained: "Lives here too. She was a gunner on top of a Stryker. Her nickname was the 'Meghanator.' She could shoot, drive, fix vehicles, and pull balky troops out of the hold. She's married to Samantha Hardy. Sam was an MP. Both of them could come in handy."

When Danny met the Meghanator, she was with Samantha. They were not what he expected. Danny introduced himself.

Samantha was taller by a few inches with long blonde hair and skin that seemed translucent. She was beautiful. So was Meghan who was muscular, stocky, and dark. Her auburn hair framed green eyes that bored straight through him and seemed to say, "I'm sizing you up, buster. I want to know what you're made of before I waste my time."

39

OVER DINNER, DANNY TOLD CLOVER WHAT HE HAD SEEN AT SUPERSTITION PASS, HAD HEARD AT THE MEETING, AND WHAT PLANS WERE HATCHING BUT SAID SHE NEEDED TO KEEP EVERYTHING TO HERSELF. She agreed. They talked about the hard choices residents might face.

In addition to her incredible beauty and amazing intelligence, Clover also was an extraordinary cook. She had an Italian stew, freshly baked bread, and some carrot concoction that was delicious.

"Any of your peanut butter pie around?"

She put on her mischievous face. "Not tonight, but if you want dessert, I'll be here."

He told Clover he had a few good dishes of his own in *Goodman's Secret Book of Stuff to Cook,* even though he didn't have all the right ingredients.

"Not just noodles topped with mice?"

"No. I can do other one-pot glops, but at the right time and in the right company, I can slow-cook a turkey, grill kebabs, make a standing rib roast, and put together a few Kashmiri curries. I tend to live primitive on my own. Lately, it's been Spam and ramen."

"I'd like to try one of those curries."

"If I can find the ingredients, I'll make one. I got fond of them in Kashmir."

Then it occurred to him that all their meals would soon be leaner. Supplies would run down and people would hoard.

That evening they sorted out their living arrangement. They would sleep together and share the bathroom. He could make use of a small room to store his gear from the cabin and set up a writing table next to the room where Clover painted.

They were comfortable. Wrapped in each other's arms, Danny slept without dreams.

40

FOR THE SECOND MORNING IN A ROW, DANNY MET HARLAN MORGAN FOR COFFEE. Jeffers and Ashkin were coming soon but the two of them were early. In fact, they were the first people at the café.

"Morning, Harlan."

"Morning, Danny. Ready to talk shop?"

"Yes, sir."

Thelma brought coffee and asked if they wanted breakfast. They decided to wait for Peter and Ian.

"You can knock off the 'sir' stuff. We're not in the service anymore. Where were you stationed, Danny?"

He gave Harlan the abbreviated version of his military career. Harlan grinned and nodded. Like every jarhead, both experienced Marine Corps training the same way—the climb up what recruits called "Mount Mother Fucker" with a heavy load of gear and weapons, and drill sergeants harassing them all the way.

"Were you an officer?"

"I had the option since I was a college grad but decided to remain an enlisted puke. After San Diego, I went to Pendleton for infantry school and ended up in a squad as an everyday rifleman."

"How did you wind up in South Asia?"

"Some higher up sent us to Pickel Meadows Mountain Warfare Training Center for more instruction and before I knew it, we were packed off to Kashmir. I managed to avoid any write-ups, got promoted, and after several weeks in the hills, accidentally ended up as fire team leader, and occasionally as a platoon leader, but only because others kept getting killed."

"How did you exit?"

"An IED exploded. I got medevaced to San Diego where I healed up and got a medical discharge. That's my military career in a nutshell."

"What actual unit were you in?"

"Part of the time I was attached to an air-ground task group with some of those expeditionary gents."

Harlan said, "I always thought those task forces were overdone—not tactical enough, and too much air support for ground fights."

"Those planes and choppers came in handy when we were in tight spots."

Harlan asked about those, and Danny told him. A fight in the Vale of Kashmir, another near Baglihar Dam on the Chenab River, and then the second battle of Srinagar which was with some Brits and Canadians.

Harlan asked, "And afterward?"

"After I healed up, I got married, went to law school, and joined a firm. Neither marriage nor law quite worked out. There's a longer story there about how I ended up in Duck Springs, but that's for another time. And speaking of longer stories Harlan, when we have time I want to hear how America got stuck in The Sandbox for so many decades."

Then Harlan asked Danny what he thought about yesterday's meeting.

"Truthfully?"

"Tell it like it is. I've always despised wishful thinking and suck-ups who told me what they thought I wanted to hear. When they did that, they monkey-wrenched the gears of hard decisions."

Harlan had little tolerance for hypocrisy and bullshit.

"Harlan, what I saw at Superstition Pass was the work of cruel people. I'm guessing some of them are psychos or high school losers. It was unnecessarily violent and intentional. The Owls couldn't have been a military target or threat. I think they just wanted to spread fear."

"They seem to have any professionals?"

"Hard to tell. They may have some ex-military among them, but I'm guessing most of them are feral locals who are bored and easily recruited because they're looking for kicks."

"I suppose we'll find out soon enough. I have a bad feeling about what's coming."

"Harlan, I don't know how strong or organized they are, but if the NADF has any force and decides to come through here, we'll be doormats. They are going to wipe their feet on us unless we run or organize for a fight, which we aren't set up for. This is a nice little town. It might be better if we evacuate."

"We could get flattened even if we leave," said Morgan.

"Right. Eight-hundred people, maybe more from outlying communities, and mostly civilians, all on the run? If the NADF troops are organized, they would catch us."

Ashkin walked in, went to the counter, poured a coffee, and sat down. Jeffers followed a few minutes later.

"Peter, Ian, Danny, let's have some breakfast, then we'll go to my place and talk in private. Breakfast is on me."

Over pancakes and eggs, there was more speculation about what might lie ahead. They talked softly as some of Pops, Thelma's, and Clover's regulars drifted in and they started getting curious looks. Most people in Duck Springs already knew there had been a long meeting at Alberto's house two days before and had their beaks pressed to the glass, sniffing around as to what was going on and ready to gossip.

Mayor Hernandez would need to tell them. Soon.

41

WHEN EVERYONE ARRIVED AT ALBERTO'S HOUSE, HERNANDEZ ASKED THEM TO LISTEN CAREFULLY.

"We have difficult choices. Yesterday, after everyone left, I asked Harlan and a few of our friends with military experience to outline some options. Most of you don't know him that well so let me do a proper introduction."

"Harlan Morgan was a decorated Marine Corp major general who led actions in Afghanistan and what is now Kurdistan and what was then Syria and Turkey."

Harlan was embarrassed.

"After retirement, he taught tactics at the Marine Corps War College at Quantico. If you haven't seen it for yourself, he is brilliant, humble, and studious. He's written books, one reinterpreting *The Art of War*, the other a takeoff on one of Sun Tzu's chapters called *The Sheathed Sword Strategy,* which is all about winning battles without kinetic fighting. Harlan, tell us what you think."

Harlan stood up and walked over to a corner of the living room where everyone could see and hear him. People leaned in when he started to talk.

"Thanks for those gracious words, Alberto. When people introduce me like that, I always wonder if I'm dead."

Chuckles rippled around.

"All of you heard Danny's report about Superstition Pass. Truth is, we don't really know exactly what we are facing. We just know good people, all civilians, got killed. It could be a pretty disciplined force of NADF soldiers out there, or a bunch of jackals dressed up playing soldier. My guess is a bit of both, but it's just speculation. We have no idea who they are, where they are, and how disciplined and well-armed they are."

He paused, sipped from a glass of water, and continued. "We also don't know much about their supposed leader, Herman Matthews. I learned the hard way not to underestimate amateur zealots. Fanatics may have actual soldiering backgrounds or they may be playacting. Either way, we need to do two things. We need to get to Bradford and see what's there and we need reliable intelligence. Until then, we are guessing."

He waited a beat, then said. "We also have to consider some basic choices, none of which are pleasant and all of which need deciding soon. One choice is just ignoring what's happening, minding our own business, and hoping they won't bother us on their way to somewhere else. Unfortunately, a wish is not a plan.

"A second choice, is we pick up, leave town, and run. A third is to try to negotiate terms and surrender Duck Springs to them if they come. A fourth choice is to prepare for a fight with whatever we can muster. A fifth is to do some combination of all of these."

He turned to Alberto. "Mr. Mayor, I have a few ideas on how each of these scenarios could develop, but until we have better information, they won't help."

"Thanks, Harlan," said Alberto. "Questions?"

Cynthia McDonald was wearing clean burgundy scrubs. She raised her hand. "General, we've got retirees here and some are frail and vulnerable. A few have cancer or kidney conditions and need infusions. We also have kids, some who are deaf or blind. What's best for them?"

"I can't answer that," said Harlan. "At the moment we are just starting to see the threat, but frankly, without more information, it's hard to know what the best course is for anyone."

Ted Cingcade asked, "Harlan, what odds would we have in a fight? I mean realistically."

"Again, we need intel. The NADF could be a real army or a bunch of mosquitos and ticks. We can make better estimates if we get a fix on who is out there. I need to be clear: Fighting is not an automatic recommendation. Even though I'm a military man, I hate fighting. I would rather have a beer and write books criticizing other people's battles."

Then Brian Jankowski asked, "If we evacuate, you have thoughts on where we would go and how we would get there?"

"I can't answer the first question, but as to the second, we would need your semis and every other car, truck, tractor, bicycle, and motorcycle that runs."

"You'll have mine if you need them. I can't use them anymore," said Jankowski. "Too dangerous for rigs and drivers."

Alberto stood up. "Harlan, thank you. To summarize, we have four things to do. First, we have to see what's at the abandoned base. Second, we need more information on what we are facing. Third, we have to let people in Duck Springs know what's going on without creating a stampede and fourth, we need to see what skills we have here in town. If you work on the first two Harlan, I'll get three and four done."

42

HARLAN WAS ON DANNY'S MIND. Watching him at Alberto's house, he studied the way he calmed people but also confronted hard realities. It brought to mind books and manuals on leadership. Danny thought you could study leadership ad nauseum and still never get to the core of it or predict who would be good, bad, or mediocre in the middle of a human storm.

Churchill's strength was fervor and passion. He once told others that leadership is just moving from failure to failure with enthusiasm. Gandhi had a fierce moral fiber developed in South Africa when he was subjected to narrow-minded prejudice. He applied what he learned to achieving India's independence. In the run-up to D-Day in WWII, Eisenhower was a master logistician and negotiator. He came out of supply and saw things in terms of purpose, teamwork, and execution.

Danny saw glimpses of Alberto's power too. Alberto was everyone's cheerful buddy but morphed into a serious mobilizer when moments turned tough and every choice seemed imperfect. He had been good-hearted and casual in the time Danny had known him. Now, he was quietly fierce.

Over the next several days, Harlan and Alberto convened small huddles to discuss particular problems. Without saying it, they were preparing for the worst. They had Ted Cingcade and Brian Jankowski inventory fuel, generators, batteries, and the prospects for finding more of everything. They asked Cynthia to make a list of what first aid and medical equipment she had on hand and whether she knew of any doctors who lived nearby they could recruit. They approached Pops, Thelma, Slim, and Clover to work on food and water and asked Izzy Watts to put together a special *Chronicle.*

Izzy said, "No electricity, no ink, paper, or printing press? No *Chronicle.*"

"Izzy," said Alberto, "go see what Maynard squirreled away in that back room. We need some kind of Paul Revere ride to let people know what is happening. We have to get the word out, and soon."

Harlan started planning the expedition to Bradford, and Ian Jeffers and Danny were tasked with developing spy missions to assess the NADF's strengths and weaknesses.

43

THE NEXT EVENING CLOVER AND DANNY WENT TO KENNY AND YOKO'S HOUSE FOR DINNER. The Miyamotos invited two other people—Daisy Yoshimoto, Yoko's sister who had come to stay in Duck Springs, and Masaji Hiraoka. The Miyamoto house was another Northwest affair, a log box but with a Japanese interior. One of Clover's larger colorful paintings hung in the living room—a deep, magenta-colored flower in full bloom with drops of dew rolling down the petals and a soft sunrise in the background. Clover said it was a bearded iris.

On either side of the painting were two vertical scrolls with calligraphy and small red stamps in the corners. The scrolls were simple and free of other adornments. Later, in a quiet moment, Masaji explained them as examples of *Wabi-Sabi*, a Japanese outlook built on being comfortable with flaws, uncertainty, and paradox.

He said tolerance of contradictions was part of life's inscrutability. Danny liked that. Camus would have liked that. Thoreau would have, too, if he wasn't too busy scolding everyone else.

Masaji recited another Japanese proverb, *Shikata ga nai.* "It cannot be helped." That is where the true strength of perpetual imperfection lives, he said.

Yoko was wearing a kimono. Squints had on a *yukata*. They showed everyone around their property with its tidy fields of fruit trees and berry bushes. Inside their long, impeccably organized work shed were fruit presses, cooking pots, and bottling machines. Tools were mounted on pegboards. A tall window looked out on two cherry trees.

The Miyamotos also had a small outbuilding near the house with a water line running into it and wooden floor slats. It had an ofuro, a Japanese hot tub, which Kenny invited them to use before dinner. It was small, made for one person at a time.

Separately, one by one, they stripped off their clothes and scrubbed down with bristle brushes and rough washcloths at a cold-water faucet before slowly entering the scalding water. As Danny boiled himself, every muscle in his body relaxed, and his perpetual monkey mind slowed.

The dinner was ridiculously perfect: smoked trout with veggies lightly soaked in soy and sugar, but somehow still crisp; rice, tea, and small cookies that Yoko baked. There was background flute music. Daisy and Masaji sat next to each other, nibbling at the tasty food and talking quietly. She poured his tea. Danny loved the veggies.

After dinner, Masaji asked Danny if they could talk privately.

Masaji was tall, broad-shouldered, thickly muscled, and extremely economical in his movements. He said he grew up in a military family and had spoken with Morgan and learned about the meetings and reconnaissance missions they needed. He wanted to come along if Danny was involved.

Danny started to object but Masaji stopped him cold.

"Danny, you don't know me. You assume I'm a bookworm making poems to hang in bottles. Before I came here, I was a professor, and before that, a long way back, I was in the Army and part of a Long-Range Reconnaissance Patrol."

"You were a scout?"

"Yes. I have other training too," Masaji said. "To be clear, I detest violence. I had hoped to never again engage in fighting, but I'm not a pacifist. I once met a Zen monk who lived near the ocean in Hawai'i and drew pictures and wrote poems. He had an ink drawing with calligraphy that said, IF THE FISH TURN SOUTH, GO SOUTH."

"My fish have gone south. I'm pretty good with knives and small arms, and I know how to slip around in the woods. I want to join Harlan, you, and the others and deal with whatever is coming."

"It's up to Harlan."

Masaji laughed. "He's already agreed."

Later, most took one more turn in the ofuro and drank too much of Squints's special-occasion sake. Eventually, Danny and Clover headed home and Masaji and Daisy left together.

44

LOVE'S INTENSITY IS NEVER CONSTANT. It runs hot and passionate some days, cools down on others, then suddenly roars back before drifting away on other errands. But the pure joy of it is falling head over heels in love with the same person repeatedly as you gain comfort with their habits of the heart, the textures of their personas, and the contours of each other's bodies. Love, someone said, is an inside job.

That afternoon, Clover and Danny were in a gilded moment. They were famished for touch. When Danny pulled her to him, she hugged him back with fierceness, as if their time on Earth might be short. In his arms, her body rose, their mouths and bodies clenched, and they slowly submitted to the pull of stars and fused into a nova.

Later, in the twilight, they walked around town holding hands. They greeted others with smiles. No one seemed surprised.

Except Danny.

45

THE NEXT DAY ON HIS WAY TO MEET IZZY, HE BUMPED INTO TINY PORTER, WHO STOPPED HIM IN THE STREET AND STARTED CHATTERING AWAY.

"Morning, Danny. Hear about the coyote?"

"What coyote?"

"Mabel Wolff has a border collie named Pancake that had five puppies. The dogs were out playing in the sun. Just as Mabel was running her flag up the pole, a coyote raced in and grabbed one of the pups!"

"Thanks for letting me know, Tiny."

"Danny, you ever notice how dog noses are always wet and ours aren't? Funny thing about that, don't you think? They can sniff stuff miles away and analyze smells fifty times better than us."

"Tiny, thanks for that info. I like dogs, but I need to go meet Izzy."

"Oops, sorry about that." He gave Goodman a toothy grin and said, "I'll catch you later!"

Maynard Porter's print shop and junk room was attached to his house. The multilith press was full of cobwebs, roaches, and a desiccated rat carcass. The sheet feeder was broken and the ink containers were empty. Even if they had good electricity, that option wouldn't work.

Izzy said Maynard would have spanked Danny for calling his stuff junk. He believed his items were "Heritage Machinery."

Scouting around the shop they found an old platen press, an aging IBM Selectric typewriter that wouldn't work without juice, a hand-cranked duplicating mimeograph, some old-time telephones, an ancient clothes iron that may have weighed twelve pounds, and a couple of old Underwood and Olivetti typewriters. The Underwoods and Olivettis were operational and the mimeograph might work if they could find ink and paper, which they did. There was enough for one run if Iz was careful.

Izzy said, "I'll get this old gizmo ready. You like to write stuff so you draft a one-pager. We need to run off a thousand copies if we can."

"How do we deliver them?" He noticed that Izzy's California-flavored lingo of "babes, dudes, and good vibrations" had been abandoned . . . for the moment.

"I can get help from Gloria, Penelope, maybe some of the others who just came to town, plus a few who have cars or motorcycles. We won't be able to deliver to the farthest outlying places, but we should be able to get to everyone in a fifteen-mile radius. We can reach people around here and then rely on their word of mouth."

Even though Izzy sometimes talked like an idiot, he was smart and had spunk.

Danny started drafting what might be the final issue of the *Duck Springs Chronicle*. It would be a letter from Alberto in handbill form under the *Chronicle* masthead.

> Dear Friends, Families, and Citizens:
>
> Many of you know that Norma Chavez, our duly elected president, has been assassinated and attempts are being made to overthrow the govern-

ment of the United States. Our country is in the hands of renegade conspirators led by Remus P. Willard. We have also had incidents of violence close to Duck Springs in which a group that calls itself the New American Defense Force has killed nearby citizens.

We don't know much about the NADF and plan to have more information soon. In the meantime, I have asked council members Ashkin and Hart, our neighbor and friend, General Harlan Morgan, and others to help assess the situation and organize for several possibilities. The names of the Duck Springs citizens working on preparations are listed on the back.

We will be reaching out to meet with you and your neighbors in your homes and hope you will quickly host small gatherings where one or two of us can come and give you more information. We will also be calling a meeting soon to see who else in town can pitch in for the work ahead.

In the meantime, I ask you to do the following: keep calm; don't waste food, water, or energy; and help alert others without creating panic.

Wishing all of us God Speed,

Alberto Hernandez
Mayor of Duck Springs

After Izzy added a few edits, Danny dropped it off at Alberto's house and headed back to Clover's.

After Izzy and his fleet delivered the handbills, some people left town and Harlan launched the convoy to Bradford.

46

ON MAY 31, 1918, A SECOND LIEUTENANT NAMED BRADFORD THADDEUS ROMAN FROM KEOKUK, IOWA HAPPENED TO LEAD A PLATOON OF SOLDIERS AGAINST ADVANCING GERMAN TROOPS AT CHÂTEAU-THIERRY. Roman's actions, blunted a major spearhead of the Kaiser's army.

The German spring offensive was aimed directly at Bradford's position. Their bombardment alone rattled the Americans, most of whom were green. Roman made a decision to retreat before the Germans got to them but, in the process, was confronted by another German unit coming up behind them.

Seeing the Americans, the Germans opened fire. Roman's unit fired back, and Roman raised his weapon just as he stumbled on some debris. As he fell, he caught a round from a German rifle in his left shoulder and, in the process, saved the sergeant behind him from what would have been fatal.

Roman got up off the ground and charged. It was stupid, suicidal, and unexpected, but Roman's assault against a far bigger force ended with the capture of two companies of enemy soldiers. Roman won a Medal of Honor and went on to a distinguished military career. When someone later asked him how he won the nation's highest military award he said, "I tripped."

The Bradford T. Roman base was established in 1939. Its original purpose was to stage small exercises for all combat arms. At its height after WWII, armor, infantry, airborne and artillery units used the facility for exercises. As needs changed, it specialized and became a training area for a Stryker Brigade that could practice maneuvers in high-desert, rolling terrain. Though the base was a small gem, the facility was downsized. Even abandoned, it had usable buildings and equipment, and even barbed wire fences with razor coils on some stretches.

The little convoy from Duck Springs drove up to a weathered sign that read: THE BRADFORD THADDEUS ROMAN UNITED STATES ARMY MILITARY TRAINING FACILITY. RESTRICTED AREA. NO UNAUTHORIZED ENTRY.

Harlan was in the lead, wearing fatigues and aviator sunglasses and looking top brass. Ian was next to him and Danny was in the back seat with Brian Jankowski and Vern Craft. Meghan, Clover, Pops, and others were behind in pickups and vans. No one was in sight when they arrived. Morgan got out, walked over to the gate, picked up a phone and pressed a button. It rang twice before a voice came over the tinny speaker.

"Corporal Louis Bennis," the voice said. "This is a restricted area. How can I help you?"

"Corporal, this is General Harlan Morgan, First Battalion, Ninth Marines. Put me through to your commanding officer."

"Captain Tucker Jones is in command, sir. I'll request he come down."

"Good. Now get out here, open the gate, and let us in. It's starting to rain. Tell Captain Jones we're here to relieve you and General Harlan Morgan needs to meet with him."

"Sir, yes sir."

Five minutes later, Captain Tucker P. Jones who hailed from Chicago let them in and he, Corporal Bennis, Harlan, Ian, Vern, and the others headed into a small office to talk before they fanned out to scope the base. Jones was a lanky, sandy-haired man who looked to be in his late thirties. He had piercing blue eyes under bushy eyebrows. The uniform that might once have been starched and crisp was rumpled, but he stood to attention and offered a smart salute.

What they learned was this. The training facility had been downsized long before Willard's coup and had been on a list of potential base closures for two decades. Most of the small detachment of remaining men and women who were stationed there abandoned the facility when word came that Washington DC had fallen. Jones, Bennis, and a dozen others stayed.

In its best days, regular Army and National Guard units and a few special ops teams used the facility for forest and high-desert training. It was roughly 75,000 acres; not that big as training areas went, but useful in its time.

There were flat areas for live fire exercises, covered areas for troops and vehicles, observation bunkers, a short runway and chopper pad, concrete buildings with offices and classrooms, a mess hall, a maintenance building, several dormitories, a sickbay, an armory, and a small airstrip. There were a few vehicles sitting near a fuel depot, including some Strykers.

They explained what was happening in Duck Springs and the possible impending fight with the NADF. After a discussion, Captain Jones said, "Nobody has been around here for months, sir, and we've had no contact with any superiors. Take whatever you need, on one condition."

Harlan arched an eyebrow. "What's that?"

"We help you load up, burn the rest, and go back with you."

Vern turned to Ian, and said, "I like these guys!"

Clover, Cynthia, Meghan, Vern, and others fanned out on scrounging missions. In addition to Captain Jones's left-behind soldiers whom they dubbed "The Lost Battalion," they found food, gas, medical supplies, a fine assortment of small arms, drones, including some interceptor drones, and all the ammunition they could carry.

Meghan was ecstatic, bouncing up and down on the balls of her feet, her eyes twitching with excitement. She had found a half-dozen eight-wheeled Strykers, two with 105mm canons, others with .50 caliber machine guns. They were in working order and were stocked with ammo. She also found several transport trucks, some mobile fuel pods, and five Humvees.

Clover and Cynthia found food and medical supplies, and Ian found maps. They were about to start loading everything they would haul back when Harlan stopped them. While they had been scouting the base, he had been in a long huddle with Captain Jones. Harlan turned and put his hands up as if he was stopping traffic. "Hold up," he said.

The plan now took a completely unexpected U-turn. Instead of trying to fortify and arm Duck Springs, Harlan said, let's bring the whole town here, at least those who will come. Captain Jones had agreed but Harlan asked him anyway in front of them.

"Can you put up eight-hundred citizens from town? Only a few have military experience, and even fewer have been in combat."

"General, it would be an honor. With enough hands, we can organize bulwarks, sentries, and outposts. And speaking personally, I wouldn't mind giving the NADF a few licks when they show up."

Danny, Ian, and the others were stunned.

47

BACK IN DUCK SPRINGS, ALBERTO AND HARLAN CALLED THE LEADERSHIP GROUP BACK TO HIS HOUSE. They were evolving into something like a Jedi Council out of the old *Star Wars* movies. Alberto was Obi Wan Kenobi, Harlan Master Yoda, and everyone else was a talented Jedi warrior ready to help fend off the Empire.

Danny and Harlan met for coffee before the Jedi meeting for their Sandbox talk. Goodman wanted to understand how the United States had gotten so mired in Kashmir. Harlan connected the dots.

Despite the overblown rhetoric of "American Exceptionalism," the United States was more like Pakistan than most people understood. The Indo-Pakistan War in Jammu-Kashmir, he said, was just the latest set of aggressive moves inside Pakistan and the United States. In many ways, the two countries were mirror images of each other.

Both were failing states. Both had massive economic inequalities amplified by homegrown despots cut from the same cloth. Remus Willard and the self-anointed Ifram Mahdi both confidently claimed to be saviors. Both had cult followings, developed propaganda factories, created a mythology of restoring order, rigged elections, and orchestrated the disappearance of rivals.

The Jammu-Kashmir confrontation, said Harlan, was just the latest in a long line of invasions and occupations that sucked the life out of the "United States." The Sandbox was an elongated World War III. The conflict started in Kuwait and Iraq in 1990 by Bush the first, then continued in one form or another through the terms of Clinton, Bush the second, Barack Obama, Donald Trump, Joe Biden, and all the others leading up to President Chavez.

"War is God's way of teaching Americans geography," said Harlan quoting Mark Twain. "Hotter or cooler, our WWIII started small, then spread in waves that gobbled up countries like a giant python. First came Iraq, then Syria, Iran, Turkmenistan, Kurdistan, Azerbaijan, Armenia, and Uzbekistan. And then, more recently, countries in Africa bordering the Sahel: Mali, Burkina Faso, parts of Algeria, and Niger.

"What does it all mean for what we are doing now and what the future holds for the United States?" Danny asked.

Harlan sipped his coffee.

"I think we are a jumbo cargo ship floundering in extremely stormy seas. If we can get past Willard and the NADF, which isn't guaranteed, the country may eventually right itself and return to enduring fundamentals. At the moment, that's a big if."

After an hour, they left for Alberto's house.

48

WHEN THE JEDIS CONVENED, THERE WERE FRESH DEVELOPMENTS. The biggest surprise was two new refugees with several people crowding around them.

"Friends," said Alberto as he opened the meeting, "thanks for all your hard work, which we can discuss in a few minutes. First, for those who don't know them, I need to introduce two special people."

He pointed to a tall, Scandinavian-looking man wearing a dirty gray mechanic's jumpsuit and a blue baseball hat. He was six feet tall, had a square jaw, a scruffy beard, and a head of thick brown hair streaked with gray. Danny reckoned him to be in his sixties. He was Marcus Longborn, Duck Springs' native son, former VP, and now president in exile.

Standing next to him was a distinguished looking Black man named Christopher Knox. Shorter than Longborn, he had white hair, dark skin, and eyes burning with ferocity under a large, furrowed forehead. Knox was known as a powerful orator whose speeches had withered opponents in debates and launched him up the political ladder. Before the coup, he served as Speaker of the House, third in line of succession to the president.

The two of them were accompanied by Longborn's wife, his daughter, and two Secret Service agents. All of them had crossed the Canadian border at night on a back road near Huntingdon, British Columbia.

What they said was stunning. Longborn, Knox, and others were attacked at the same time as the president. Longborn, his voice strained, said Norma Chavez survived but was killed later at Blair House getting ready for a meeting with a delegation from France. Once Chavez and her service detail were gunned down, Blair House was torched.

Knox's wife and two boys were killed when their home in Bethesda was attacked by a dozen drones. Knox never flinched while Longborn described the massacres.

Forces deployed by Willard and Brody simultaneously attacked congressional leaders in their Capitol offices and conference rooms. Bombs had gone off, senators and representatives fled or were shot down, and many government buildings in DC were shattered. Air Force One and Marine One were both destroyed.

Similar fights took place at key defense sites, power plants, the national energy labs at Argonne and Oak Ridge, and a dozen military bases around the country. The Executive Office building, one of the Trump towers, and most of Union Station had been attacked and blown up; Reagan and Dulles Airports were in the hands of Willard's people. Longborn, Knox, and a few others had been secured by a team of loyal Secret Service agents and flown to Canada where they received immediate asylum.

"Even there," continued Longborn, "Willard's people tried to hunt us down. In fact, one of my service agents, a wonderful woman named Patti Gannon, was killed, shot down while she was having breakfast. Prime Minister Maclean has been extraordinarily supportive and I will forever be grateful to him. He sealed Canada's southern borders, provided security, moved us around, sequestered us in rural British Columbia, and helped us covertly get to Duck Springs."

After Longborn finished, Knox spoke, his voice had never lost its deep North Carolina drawl. He spoke slowly and with sadness, sorrow was etched on his face but his words were defiant.

"Thank you for taking us in, Mr. Mayor. These are terrible times for our country and for the loved ones of thousands of people who have already died, including beloved members of my own family. More deaths are inevitable. My spirit grieves, but it isn't broken and never will be. We will set this right so our children and theirs never live under the tyranny we had when we broke away from England. Now, we have to do it again."

Longborn stood up, took back the room, paused before he spoke, and choked back emotion. "Our country as we knew it six months ago no longer exists. The next few months will determine our fate. Chris and I are single-minded. We will resist, with our lives if it comes to that, but we also don't want to set up you fine people in Duck Springs as targets. We know we will keep being hunted. We expect it. We intend to stay here for a few days and then move on and link up with groups fighting in California."

Alberto turned to Longborn and said, "Marcus, this is your home. You and I grew up here. You and Speaker Knox must stay. Forever, if that's your desire. We need you."

"They killed many good people," Longborn said. "Willard's goons struck with amazing speed and coordination, but that would have been the work of Eugene Brody and his subordinates. Personally, I think Remus is an old racist moron and a wing nut but he's probably a pawn for Brody, who seems smarter and more pernicious. Please know that Chris and I are fighters. We are the United States government in exile, and we will reinstitute our rightful democracy. Or die trying."

Questions followed. People were hungry for details driven by both curiosity and fear. They worried for loved ones in other places and fretted about their own safety.

Harlan asked, "How strong is the NADF and what's left of the United States military?"

"Hard to know. Before the coup," said Longborn, "FBI reported there were more than two thousand hate groups in the country, many of them with small militias. The coup couldn't have happened without amazing organization and pre-positioning, especially considering the NADF's ability to neutralize our intelligence, military, and police services."

Knox chimed in. "On your second question, General, there are likely a lot of loyal units left, especially in remote areas. We also think our forces will be rudderless without a civilian or military command structure. And we know from Canadian sources that many of our key assets were destroyed by our own people rather than letting them fall into the hands of the gangsters."

"What does that mean in terms of priorities?" asked Ian.

"We have to establish secure communications in the West," Chris answered, "and then expand it east and south across the country. Once we have that, we can begin to mobilize a coordinated resistance. I have every confidence that will happen, but at a cost. Meanwhile, we need leadership everywhere. The biggest weapon the NADF has is its ability to create paralysis in the face of fear."

Alberto asked, "Can you tell us anything about the NADF here? We know there's a unit near us because they killed people close by, but we have no idea how strong they are."

Longborn said, "I wish I could tell you but we just don't know. If I were to hazard a guess, I would say they have some dug-in groups here. Before all this happened, I saw FBI reports on the paramilitary and survivalist groups in the Northwest. There weren't that many, but the ones I knew of attracted ugly customers. Like Harlan said, I expect they are composed of a lot of dropouts led by a few professionals."

The discussion continued. Each assessment group provided a report. Longborn and Knox listened.

The reports were not promising.

Izzy Watts said the last issue of the *Chronicle* with the letter from Alberto had gone out. Izzy urged everyone to hang onto their copy.

"It's a limited edition, dudes," he said with excitement. "It will be a collector's item."

"If there's anyone around to collect them . . ." somebody muttered.

Pops, Thelma, and Clover said they weren't yet ready to report on food and water and suggested they might call a few people now that Alberto's letter had been published.

"Slim will have a few things at his store," said Clover, "and we have some bulk items at the café, but people will quickly become hoarders and probably won't tell us what they really have. We're interested in the essentials: flour, salt, sugar, cooking oil, cans, and packaged goods."

Ashkin and Craft reckoned half the residents of Duck Springs had a sporting rifle or shotgun. A few people might have some museum-quality Remingtons or Winchesters. Craft, always ex-military, said to the group, "We want to do a better inventory now that Alberto has the town on notice. The bigger problem," he explained, "will be ammunition. We simply don't have much."

Cynthia was gloomy and didn't pull her punches. "Look, there wasn't that much at Bradford. We found a lot of litters, splints, bandages, crutches, and a few boxes of meds but we really don't have enough medical supplies. And we've got no doctors. We can probably recruit a few people who were nurses or med-techs somewhere in their past, but the truth is, we are screwed if we have a massive influx of traumas."

After some back and forth, Harlan stood again and addressed the group.

"The absolute first thing we must do is to get better intel. Let's find out as much as we can about who is out there and what kind of threat they pose. To do that, Ian and Meghan are going scouting in one direction, Danny and Masaji another.

"Most of you may not know it, but before Ian joined the Forest Service and was stationed in Duck Springs, he was an Army Ranger and sniper." Ian blushed. "Meghan was a lieutenant and commanded a Stryker group and Danny fought street-to-street in Kashmir. Masaji served as a United States scout and is very experienced. Once we know more about what we are dealing with, we'll reconvene.

"General," Ian said, "give us a few days since we may need to circle out a distance."

"Do it," said Harlan, "and come back alive."

"Roger that, General."

"And don't call me General. I'm Harlan."

49

LONGBORN AND KNOX WEREN'T THE ONLY NEW ARRIVALS LOOKING FOR SHELTER. Others drifted into town—some from Seattle thinking they could hide out in Duck Springs. People craved safety.

Among the newbies were three malnourished Owls from Superstition Pass, including a man named Paul Chang. The newly arrived Owls had an ecstatic reunion with Alyssaranda Gibson and Masaji Hiraoka. They saw Shane, Cloud Watcher, and one of the women and her teenage son stand up to the thugs and get killed, then bolted. Since then, they had been living in the woods, staying in abandoned hunter cabins, scrounging for whatever food they could find, and eluding NADF patrols.

A tall, handsome Hispanic man also rolled in. His name was Julian Maximo Hernandez, Alberto and Heather's son. He'd made his way to Duck Springs from Eugene, Oregon where he had been finishing medical school.

"Max!" Alberto shouted.

Heather ran toward him for a hug. "I'm so glad, so relieved." It was a jubilant moment in an otherwise dark hour.

A man named Titus Fontaine from Seattle sought Danny out. He was a friend of Danny's brother and handed him a letter. The essence of it: Josh, Sharon, and another couple had made it to Tillamook and were living near Cape Meares on the coast. They were safe.

Eric Abbott showed up with his wife and three children. He introduced Danny to his wife Jane. He had two beautiful young girls, Mindy and Vicki, and a tall older boy named Dexter.

Eric and Danny shook hands warmly and he said, "I decided to make a house call, and I remember you said you might be able to use a dentist up here. How's that root canal? Any problems? I brought my instruments." He showed Danny his torture tools.

Two other desperately needed arrivals were Mohan and Laxmi Das, two young South Indian doctors from Seattle. They were warmly welcomed, especially by Cynthia.

At home over sandwiches, Clover said, "We were able to find everyone homes close to town, but there is one other surprising arrival. Come over to the café after we eat. There's someone you need to see."

"Who?" he asked.

"You'll see." Clover's face was mysterious. He pried but she clammed up.

It was Julie from The Ars coffee shop in Crockett City. She had dyed her hair brown, removed her hardware, and shed her goth clothes. She wasn't how Danny remembered her. She looked small and bedraggled now, like an eight-year-old who just discovered the world can really hurt you.

"How are you Julie?"

She looked away. "Fine," she mumbled.

But she wasn't fine. All the edgy, against-the-grain cockiness that he had admired at The Ars was gone, and she looked like she needed food, a bath, and sleep. Clover raised her eyebrows, signaling Danny not to press the matter.

What he learned later explained things. Clover spent time with Julie at the café, feeding her a bowl of tomato soup and a jumbo toasted cheese sandwich that she couldn't finish. Slowly, gently, in fits and starts, her story came out.

Julie's last name was Roth. She was picked up by an NADF goon squad, raped, beaten, interrogated, and detained with a dozen others at a makeshift prison camp north of Crockett. She was held there for two weeks until she and another girl made a dash for the woods. The other girl was shot in the back. Julie hid under piles of wet brush and behind boulders, then slowly made her way to Duck Springs looking for help.

"She needs time," Clover said, "but she'll recover. Underneath all that big talk in Crockett and the scruffiness and anguish you just saw at the café, she's a tough kid."

"Those monsters will haunt her the rest of her life."

"Most women have stories like that," said Clover. "Not always as harsh as Julie's, but all of us have fended off men who were trying to grope us, or do worse."

"That ever happen to you, getting groped?"

"Only by you," she said with a sly smile, "and that's because I let you. The other morons who tried? I broke their arms."

Her eyes were twinkling.

50

THANKS TO THE FINAL EDITION OF IZZY'S *CHRONICLE* AND A WORD-OF-MOUTH CAMPAIGN, THE CALL WENT OUT FOR ANYONE WITH MILITARY EXPERIENCE TO COME TO A MEETING. Folding chairs and long tables were set up in the basketball court at the community center and Slim, Thelma, and Mo provided a meager selection of cookies and water at a back table. Eighty men and women arrived—more than expected.

It was an odd assembly—only twenty or thirty of those who showed up had actual combat experience. A few were soldiers who had been in one or another of the older Sandbox wars. Some were younger and might have been in Kashmir. Others had some kind of training—cooks, supply managers, administrators, logisticians. There were a few who took ROTC in high school or college and a couple who just liked to go to meetings.

Danny was at the door directing people to tables. When Amos Arnold walked in and Danny asked if he had served, he said, "Kind of. I grew up in the projects in Chicago. We had our own wars and little armies. We wore colors and had zip guns and a few serious weapons. I know how to scrap on the street if I have to."

Then, Thomas Quinn and his dogs, Rosa Parks and Ladybird Johnson, trundled in. The dogs were panting and sniffing, saliva drooling off their chops, tails wagging, getting petted by everyone as Thomas rolled by. He and Danny nodded to each other, and he said, "My trigger finger still works." He smiled and winked.

There were many people Danny had never met and others he vaguely recognized. An older woman named Gwen Kent, who did a tour in the army, and a talkative Black guy named Otis, who, until a few years ago, was in the Oregon National Guard. He'd been a medical tech and said in WWII his grandfather had been a tank driver.

He told Danny a lot of rural Dutch people had never seen Black soldiers. Kids would come up to his grandad and run their fingers along his arms to see if it was paint. Grandad would tell them that they were white guys who had been dyed black for night fighting.

A few others showed up, including one of Thomas's buddies. He had a wrinkled, well-grooved face, and he wore his white hair in a mullet—short in the front, ponytail sticking out from a knit watch cap in the back. One of his hands was missing.

"I was a SEAL," he said. "A special op to rescue hostages in Egypt. Didn't quite go the way we planned, but we got most of the innocents out and knocked out the bad guys."

"Thanks for coming," Danny said, "I think we will need every man with combat experience." He watched him and Thomas go into the room.

One of the most debilitating shadows a man can have is feeling worthless. Danny felt some of that. Some guys he knew had paid with legs, eyes, and arms. Others would never talk about any of it. But unplanned obsolescence leaves a trail of pain. If you were lucky, you found a way around it or a navigator or trail guide like Clover who could get you past the landslides and washouts. Or, maybe a couple of smart dogs like Rosa and Ladybird, who gave unconditional love and helped Thomas every day.

Izzy and Penelope appeared. Izzy was carrying a pillowcase, and when he saw Danny, he started right in with some "dude" talk, but Danny cut him off. "You don't have military experience. What are you doing here?"

"Penny and I want to help. We found Uncle Maynard's old guns." He opened the sack. "Teach us how to use them, and we'll help."

Danny opened the sack and saw two pistols. One was an ancient percussion gun, the other, a Colt Walker. Both were rusted with the grips falling off. There was also a box of cartridges.

"Izzy, these things haven't been fired in years. They're collector items. Put them back with Maynard's other stuff. You try to use these, they'll take your eyes out."

"OK, but we want to help."

"If you're serious, put on your running shoes and help us take inventory at some of the tables when the time comes later in the meeting. We need a record of who has what experience so Morgan and Hernandez can get things organized."

When everyone was settled, Alberto stood up and went to the podium. A few Jedis sat behind him. He thanked everyone for coming and then summarized what was known so far. He didn't mince words. "We are up against terrorists who have overthrown our country. They are killers."

He summarized what happened at Superstition Pass and talked about the risk of Duck Springs getting completely waxed. Next, he introduced President Marcus Longborn and Speaker Christopher Knox and asked Marcus to speak.

As Longborn was stepping up to the podium, Crazy Mary came in. She had a bright-yellow blouse on, but nothing else. "We are all going to die," she said, wide-eyed with fear. "All of us. Me too!"

Cynthia gently took her by the arm. "Mary, come with me and let's get some cookies." Mary relaxed and went with Cynthia to the snack table.

Then Longborn started to talk. "Friends, I wish I could have come home at a happier moment. And Mary, you are probably right . . . some of us may die. Truthfully, I have forgotten how much I miss this place. When I was growing up here, Duck Springs was a dinky little town in the Washington woods—a place where people from Seattle came to refresh themselves in the summer, and where we were just the 'locals.' Many of us remember when doors were never locked and people felt responsible for other people's kids when they played in front of their house." He paused and nodded with the crowd.

"Our worst days here were better than the best days in most other places. I fear those days are gone, or at least on hold. I know we have practical matters to discuss but let me tell you why this is such an important moment. We have to fix this attempt to destroy all the little places like Duck Springs. We have to hold on and fight back hard."

He had a cold, so he paused, coughed, and blew his nose with a loud honk.

"You all know the United States began with some pissed-off colonials. In 1773, bundles of highly taxed tea from England were thrown in the water. The instigators of the breakaway thought that free and independent individuals, working together, could live without despotic monarchs. They pledged to do that, despite their ferocious differences of opinion."

He sneezed again. "Pardon me. I'm allergic to certain NADF goons who are trying to kill me."

People laughed.

"Those colonials made a covenant. Unlike life under King George, they opted for a democracy that took votes, even in the face of heated disagreements. Everyone would give up the freedom to do anything they wanted and accept the restraints of an elected majority. In exchange, there would be guarantees and protections."

Another sneeze. "Those rotten NADF people must be getting closer!" He shook his head and continued.

"Freedom of the press. The right to assemble. Free speech. The right to peacefully protest. And your right to practice whatever religion you want. Peaceful transitions of power and the resolution of differences of opinion by courts under the rules of law.

"That's what is being tested now. Around the country democracy is on the run, but that tide will turn. It must," he said emphatically. "But only if people step up and push back. I believe that has started."

He paused and pointed to Knox. "Know this: my duly elected friend and colleague, Speaker Knox, is now second in line to the presidency. We are here together to the end."

Applause erupted as Longborn sat down. Pops whispered to Danny, "He's not Mucus Dickbrain anymore."

Harlan Morgan stood up. Ramrod straight and formidable. He gazed around the room for a long time before speaking. He knew silence and a soft voice often conveys more than words. Some of the men and women he looked at had known violent combat. Others, who had not, were willingly stepping into the fray. Now he offered no fancy introduction, no honorific "ladies and gentlemen" or "thank you for coming."

He had given a lot of thought to what he was about to say, and he began by asking everyone who had been in combat to stand. About a quarter of the room got up. He saluted them and then briefly explained the situation.

Throughout the 1980s and '90s, and continuing right up to the moment the NADF emerged, the United States had been involved in hundreds of military missions. Older people remembered the battle of Mogadishu in Somalia. Others were familiar with special operations that went on in Grenada, Haiti, Liberia, Uganda, Colombia, Syria, and Sierra Leone.

"The United States became the policemen of the world. Now, we have to police ourselves."

He reported what was known about O'Reilly, Matthews, and the armed thugs who were gathered not far from Crockett City. He said many of these people were amateurs but cautioned not to underestimate them. "They are fanatics!" Harlan said.

He spoke about the trip to the Bradford military training facility and the equipment and supplies they had found. He talked about evacuating and being as fully prepared for the NADF as the town could get, about staying disciplined and brave, and about trying, if at all possible, to avoid a fight. "But," he said, "everyone may be asked to do that."

Then, he outlined the strategy.

"This afternoon, we are going to put up roadblocks going in and out of Duck Springs as we get ready to move. If the NADF shows up while we are doing this, we will hold them off until most of you are on your way to Bradford. The base is protected and defensible, and we will stand a much better chance of surviving if the thugs attack there, which they are likely to do.

"So, when we are done tonight, all of you need to mobilize and help pack up your kids and pets and as much food and gear as you can carry. We are going to slowly start moving everyone."

The room stirred and there were little ripples of talk at every table. What followed was a replay of all the questions the Jedi Council had wrestled with. Alberto stepped up and asked for attention. "The floor is open for questions now. Hold your comments until later, and please, no sneaking in a short question after some long-winded comment."

The first question came from a big, barrel-chested guy in his thirties: "How do we know they will attack us?"

"We can't be sure," Harlan said, "but we know they want to capture and kill Marcus and Chris who are the last pieces of our legitimately elected American government. They have taken over

Crockett and other cities and there is no reason to think they are coming here as friends."

Another question from a concerned dad: "I have four kids. Is there room for everyone at that Bradford place?"

"Yes," he said. "It won't be as comfortable as your own home, but we'll make it work."

Then Maurice, an old-time resident, asked, "What if someone doesn't want to leave?"

"Nobody is forced to go. People can stay or head elsewhere if they choose. Not advisable," said Harlan, "but we aren't the NADF."

The questions went on, some answered by Alberto and Harlan, others by Cynthia or Ian or one of the other Jedis. Then Harlan took the room back.

"Our next step tonight is this. We've posted signs on different tables for Medical, Equipment and Supplies, Fighting Units, Fire, Day and Night Sentries, Communications. We have people ready at each table. We want to quickly inventory who has what kind of skills or experience, and what you can do here and once we get to Bradford. And finally, I need to stress self-control. We may or may not have much time, so we have to be ready to move carefully and at the right pace. Please sign up at the table where you think you can help the most. Talk to the leaders at each table and get to know your comrades. Your lives will depend on each other."

Formalities finished, people went off to different tables. The meeting lasted five hours. Most stayed longer. The mood was somber but no one seemed in a hurry to go home.

Izzy came up to Danny and looked him in the eye. "Danny, the other messengers and I have been talking." His eyes were clear. "We are in it with you."

Then he and Penelope drifted off.

51

ONE OF THE EARLY CONVOYS TO LEAVE DUCK SPRINGS FOR BRADFORD ROMAN WAS LED BY THE LOST BATTALION'S CAPTAIN JONES AND CORPORAL BENNIS. It was a line of cars and trucks carrying 150 townspeople, mostly women and children, along with baggage and supplies, some of which were in a dusty truck from Ted's quarry. Jones and Bennis would supervise their settling in at Bradford.

They helped get the old and young aboard, and Grant Terwilliger rode along with them, armed with a light machine gun in case the NADF showed up. Grant spotted a drone dropping down to have a look and pointed it out to Bennis, who shot it out of the sky.

Over the next two days, more trips carried additional people to Bradford, and ten more NADF drones were picked off with a few interceptors they had. A few of the NADF's landed in town.

52

VERN CRAFT AND THOMAS QUINN, THE ARMS AND AMMO EXPERTS, HAD AN IDEA AND MET WITH HARLAN.

"General, sir," said Thomas, "we think the NADF will try to bust through and assault us with armored vehicles. Won't surprise us if they have some heavy Humvees and a few Strykers. Maybe even some small tanks."

Harlan winced at the words "general, sir" which he found ever more tiresome. He told them that.

Thomas and Vern were trained in military courtesies. It was hard to shake habits sergeants had drilled into them. In their geometry of command, formalities were essential.

"We understand your defense, but how about we stick a few arrows into O'Reilly with some simple petrol firebombs? If they come at us in covered vehicles, we burn them. Even civilians can throw bottles, and Vern and I can prepare a lot of them, especially if we can get enough empties from everyone's secret stashes."

"I like it," said Harlan. "I'll contribute mine."

Vern, Thomas, and the dogs headed to the Quinn home, where the two old soldiers started filling bottles with gasoline and inserting kerosene-soaked cloth wicks. They added some

Tide detergent to a few of them, along with detonator cords. That turned them into crude napalm bombs. Both of them were itching to pee on the NADF and not be obsolete.

53

SOME NEW ARRIVALS BROUGHT MORE DISTURBING NEWS. NADF patrols were increasingly present on the roads out of Crockett City. They heard about others who, before getting to Duck Springs, skirted small NADF encampments or saw them while they hid in the brush. They also learned from one of the Seattle arrivals that sporadic Canadian broadcasts were coming through and reporting pockets of resistance emerging in other parts of the country. Something bigger seemed to be developing around St. Louis.

When Ian, Meghan, Masaji, Harlan, and Danny gathered at Harlan's to further plan reconnaissance, they had interviewed all the new arrivals, and with Clover's help, talked with Julie, who seemed to be recovering. Julie's progress was largely due to Clover. The two were getting close.

Morgan spread a map on the table. His home was full of books, photos, and a few knickknacks. Danny noticed he had his own row of Camus's writings with bookmarkers sticking out.

"Folks, we have no hard evidence of anything and a lot of accounts are unreliable. Still, they have a certain value. We can spend a lot of time running in circles, but at some point, we have to make calculated bets. I would like to try something I think you'll find interesting."

What he did next was run an exercise used years ago to find a lost American nuclear sub called the *Scorpion* that had inexplicably gone down in the middle of the Atlantic in a 60,000-square-mile search area. The method was quirky, based on a Las Vegas betting system.

It worked like this: Everyone pooled information by verbally sharing all the bits and pieces of gossip, conjecture, or info they had picked up from anyone. Then, they stepped back and reviewed Morgan's map together so they all were familiar with the geography. Next, they each wrote down their best private guess as to the longitude and latitude of the NADF's main encampment. Morgan collected the index cards and, one by one, read off the private bets on the NADF's coordinates. When Ian marked them in pencil on the map, they formed a diamond shaped rhombus.

The locus was not far from a small town called Caldwell, about forty miles away. That was the area Danny and Masaji would scout. Morgan told them that the whole process they had just used was a simplified version of Monte Carlo Analysis and the Navy and Coast Guard had developed sophisticated AI versions to look for missing vessels and enemy positions using satellite data.

"Good hunting, gentlemen," Morgan said. "We need reliable information, and we need it soon." Then he added, "Come back alive."

54

"I LEARNED NEVER TO TEST THE DEPTH OF THE STREAM WITH BOTH FEET," SAID HARLAN AS HE SENT MASAJI AND DANNY OFF IN ONE DIRECTION, AND IAN AND MEGHAN IN ANOTHER. Danny and Masaji's particular job was to avoid contact but to check out the NADF around Caldwell.

Danny and Masaji set off in an old but well-tuned Datsun station wagon with winter tires and extra jerricans of gas. It belonged to Vern Craft, who had stocked it with a few hand grenades. "Make sure all the parts are still attached when the car comes back. You know . . . engine, roof, wheels, that kind of stuff."

Clover and Daisy saw them off. But every passing moment can change the situation and no matter how high-tech it gets, war on the ground always turns primitive. It is full of pagan instincts that always threaten to overwhelm reason and bring out primal compulsions: bloodlust, hate, revenge, the need to win at ever-steeper costs, and, most of all, an overwhelming craving for retribution. Those can motivate you in the fray but become your worst enemy when irrational thinking or slow reflexes take hold.

Harlan had once written how old warriors like Sun Tzu, Miyamoto Musashi, and Carl von Clausewitz knew this. They were intuitively aware of the binary warrior brain but two brilliant Israeli psychologists, Kahneman and Tversky, both army veterans, proved it.

System 1, they said, is rooted in the brain's amygdala. It operates fast and is made of sudden instincts. System 1 blinks flashing lights and tells you to run, hide, or fight. Sometimes, the alarm bell is right but sometimes, the amygdala gets things wrong and hijacks System 2, which is slower, interpretive, and uses analysis, reason, and foresight.

You see something long and brown on the ground and it appears to move. Or is it your imagination? Humans crave certainty, and when that's not present, we invent it. System 2 says: whoa . . . let's check this out, maybe study it. System 1 demands a quick choice: snake or stick? If you guess wrong, you can die. System 2 deliberates and thinks things through. That can kill or liberate you.

Masaji and Danny made their way in the Datsun, then moved on foot. What they saw confirmed Harlan's hunch that the NADF was getting ready to move. The camp was slovenly but appeared to be mobilizing. Tents were being struck and they saw Humvees, field vehicles, personnel carriers, mounted patrol jeeps, and an eight-wheeled Light Armored Vehicle mounted with a chain gun. They saw two anti-tank guns and at least a dozen armed drones. There was a small pile of machine guns and mortars, and several men checking boxes of shells and ammunition.

Masaji went off to scout closer.

55

DANNY WAITED AND WATCHED, THINKING ABOUT A POSSIBLE REPORT TO THE JEDIS WHO WERE PREPARING DEFENSES TO COVER THE RETREAT TO BRADFORD. Looking at the NADF's firepower, he feared any real fight would be a quick lost cause.

Twenty minutes after Masaji left, Danny was still on the ground at the top of the overlook, scanning the camp. He heard a rustling in the brush. Snake or stick? Then a voice said, "You there, stand up and put your hands over your head." Snakes.

Two men wearing black shirts and red scarves were standing over him, rifles pointed at his midsection. He stood up. They stripped away his knife, pistol, and binoculars, and did a quick frisk. The bigger one, a beefy blond-haired man three inches taller than Danny, said, "Who the fuck are you? What are you doing here?" When Danny didn't respond, the guy hit him hard in the solar plexus with the butt of his rifle, while the other one punched him in the face.

He couldn't breathe.

"I'm going to ask you one more time, who you are and why you are here. If you don't answer, I'm going to shoot you right between your fucking eyes." The bigger one unlatched the safety and raised his piece.

Knocked to the ground and kneeling, Danny was trying to catch his wind. The tall one raised his rifle and pointed it at his head. Just then, there was a blur of movement. Danny saw him grab his throat, and the shorter one doubled over with a massive wound in his midsection. When that guy looked up, his throat was cut before he could speak.

Then Masaji helped Danny stand. "Let's get out of here. Fast. We're in the middle of an NADF camp. They're everywhere and they're swarming. There are more patrols on the hill. Looks like I got here just in time."

He glanced down at the men he killed, hung his head, closed his eyes, and whispered to someone, "forgive me."

Danny retrieved his gear and looked at the dead bodies. Both covered with blood. Masaji had come in like a torpedo.

After Danny's breathing returned to something near normal, they set off. He was still wobbly as they inched their way back to the Datsun and headed to town. They would report that the NADF outside Caldwell was mobilizing and on the move.

For where, they couldn't tell.

56

MYRON SHAPIRO'S LECTURE HALL WAS PACKED. He was painting a phosphorescent flower while Josh and Sharon cooked a fish and Sam Johnson frowned and told Danny he was a dumb shit. Izzy and Penelope were frantic because the *Chronicle* wouldn't print, and Lilly Frizell said, "Where's my money?" Maynard slumped in his chair. Four men with turbans fired submachine guns. Ten-year-olds screamed.

Then the phone rang. But it wasn't the phone. It was Clover's metal spoon scraping the side of a pan of French toast. Danny could smell some coffee she must have hidden, and he heard the sizzle of egg-soaked bread frying. Clover had a blue robe on and was standing like a stork, one leg bent and off the ground, crooked against her other knee, hips tilted, making breakfast, humming to herself.

His dream evaporated. He brushed his teeth and stared at his sorry reflection. Masaji and he had gotten back at two a.m., exhausted. His short hair was sticking out in all directions and his face was swollen and smeared with dirt and blood.

Clover stared at him for a long minute. "I'd say good morning, Sergeant Sunshine, except you look horrible. Plus, you were thrashing around in your sleep again. Go wash, shave, and brush your hair. Rosa and Ladybird look better than you after they've been rolling in some dead thing they found."

Once he cleaned up, he ate breakfast and savored her coffee. It was ten a.m. He rarely slept past five a.m. but must have needed the oblivion. Clover went off to work and Danny flopped back down to sleep. His rest was short lived.

There was a knock on the door—Izzy and Penelope were there. "Harlan called a meeting. He wants everyone there, you especially. By the way, you look like shit."

57

WHEN THEY ASSEMBLED, CYNTHIA CAME OVER AND INSPECTED HIS EYE. "Nice shiner you got there, Danny-Boy. Clover do that?"

After everyone was there, Harlan said, "I wish I could give you coffee, but I'm out. My nights are just as pathetic too. My wine and cigars are almost gone."

Ian, Meghan, Masaji, Brian, Alberto, Izzy, and the other Jedis were there. In case Danny needed another reminder, Vern said, "Danny, you look like crap."

"Our immediate mission," said Harlan, "is to get Duck Springs moving to Bradford, and, at the same time, stay ready for offensive strikes from the NADF. Let's get reports from each of you, then we'll talk about next steps. Ian and Meghan, please start, then Danny and Masaji. Then I'd like to talk about how to cover our retreat to Bradford."

Ian and Meghan reported that over two long days they had scouted west nearly to the Western Crest Trail by car and foot. They found a few homes, some with dead people—in two cases, entire families, including small children. Then, about twenty miles due north of Duck Springs, they found several NADF camps with maybe a hundred soldiers each. They had small arms and some stationary machine guns. They also saw pairs and trios of NADFs circling the perimeter, and small patrols coming and going.

Harlan said, "O'Reilly is flanking us."

Masaji reported their observations. He told them the main camp was heavily armed with vehicles and weapons and were mobilizing.

Harlan asked for Cynthia's report.

"We are as ready as we can get. Bradford has additional supplies and instruments, and there are enough cots and beds that we can set up a surgery and burn unit. We could use more personnel. Our two new doctors, Mohan and Laxmi Das, are wonderful, and Eric Abbott can deal with some mouth and facial injuries. We have Maximo and a few former medics and techs, but if we have simultaneous mass casualties in the hundreds, we'll be overwhelmed. We just aren't equipped for that."

"Brian, what's the status on our roads in and out of town?"

Jankowski took off his hat and ran a hand over his bald noggin. He said the barricades at the north and south road entrances into town and a third along the river were, for the moment, reasonably strong. Lines of vehicles, including his semis, had been set up and some trucks had been turned on their sides.

"Frankly," said Ian, "the place we are most vulnerable is up above. We have a few people camped at the top of the escarpment where the falls drop down into town but they are just lookouts. If we get attacked from above and below simultaneously, we are in for it."

"You're right. We'll try to fix that," said Harlan. "Peter, how about fighting units and deployments?"

Ashkin, always precise, reported that beyond the veterans, they had thirty-seven civilians acting as watchmen and 139 people who were capable of serious fighting.

"Everyone we've recruited is organized into a unit or squad. Some are on the roads manning Brian's barricades. Others are in reserve in the middle of town. But I've got to tell you, Harlan, some of these folks have never been in a fight and will be pretty weak."

Vern was next. "Ammo is still a problem if a big assault takes place before we get to Bradford. Thomas and I and a couple of nice recruits from the meeting have modified what we can, but we'll be up against it. On the upside, we have several hundred Molotov cocktails ready. And if you drink up the rest, people, we'll add more!"

Pops jumped in, "I have a few left. I was saving them for evening anesthetic purposes but you'll get the empties." There were laughs, then Harlan asked Grant Terwilliger about fire preparation.

Grant kept it short but ended with humor. "We are as ready as possible," he said, "but my team wants pay raises, health benefits, and better retirement. We are taking it up with the union."

"Izzy, communications?"

Izzy puffed up. He seemed proud to be in a room with serious people. "I've got more than fifteen runners and couriers. They'll be available to each unit leader."

Danny thought, *Thank God, no "babes" and "dudes."*

Harlan took the floor again. "Thanks to all of you. I've been meeting regularly with Alberto, Marcus, and Chris to gauge morale. So far, things are fine and most people are packing. We have the blockades that will keep the bad guys out but they also keep us in, which can be dispiriting, especially with food and supplies dwindling."

Vern said, "We may be eating cat food soon. Hell, we may be eating the cats. Won't be my first time. A bit bony but fair eating if you add a lot of garlic and onion."

Harlan shook his head and then continued. "We need to keep packing. Cynthia, I'd like you, Peter, and Pops to get people on vehicles and moving. Jones and his people from Bradford can help with some of their covered vehicles. Maybe Ted can use one of his big quarry trucks.

"Ian, can you organize a few combat-ready people on a raid, scout west and north, hit them where you can, and station our people at the top with more weapons? We are most vulnerable there, especially if an attack comes from the camps you scouted. Still, it would be good if you could give them a kick in the teeth. See if you can knock off some of their patrols, or whatever you encounter if they aren't bigger than you can handle. And come back alive.

"Meanwhile, at the right moment, I want to stick darts in O'Reilly and the NADF and cover our retreat to Bradford. Maybe we do that with Vern and Thomas's brews if the little plane works. If they disable some of their vehicles and bigger guns it would improve our odds significantly. Vern, you up for joining the party?"

Without missing a beat, Vern said, "Delighted. I've been itching to get into this. I've slowed down a bit, but I'll see if we can take out a few of their positions and maybe get a shot at O'Reilly or Matthews."

"Vern," said Grant Terwilliger, "you're a fucking Rambo!"

Vern grunted. "I only wish. I'm older and fatter, but I'm still on this side of the grass and Thomas is game. Rosa Parks, and Ladybird Johnson can take care of the shop while we are off. The dogs work harder than either of us."

Before the meeting broke up, Harlan had one more thing to say. "Folks, up until now the NADF probably thought Duck Springs was home to the Flintstones."

Izzy turned to Danny and whispered, "What's a Flintstone?"

He sighed, "Before your time. Almost before mine."

Harlan said, "O'Reilly and Matthews will have spied on us just as we have on him. He'll look at his own reconnaissance and surmise we are weak. Which is good. But all that changes once we get aggressive." His message was sobering.

"I want each of you to make sure you have seconds, thirds, and fourths in command in the event you are disabled or killed. Make sure your units know that. Ian, and then Danny are next in line to me.

Before the meeting broke up, Danny asked him who would be the best fourth if he went down.

"Meghan," said Ian.

"I agree. Let her know," nodded Harlan.

Danny headed home and flopped into bed.

58

WHEN DANNY AND MASAJI STOPPED AT VERN'S GUNS, AMMO, AND ARCHERY STORE TO PICK UP AMMUNITION, VERN HAD THOMAS QUINN WITH HIM. Quinn adroitly rolled himself around in his wheelchair. The dogs often pulled him around town, but he could navigate some stairs and even a few trails if they weren't too rough or vertical.

It wasn't surprising that he and Vern were close friends. In fact, they were partners in various little adventures. Vern was a tech-weenie who spent years in the Air Force fixing shot-up fighter planes. Thomas could fix anything. People stopped by with broken fans, jammed coffee grinders, and ancient pickups that were listing to one side. Most contraptions left better than they entered. A few went onto a scrap pile that could be cannibalized for parts.

When Danny first met him, he said, "Pleased to meet you, Tom."

He said, "I prefer Thomas." Each, in their own way, were village cranks but real contributors to the town's welfare. Thomas was gruff and obstreperous. His two Labrador service dogs were always with him. You could tell he loved them, they loved him, and they were used to being at Vern's store. Like sled dogs, they lived to work.

After buying some ammunition for his 30.06, he said goodbye. He wanted to get back to his cabin and retrieve the last of his food and books.

When he pulled up, he could see the cabin had been ransacked. The potbelly stove was knocked over and Danny's remaining clothes, pots, pans, and lanterns had been trashed. There were bullet holes in the wall. Stumpy's head was gone and what was left of him was splayed out on the porch in a pile of feathers and sunflower seeds. Someone had also tried to torch the place. One wall was charred but too wet to burn.

Danny rummaged around and salvaged a few items, then got back in his car. He was preternaturally calm. When his work at MCS took adverse turns, or opposing counsel acted badly, which happened often in serious lawsuits, Sam Johnson would laugh and tell him revenge is a dish best served cold.

"Fuck 'em," he would say. "You'll have the last word when you win."

59

THERE WAS A LITTLE NEWS COMING INTO DUCK SPRINGS FROM A STATION IN VANCOUVER. The newswoman reported that local resistance groups were engaging in sporadic fights in Boston, Atlanta, Sacramento, St. Louis, and New Orleans. Details, she said, were sketchy.

If the news was true, the NADF had consolidated the militias and paramilitaries and were trying to complete their takeover, but some Americans were fighting back. In between the sound of static, there were other bits of reporting before the signal faded.

60

CYNTHIA WAS BLUNT, AND EVERYONE LISTENED. "Assuming we are in for a serious fight, we could use five or ten more docs plus an emergency room, an MRI, a CAT scanner, ventilators and a bunch of ER nurses." What she didn't have was some kind of fairy dust to sprinkle over everyone's quiet but growing premonitions.

Danny thought hard about the conversation. He could feel the pessimism which was starting to edge up toward panic. Fear sometimes goes viral and contagious, becomes psychogenic in small groups, and can turn into mass hysteria. Maybe some chemical that regulates everyone's equilibrium gets disrupted and compounds course out of glands and pool together. Suddenly, fear blossoms.

When Camus wrote *The Plague*, some took it literally while others thought it was a metaphor for the spreading Nazi threat. Either way, denial, wishful thinking, bureaucratic procrastination, and heroic attempts to find a serum were part of Camus's narrative. He said none of it mattered. The virus didn't care what anyone thought.

In Srinagar, Danny saw how sudden overwhelming violence could lead to breakdowns in the structures and orderings soldiers carry in their heads. Balloons popped, there was deflation, and everything they had been trained for fell away.

He knew the odor and taste of it firsthand from Kashmir. The disorientation arose again in law school when he sometimes experienced a sudden dread that he couldn't cut it. That same kind of fear returned during his descent into The Troubles, when he was losing everything and afraid of being caught by the Frizells, Judge Arakawa, Kirsten, and the loan sharks.

Now it was here again, the shivers, stepping on soft ground and wondering if it might be deeper quicksand and if Duck Springs should just cut and run. Then he told himself that Harlan was right. You always run into trouble when you avoid hard realities. The town really wasn't set up to fight or run from an army of 2,000. Whichever way they moved, death would follow.

"We now know for sure a former army sergeant major named Ned O'Reilly is leading the local NADF army there," said Harlan. "I met him years ago and, frankly, he's a vicious piece of business who retired before he was drummed out of the service for insubordination and behavior unbecoming. He's very intelligent but emotionally unstable. His adjutant and number two appears to be Herman Matthews, who knows this area. Cynthia talked about him before."

Then he turned to Longborn and Knox. "Mr. President and Mr. Speaker, we are confident that O'Reilly and Matthews know you gentlemen are here."

The Jedis started chattering but Harlan stopped them. "We still have a few days to get everyone to Bradford but we don't have weeks to dither. We are almost at the fork in the road where everyone in town has to exercise their final choice. People either leave now or take their chances understanding we are in for a scrap. Alberto, you need to lead the town to their decisions. I have to prepare the logistics of a defense."

Alberto turned to Longborn and Knox. "Gentlemen, we need you to keep inspiring and rallying us. If we are to restore government, it has to start here and now. If we fight, we need you to help us, not just as symbols but as a part of a real resistance. We need to show O'Reilly's thugs they are in for a serious ruckus, and we need Mabel over there to run her flag up the pole at the post office even if we don't have any mail coming in."

Danny vaguely remembered some lines from Yeats about falcons that could no longer hear their falconers and a center that couldn't hold. But William Butler Yeats never met Duck Springs. If he had, he would have seen the flip side. Every member of the Jedi Council was sticking together.

61

THE DARKEST MOMENTS OF DANNY'S PAST, WHICH HE HAD NEVER SPOKEN OF, CAME BACK IN DREAMS. They crept in at night and tangled like weird fish pulled up from the deepest part of the abyss. His dreams were full of zombies from Kashmir. Waking up, he could recall people, body parts, gun chatter, explosions. The details always faded unless he wrote them down.

Not so with Clover. She was fresh water for people like Danny wandering in their own deserts. But Clover wasn't always sunlight either. She had a few vexatious gremlins of her own that resided just below her lovely epidermis and who, once in a while rose up and bedeviled her.

One of her fixations was fastidiousness. She was excessively organized and a neatnik perpetually cleaning, puttering, rearranging, and fussing with all the stuff in her house and at the café. Danny now knew many of her looks, including the one called "Clean up your shit," but he much preferred the one that said, "Come hither." There were others he loved too. Her melting face of contentment. Her bubbles of joy. Her sudden wide-eyed curiosity. And he absolutely adored the edgy, funny double entendres that sometimes rolled out of her.

Like a schoolmarm with a slightly upraised eyebrow, Clover was still the perfect complement to Danny's sloth and squalor. In the Marines, he had learned to keep his food, clothes, and weapons clean, but surroundings didn't matter much. He became accustomed to working in fetid conditions. He could stay personally tidy but oblivious to the garbage, blood, and grime of a battlefield.

Danny came back from a Jedi meeting to find Clover in a rare bad mood. He could tell instantly. The kitchen was full of smoke and there was a spill on the floor from some sauce or soup. She was frosty and tried to smile but it was a grimace.

He would have dismissed it all and carried on, but he knew Clover was excessively harsh on herself when something she was responsible for went wrong and didn't meet the high bar she reserved for herself. When things went bad, she wanted privacy.

"Go away for a while," she said. "I'll be OK later."

Danny started to object but her left eyebrow arched up a few more centimeters and her eyes got flinty.

"Go away."

He had seen a few of these moments. They lasted an hour or two.

"I'm going to General Morgan's for a little while to talk about the evacuation unless there is something I can do here."

"No, go. I'll be OK. We'll eat late. It's very fashionable in Buenos Aires."

He walked into the room where most of his stuff was still in boxes. He grabbed the two volumes of Camus's journals, the *Carnets*. One was from 1935 to 1942, the other from 1942 to 1951. They had been translated from the French and published in London. He bought them thirdhand in a sidewalk bookstall in New Delhi and treasured them

He also wanted to lend them to Harlan and talk with him about Camus, Sun Tzu, counterintelligence, their situation, and the coming fight. Somehow, he sensed but didn't understand the mysterious intersections of all the puzzle pieces: war, peace, philosophy, tactics, and Duck Springs. He needed to connect dots.

Camus still fascinated him and got him thinking about fascism, the call to fighting, and his own vacillating self. Here was what Camus scribbled in his journal in 1940 while the Nazis were murdering people:

> The temptation is a permanent one. Should we resist or give way? Is it possible to live a monotonous, repetitive life while perpetually haunted by the thought of a work to be created, or should we adjust our life to this work, follow the lightning flash?

Camus saw humans as imperfect sums of the choices they make in a world that is relentlessly unfair. There are always hard decisions. The only way to deal with all of them was to exercise your own freedom until freedom itself became an act of rebellion.

Danny had his own ideas. Camus's big question circled around the prospect of killing himself. Danny was beyond the suicidal impulses that had brought him to Indian Creek and Duck Springs. His thinking now centered on killing others.

62

HARLAN OPENED THE DOOR. Like the way he dressed, like the way he seemed all the time, Harlan's house was a neat affair. Rough logs on the outside, a pine paneled interior with endless bookshelves, a large oak desk, a clean kitchen, and a working fireplace. He was smoking a skinny cigar.

"General, I know things are getting urgent but do you have a few minutes to speak with me?"

"I do, but for God's sake, stop calling me General unless you want me to start calling you Staff Sergeant every time we talk. You like cigars? I have a couple last special-occasion Cubans and can offer you a glass of wine or even some hair of the dog."

Even though the town's situation seemed precarious, he was as relaxed and off duty as Danny had seen him.

"I enjoy a cigar now and then but want to make sure I'm not intruding."

"You're not. Come in and sit down. I can use some company." He handed Danny a stogie and a glass of wine.

"*In vino veritas,*" he said, raising his glass.

Then he pointed Danny into an easy chair. An exceptionally ugly and overweight tomcat with one eye sewn shut immediately jumped onto Danny's lap and started purring.

"Ignore the cat. His name is Bela Lugosi. He tangled with a raccoon or coyote, which is how he got torn up. He's not much to look at but keeps the mice running."

"What's a Bela Lugosi?"

"Not what . . . who. Lugosi was an old movie star; he played mummies, vampires, and ghouls. Way before your time, Danny. What do you have there?" he said, eyeing the books.

Danny explained that he remembered him talking about Camus and thought he might like to look at *Carnets* when he had time. "These are my prized books. I couldn't part without them when I left Seattle."

He thanked Danny profusely and said he was eager to read them. What followed then was a long exchange of ideas touching on the move to Bradford, philosophy, politics, battle plans, and Harlan's own writings.

Then they talked more specifically about what they may be facing.

"Harlan, I think you wrote about this in *The Sheathed Sword*."

"You actually read it and stayed awake?"

"I did. You started with Sun Tzu's admonition that the highest and best strategy is always breaking the enemy's resistance without fighting. Do we have any chance of that?"

"Maybe," he said. "You know, I saw something interesting on a walk by the Green before all this NADF business started. I saw a large eagle attack a red-tailed hawk but, before he could finish the job, a second hawk materialized and they started badgering the eagle until the eagle took off. Maybe we are those hawks."

"You think we can actually mount a defense?"

"If we do it right, and if we are ready to tough it out with them. We have to let the NADF think we are yokels while we quietly stiffen up and, at the right moment, fight them in our own way."

"You think folks here can do that? I'm not so sure."

"Nobody can be sure. A famous boxer said everyone has a big plan until they get punched in the nose the first time. That's as true for us as it is for them."

"Isn't the only real alternative to cut and run?"

"Probably, unless we send someone out to assassinate O'Reilly and his best officers, which isn't out of the question. I'm guessing he thinks we are weak. Which is fine. Before O'Reilly knows different, we can hit him and look for an opening to end the whole thing."

"We would need a hotshot sniper," said Danny. "I think Ian Jeffers did some of that, though he hasn't said much about his time with NATO."

"He won't talk much about it. Some of this is like billiards. If we are going to fight, we need a strong break shot that busts up the table, then some excellent bank shots that put the right ball in the right pocket at the right moment."

"Unless the town surrenders."

"That's always an option, but the NADF will execute Longborn, Knox, Alberto, me, you, Ian, and anyone else they consider a threat."

"The big decisions Duck Springs must make," he continued, "are both military and political. I'm not good at the politics. That's Alberto, and under that good-old-boy exterior, he's tough and savvy. I know something about fighting. You, too, Danny, you've been there. Alberto knows Duck Springs politics."

"I fought but I was never involved in big decisions. Just followed orders."

"You are now, Danny. The Army and Marine counterinsurgency manual I worked on with others back in the day was in a sequestered think tank at RAND Corporation. We worked out a lot of scenarios to deal with the different faces an enemy presents, but mainly we wanted to modify the old doctrine of engaging in battles with conventional fighting forces."

He paused and relit his cigar.

"Does that apply here?"

"In part. If it comes to a fight, we will need to defeat the NADF by convincing them we are unprepared, then become an armadillo. It's a variation of the Swiss redoubt strategy."

"What is that?"

"We'll control as many crossings and entrances into town as we can, create passive and active barriers, make sure we have small, flexible fortifications, and send out small forays to inflict scissor cuts on them."

"Harlan, what's your real assessment of the NADF?"

"I suspect the NADF nationally is spread out and dealing with its own internal ideological spats. Just a hunch. The groups Willard and Brody recruited are unruly. Basically, they are bullies and led by martinets. They will have a hard time with each other. They probably detest each other. At the very least they will be prideful and jealous. I'm guessing their coalition is temporary. On the other hand, they have General Brody."

"You know him?"

"Slightly. I knew his father, Kern Brody, who was several years ahead of me at Annapolis. Brody senior made a name for himself in Vietnam and then in Iraq. He was full of himself. Pompous. Loved all the bright lights and medals. Very right wing and seriously xenophobic. At the academy, he would spend hours with other wingnuts getting liquored up and talking politics. Doesn't really surprise me that his son would take after him and that he and Willard are allies."

Danny was thinking about all this as they puffed cigars and sipped wine. Then he said, "I'm worried that some of the civilians here will be seduced into surrendering or joining them."

"I am too," Harlan said. "If they do, we have to let them. Frankly, it's the last thing they should do. It's suicide. You know the story of Melos that Thucydides wrote about?"

"No."

"Neocons like Brody love this story. In 416 BC, the Peloponnesian War was the world war of its time, a big play for political, commercial, and cultural supremacy in the Mediterranean. The protagonists were Athens and friends on one side, and Sparta and theirs on the other. One way or another, the conflict forced every island and city-state in the Mediterranean to take sides, similar to what Willard and Brody are doing. They wanted supremacy."

"What was Melos?"

"One small island. Melos had ties to both the Athenians and Spartans and wanted to sit out the fight. The Athenians, those high-minded inventers of liberal democracy, starved the island into submission, killed the men, and sold the women and children into slavery. All authoritarians believe might makes right. If we do nothing, we will be Melians."

They talked about the town's defenses during the slow, steady evacuation to Bradford and then the conversation ambled into Harlan's war experiences, a bit of Sun Tzu, and his own remarkable journey from the son of a small-town pharmacist to a senior military commander.

"It's been quite a party," Harlan said with a laugh. "And here, just when I thought it was over, along comes another dance."

"I need to get back," said Danny after several hours. "Clover was burning dinner and in a bad mood when I left, but thank you for the cigar, wine, and discussion. I hope you enjoy *Carnets*. In fact, I'm sure you will."

"If we have time, we'll do it again. I want to talk more about Camus and why you're so interested in him. Those were my last cigars, but I have a few more bottles of wine left. Meanwhile, you're lucky to find Clover and she's lucky to have you. She reminds me of my late wife Joanne."

"When we get a break, we'll have dinner with Clover. She makes amazing meals out of nothing."

Harlan smiled. He was an unusual man, full of knowledge, straight talk, and simple courage.

"Thanks, sir."

"You did it again."

"Thanks, Harlan."

63

BY THE TIME HE GOT BACK, CLOVER HAD THROWN OUT THE BURNED FOOD AND RECOVERED HER COMPOSURE. Her dark mood had drifted away and she was smiling again. They had sandwiches by candlelight. Then she informed Danny that he smelled like a cigar and needed to wash up.

After cleaning up, he recapped his talk with Morgan and shared their fears about submitting to the NADF. Clover agreed. We either fight or run. Or both, he told her. Later, she showed him a painting she was working on that was different from anything he had seen. It was six feet wide and three feet high with three separate panels. It didn't resemble the brilliant flowers she was so good at depicting. It was something childlike, abstract, colorful, and discombobulated, as if Paul Klee, Jackson Pollack, and Picasso got drunk and started painting together.

"I love it," he told her. "How much if I want to buy it?"

"If it were anyone else, I'd tell them to give me all their money and I'd give them back what I don't use. That's my new Duck Springs business model. But for you, I have a special price." Then she kissed him and he kissed her back.

64

AFTER DINNER, AND DESPITE THE LATE HOUR AND THE URGENCIES OF THE FIGHT WITH THE NADF, CLOVER CHANGED INTO HER PAINTER CLOTHES: AN OLD PAIR OF BLUE JEANS AND A FORMERLY LIGHT-BLUE SHIRT. Her clothes were abstract pieces by themselves, full of colorful splotches, drips, and spills. Clover blended primaries and swirled them into the more subtle colors the paint companies call eggshell or aloe vera. All of Clover's hues emanated from some formula in her head.

Danny loved watching her transform into a painter, changing out of one set of clothes and into another. He watched as she added squiggles and shapes and quieter shadows with soft shades. The room smelled of solvents and oils. This was Clover's lair, her private world for matters beyond words.

He watched her paint and then headed back to his little desk and *The Rebel,* Camus's discourse on organized and chaotic rebellions and the perpetual failure of both to achieve anything close to human perfection. In the end, Camus's quest wasn't political. It was moral—which, he supposed in the end, always became political.

This, from Camus: "He who despairs of the human condition is a coward, but he who has hope for it is a fool."

65

THE ANCIENT GREEKS HAD A WORTHY ANGLE ON JUSTICE. They had a supreme court called an Areopagus. Judges sat in the open air in the center of Athens, tugged on their whiskers, fiddled with their togas, and heard disputes over lies, abuses, heresies, and alleged transgressions. They listened to everyone and then made pronouncements. When the Areopagites were truly perplexed by an issue they couldn't unravel, they ordered the parties to appear again in a hundred years.

Danny thought a trial by divine judges over his own crimes in Kashmir would find him guilty much sooner. He hadn't told Clover everything about those days, knowing his retelling would show how deeply flawed he was. After gambling, blowing up a perfectly promising legal career, and failing at marriage, he wanted to accept his imperfections and become the *Wabi-Sabi* that Masaji described.

It was hard but Clover was changing him. Maybe deliverance and restoration were something the Areopagites overlooked.

That night, Clover shook him awake long before dawn. He had startled her. "Danny," she whispered, "you were tossing and kicking and then you screamed."

He was bathed in sweat and had a terrible taste in his mouth, as if Napoleon's army had retreated from Russia over his face in their stinky socks. He argued with her, to no avail. He said he just wanted to go back to sleep. She wouldn't let him.

"It wasn't a dream," he finally said. "It's a recurring night terror. Forget it. I really just need to sleep."

"Tell me."

"No, I'm sleepy."

"Not until you talk to me."

"Clover, there are things in my past, more than I've told you, incidents from Srinagar and other fights. Things that I did that I can't unremember no matter how much I try."

"You need to tell me," she said. "If you and I are going to make this work, we need honesty."

For a time, he said nothing. Neither did Clover.

"OK, I'll try even if this hurts us."

"It won't. Whatever went down, it's time to purge it."

It came out slowly, haltingly.

"Some young people I killed inhabit my dreams. Their ghosts live under stones and rotting tree trunks deep inside my head and, every once in a while, they come out and crawl across my brain."

She winced and said, "We all have those."

"Mine are different. They come out and harass me, then they slip back with all the other netherworld creatures. They hide, but they never really go away. It's like I am in an endless slow-motion apocalypse."

She took his face in her hands, and said, "Tell me."

So he told her about the incident he never talked about.

"I was a corporal leading a fire team inside Srinagar during the second battle for the city. There was no air support and no armor behind us. Our job was to capture or kill specific jihad leaders and bombmakers. We had names and addresses, but we knew the information was spotty. It always was.

"We moved past a place called Pratap Park and were going house to house looking for a notorious bombmaker named Mustafa. We moved into his neighborhood slowly, hugging walls and staying as low and we could. Suddenly, we started taking murderous fire."

He stopped. "I need water, Clover."

She brought him cold water.

"Four armed Pakistanis were on the street in front of us. Another two were on a rooftop above them—snipers. Our sergeant, Kelsey Loy, was killed. The rest of us ducked into doorways. We shot the sniper but another member of my team, Dawson from Detroit, was hit and bled out. There were three of us left.

"We opened up with automatic weapons and forced our attackers back into the building. The rest of us—Warren, myself, and John—moved in and threw a half-dozen grenades through the doorway. When the smoke cleared, we went in to mop up and sprayed the room down with automatic fire. Two Pakistani soldiers were dead, but we had also killed or wounded fourteen young boys and girls. They were anywhere from eight to twelve years old. It was a *madrasa*, a Koranic school where young men and women were radicalized. Three of them were alive, dying, and in terrible pain.

"One of them had a bullet that had gone through one of his lungs and out his back. I think his spine was severed. He was a handsome boy, maybe a little older than the others, with the first wisp of a mustache on his lip. He looked at me with frightened, pleading eyes. Another one was moaning and crying. When I turned him over, I could see he had both legs blown off and wouldn't survive much longer. And there was a girl, a beautiful girl, with a gaping wound in her abdomen and her intestines hanging out.

"In my few, faltering words of Arabic I held the boy's hand and asked him what his name was. 'Saleem,' he whispered.

"I put my left hand over his eyes and with the other put my pistol to his head and ended it. Then I did the same with the other boy. Then I went to the girl. She was barely conscious. I asked her what her name was. 'Mirra,' she said. Later I learned Mirra means Light of God."

He stopped talking and looked at Clover, caught his breath and choked.

"I still see those kids looking up and begging for life. Clover, I know there is no honor in war except what you do for your brothers in arms and how you treat enemy wounded. I murdered them, Clover. I killed them."

"You couldn't have known," said Clover, her hand gripping his.

"That's what our captain said at the debrief, but the faces of those kids keep coming back. I killed children, Clover, kids who hadn't yet grown up. I committed atrocities."

Clover looked at him, paused, and then said, "You're not a murderer, Danny. You did those things in war. War forces horrible choices. It's different from killing people from an airplane forty-thousand feet up or pushing buttons that send armed drones off to explode twenty miles away. Harlan knows that too."

"He does, but none of us ever talk about it. And the memories never go away. Those snakes and scorpions keep coming back."

"Everyone has to deal with death, and it's different for each person. There is no blueprint, Danny, no template, no owner's manual or master plan."

"You too?" he asked.

"When my parents died in the car crash I somehow blamed myself, which was stupid and senseless. Still, that loss was so unexpected and so overwhelming, I just hurt all the time. Then Thelma, who is very wise, said something that helped."

She said, "Clover, you're innocent. I've been through this. We all go through it. It's part of life, the part most of us won't come to grips with and can't reconcile because we are so hungry to live.

You really never grow up until your parents are gone. It's bitter-sweet. You are alone but somehow taller."

Then Clover reached over to hold him. "Danny, you are a remarkable man. You don't understand that, but you are deeply caring, incredibly handsome, tough in ways most aren't, and tender in ways most can't be. I don't care about what happened in Kashmir or at MCS or when you gambled."

"Maybe you should."

"I don't care about any of it. I'm not looking for perfection. There is no perfection. We both know about hurtfulness, and we both have dealt with people who are nasty, stupid, or psychotic. I still believe most people have some good in them. There are a few who don't—they are poisonous. Those venomous types come in small, medium, and jumbo sizes."

They sat wrapped around each other for a long time. Later, Clover made coffee and breakfast, and he slept again. When he finally woke up, he brushed his teeth and the two of them watched the sun come up.

66

DUCK SPRINGS WAS AN ANTHILL OF ACTIVITY, MOST OF IT ORDERLY, SOME PARTS CHAOTIC AND ANXIOUS. Clover and Danny didn't see much of each other after his nightmare. She, Pops, Thelma, Mo, and Slim were busy with a dozen volunteers figuring out how to feed everyone at Bradford.

Quite a few of the those who turned up at the veterans meeting were actually eager-beavers like Izzy and Penelope, folks with no real training or background. A few were serious hunters and brought their own guns. Harlan asked Samantha Hardy and Lou Bennis to train civilians who wanted to learn how to shoot.

At a break in their preparations, Samantha whispered to Harlan, "A lot of these people aren't going to make it if we get into some serious shit."

"We have to train them hard."

"I know," she said. "We want them to shoot the bad guys and not blow their feet off. We'll teach them whatever we can."

Vern and Thomas were working with a few civilian techies they'd recruited to expand their Molotov cocktail and ammunition piles. Grant Terwilliger was drilling new firefighters. Brian Jankowski had taken charge of road and river blocks. The road barricades, the top of the escarpment, and the shore of the Green River were the new town boundaries.

Brian's two semis were the first to be positioned on the north side, along with a road grader, a steamroller, and the town's old snowplow. Meghan had set up small-arms posts behind the barricades where her team could quickly pivot and hit other positions.

Harlan, Ian, Alberto, and others huddled whenever they could at Harlan's house, but meetings gravitated to the community center. A few people, Danny included, still went to the café, but there was no more ice cream, and the only menu item was canned tuna sandwiches.

Danny went looking for Clover, longing for a secret coffee, which she gave him. Grant Terwilliger was sitting with Diego Owens, the Catholic priest. "Goodman," Grant said, "just the man I want to see." With his big fire chief look, he commanded: "Have a seat."

Danny joined them. "How's your reinforced fire brigade?" he asked.

Both men look exhausted. Grant said, "Good team, capable people. It's equipment I worry about—hoses, hand tools, the pumper. There's not enough to go around, and what we have is old and needs repair."

"There's an interesting story going around." Grant continued, his eyes starting to gleam. "Came in from something called 'Radio Free Denver.'"

As usual, Danny could never tell when Terwilliger was starting to relay real information or small-town baloney. What ensued was pure luncheon meat slathered with lard, mayonnaise, olive oil, and butter.

"Seems like some regulars in a bar near Hotchkiss, Colorado, got together and decided they wanted to declare war on the NADF. Their spokesman, a Mr. Sean McBean, put a call in to General Brody to let him know they were coming for him and wanted to give him a chance to surrender. 'Put me through,' McBean demanded in a slightly slurred voice.

"The general came on. 'Mr. McBean? What can I do for you?'

"McBean said, 'Want to let you know we're coming for you and if you give up now, we'll go easy on you.'

"Brody paused and then said, 'That's interesting, but tell me, how big is your army?'

"McBean said, 'Well, at the moment, there's myself, my cousin Arthur, my neighbors Gerry, Murphy, Billy, and the entire checkers team from Froggy's Bar and Grill. That makes eleven of us.'

"Brody replied, 'Look, you need to know we have more than 400,000 well-trained men and women in the NADF and more joining every day.'

"McBean said, 'Hmmm, General, let me talk with the boys and I'll ring you back in a few minutes.'

"When he called back, he said, 'General, just want you to know we are now airborne.'

"'McBean,' said Brody, 'I don't mean to pry, but what exactly do you have?'

"'Well, sir, we've modified my old ultra-light and mounted it with a couple of rifles.'

"Brody was silent for a minute, then said, 'Look, Mr. McBean, we have dozens of captured fighter planes and choppers and enough drones and missiles to take Colorado off the map.'

"'General, I'll be right back.' Twenty minutes later McBean called again. 'General Brody, bad news. Sorry to tell you but the war is off.'

"'Why the change of heart?' asked Brody.

"'Well,' said McBean, 'I talked with the boys, and there's no way we can feed a half-million prisoners.'"

Terwilliger grinned and paused, his face creased with worry lines. Even through the weariness, his funny bone was vibrating.

"Grant," a smiling Danny said, "that's the best bunch of bullshit I've heard in weeks! We need you to keep us laughing."

67

THE NEXT DAY, FOUR FAST MOVING DRONES FLEW ACROSS THE RIVER AND OVER DUCK SPRINGS. Shooters with better aim than Danny took them down.

68

HARLAN GATHERED THE JEDI COUNCIL FOR A LATE AFTERNOON MEETING AT HIS HOUSE. He asked everyone for reports. Alberto, Marcus, and Chris sat in the back and listened. They were approaching peak readiness but fears were rising.

Finally, Ian said what was on everyone's mind, including Danny's.

"Harlan, if the NADF is disciplined and comes before we leave, we won't make it. We have good people here, but most of these folks are retired civilians who make jams and jellies and run little stores."

"I know," said Harlan.

But Ian continued. "Only a few people here have been around dead people stacked up like cordwood or seen friends vaporized from mines and rockets. No question, they are well-meaning, but I worry most of them will freeze or run the minute they see one of their neighbors cooked alive in his pickup."

Harlan was silent as Ian's words hung in the air. Then he answered. "I know people are afraid, and not without reason. We all are. Hell, me too. I hope with every fiber of my being that we don't have this fight, and I'll do everything I can with Alberto, Marcus, and everyone here to avoid it. But you all know the drill. We get as prepared as we can, we leave as fast as we can, we negotiate if opportunity arises, and, if we have to, we fight with whomever we have."

He turned and looked at four of the Jedis who were squeezed uncomfortably on a three-person couch.

"Ian, Meghan, and Danny, it's time to make our moves. While you try to keep them at bay, the rest of us will keep packing and leaving.

"Marcus and Chris, please keep talking with people one-on-one or in small groups. They admire and respect you. Alberto, can we get the ministers here to organize special services? I'm not really a man of faith and have never figured out whose side God is on, but I think some will be hungry for prayer."

Alberto said, "We have Diego and Roy. They will be a comfort, and we will need them in a fight. I suspect they will tell everyone to beat their swords into plowshares. Personally, I'd rather melt the plowshares down for more swords."

69

EVEN THOUGH THEY KNEW MORE INTENSE FIGHTING WAS PROBABLY IMMINENT, CLOVER AND DANNY INVITED HARLAN OVER FOR A MAKESHIFT VEGGIE CASSEROLE DINNER. Other than some Meals-Ready-to-Eat from Bradford, meat was scarce. Danny set the table and made it look as nice as he knew how. Then Clover fussed with it and added napkin rings, a vase with flowers, a warming dish, and candles.

When he showed up, Harlan brought flowers from his yard and two bottles of wine. With a grin, he said, "Don't throw the empties out. They go to Vern and Thomas for Molotov cocktails!"

They ate by candlelight and drank his wine. Harlan asked each of them about their pasts. He wanted to know why Danny left his law practice, and Danny told him the truth. Harlan listened without judgment. Then he wanted to know about Clover's family and growing up in Duck Springs. She regaled him with some of the Fiffe family story. Then she asked him about his own family.

He talked about his wife, who passed away after a long illness, and about his son Lawrence, who was a lawyer at The Hague and whom he had had no word from in many months. Harlan gave them the short version of his military career and his scholarship and writing, and then Clover pulled out a surprise.

Wonderful coffee and a peanut butter pie.

"You're in for a treat, Harlan," Danny said.

"Gentlemen," said Clover, "keep your expectations down. I didn't have all the right ingredients, but it will still go well with some coffee I hoarded."

As Danny cleared the table and began washing the dishes, Harlan headed off with Clover, eager to see her paintings. He knew a lot about art and admitted to a special affection for the impressionists. Once the dishes were done, Danny joined them.

Her three-panel work-in-progress had a long sheet draped over it. When she pulled it off, Harlan clucked and beamed. The six-foot-long, three-foot-high panels had pencil outlines and a few painted places. Certain spots had the start of color. There were blues in what would be part of a sky, white blotches that might become clouds, stalky brown fir trees in the back, and the start of gold and metallic green summer flowers. In the foreground: vegetables, fruits, and grapevines hanging on trellises.

Harlan paused, then declared, "You're painting a garden!"

"Exactly. It's the garden in my mind, the one I want to make when all this is over!"

"What's that in the far left corner?" He pointed to dark areas with vague images emerging.

"Those are the threats," she said. "Bad weather. Herds of starving pigs that will chew everything to nubs. And maybe human destroyers like the NADF or bored teenagers gone rogue."

Her mixed-media painting had its own topography of forms, textures, and colors. Eventually, she explained, she would cover it with fixative.

"These are really good," Harlan said, looking around the studio. "Some parts remind me of O'Keeffe and Miro. The closest I ever got to artistry was third-chair clarinet in my high school orchestra, though I have to say, since then I've become an appreciative audience for many types of music, painting, and writing. My eyes or ears latch onto something and rivet me, then it burrows into my mind, and I start to better understand the person behind it."

"Harlan, you're why painters paint, musicians play, raconteurs tell stories, and writers write. The endless hope that someone will see or hear them through their work."

"I'm a full-time looker-listener. It's part of my theory of being a good follower. Those of us who stand around and do nothing also contribute."

"You have music in your soul," said Clover.

"Clover, you have probably heard Danny here talk about Albert Camus."

Clover's face pinched up. "Quite a lot . . . actually an awful lot."

"I'm a big Camus fan too. Camus once told an artist friend, it wasn't his paintings he liked, it was the act of painting. I'm the same way. I get mesmerized by the doing. Your pictures do that. They pull me in."

Clover looked at both men and said, "You too? I don't get this Camus magic that you guys talk about. He was probably a good writer, but what exactly is it you two find so compelling? Especially now, in the middle of a civil war?"

Harlan said, "It's his larger story. He was always struggling to reconcile life's contradictions and find a true north. He was bold in his experimentation with big ideas. He hated small thinking. And there was an unbearable loneliness in him."

"What do you think Camus was looking for?" she asked.

"I think he wanted consolation for the evils we humans inflict on each other." He turned to Danny. "By the way, can I hang onto *Carnets* a while longer? I'm making my way through them. They explain a lot."

"Of course."

Before he left, this endlessly interesting man reminded Danny to get the empties to Vern and Thomas for their bomb factory.

70

CLOVER STARTED TO GET CURIOUS ABOUT CAMUS AND DIPPED INTO SOME OF DANNY'S BOOKS. It was hard for Danny to explain his obsession, other than that his problems and Albert's were related. Camus's full-throated inquiry into man's quandary about meaninglessness was tangible for him, especially as the NADF closed in and his involvement started to overtake more waking hours. They were the exact same moments Camus faced in Paris in WWII with Nazis killing innocent people.

In his early ruminations, Danny said, Camus concluded the world and humanity's role in it were "absurd." That was his exact word. What he meant was that sin and virtue didn't exist, and that pessimism, meaninglessness, murder, or suicide were all equally legitimate responses to life's emptiness.

"That's so bleak," she said.

Danny said. "I'm not a psychologist, but on the one hand he was raised in a poor and unhappy French family and had recurring bouts of tuberculosis. On the other, he found joy in reading, writing, and playing football in the Algerian sunlight."

"That doesn't explain things," she said.

"He was the product of two ways of life. His view about the emptiness of life came from his early years of poverty and illness.

But as WWII revved up, he went to Paris, joined the struggle against the Nazis, and wrote fearlessly for *Combat*, a resistance magazine. It was risky but had an impact.

"Even then in the middle of mounting oppression, he began to see beauty and courage in the pushback. He chronicled it in his experimental stories, plays, and essays.

"Personally, he was also full of life: multiple marriages, intellectual disputes with other writers in Paris literary salons, and endless love affairs.

"As the war developed, Albert's odyssey became more and more overtly political. He clearly understood the morality-politics connection and the horrors of war gave his thinking immediacy. But much as Camus hated dictators, he wasn't always sure about his own politics. At different moments, he was a self-described communist, anarchist, socialist, and European federalist. And, Clover, I think Camus would have fit snugly into Duck Springs because he was a searcher and experience-monger. He might have joined the Parliament of Owls at Superstition Pass and hung his musings in bottles. Or he may have written for Maynard and spent his time as a professional critic of Alberto and the council. But faced with the NADF, he would have fought."

The next night, Clover and Danny ended up in still another discussion about Camus at Harlan's house after another planning huddle for their fight. Masaji, Ian, Roy Voss, Chris Knox, and a few others were there. When they were done reviewing supplies, vehicles, and weapons, the talk turned philosophical and up popped Camus again.

Minister Voss started with: "You military guys have gone through all this. Not me. How can I help people right here in Duck Springs prepare? How do I get them ready to kill others or get killed themselves?"

"Don't assume the rest of us have figured that out," said Harlan.

With his deep, Speaker-of-the-House voice that always commanded attention, Chris Knox said, "My people have faced that dilemma ever since the first slave ship landed in 1619 and we were auctioned off to pick cotton. When we asked why, we were told it was God's will and just accept it."

Harlan said, "We still haven't come to a real reckoning on that. Albert Camus believed we always make hard choices in the jaws of an irrational world. Isn't that what we're facing now?"

"Actually," said Voss, "he only came to that conclusion after years of being confronted by what he thought was pointless violence. Native Algerians were fighting a vicious war to get rid of the French."

"No wonder he was despondent," said Clover. "He was French but felt Algerian."

"I read a lot of Camus in seminary," Voss said. "A strange man. He had ferocious debates with Sartre, Malraux, and argued with all of them. He even got into a fistfight with Arthur Koestler. Camus disavowed all of them and thought the existentialists were crazy."

Clover asked, "If he wasn't an existentialist, what was he?"

"He was an artist like you," said Harlan with a huge smile. "Only his pictures were stories instead of oils and watercolors. They were the interim conclusions he was coming to at different stages in his lifelong search for an enduring explanation."

Danny said, "I think Camus was a very lonely man who accepted our core biological existence but was seriously hungry for some higher ground that would give the in-between more meaning."

"What happened to him?" Masaji asked.

"He won the Nobel Prize in Literature in 1957 and died in a car crash in France in 1960. He was forty-six," said Voss.

PART III

71

HARLAN MORGAN'S MILITARY STRENGTHS AS A FORMER GENERAL WERE MASKED BY THE LIGHT WAY HE HAD WITH PEOPLE UP CLOSE. He seemed to rely on wandering around more than formal orders or chain of command. He asked if Danny wanted to join him for a quick look at the barricades and the top of the bluff. There could also be a stop at the café for some watery coffee if there was any.

They started on the town's north end. Brian had one of his tractor-trailer rigs parked in the middle of the road. He was pacing back and forth, inspecting his barricade and constantly looking for ways to shore it up. There were sandbags and logs underneath, and the semi was flanked laterally by a road grader and several pickups. It was a reasonably good roadblock.

Behind them, tucked off to the side and behind some small trees and brush, was a .30 caliber machine gun, courtesy of the Bradford armory. Five men and women were on sentry duty, and Gloria Nazzara, Penelope's sister, was there with a motorcycle if they needed a runner. On advice from a veteran who had been under sniper fire, she'd abandoned her glow-in-the-dark hairdos and dyed it black.

Harlan and Ian talked with some of the men and women while Danny chitchatted with Amos Arnold. He was carrying an old Winchester. "That gun won't do much if we get into a serious invasion but it's good for close-up fights," he said. "I recall you grew up in the projects in Chicago. What was that all about?"

Amos laughed and said, "I ran with a ghetto gang called the Cabrinis. Kind of a nasty bunch but good for self-protection in our building. We had our own colors and carried zip guns, switchblades, and knuckle-dusters. Not that I used them much. I always preferred to run and hide. I got out of Chicago right after high school."

"Where did you go?"

"I managed to get a basketball scholarship to the University of Illinois downstate in Champaign. I was a second stringer but it changed me. I studied engineering and a bit of architecture, and eventually got the hell out of the Midwest and went to work with an engineering firm in Pittsburgh specializing in Corten-B steel structures that rust a few millimeters and then harden to weatherproof. I actually made a few bucks, met Susan, who cured me of my more barbarous tendencies, had my own small firm in Seattle, and did well."

"You meet Eric yet?" he asked. "Not a lot of African Americans here. How'd you end up in Duck Springs?"

There was no look of resentment at Danny's mention of race. Instead, Amos smiled and said, "Yep, I met the new dentist. Seems like a good man. Look, I came up here summers to get away from the city. People seemed to accept us, which was rare compared to so many other places in America. We bought a small summer place and finally just moved here full time. I was able to work long distance and traveled when I wanted to for consulting gigs, which were pretty lucrative. I suspect those days are gone."

One of the other sentries, a guy named Buddy, was a former logger who had worked for Weyerhaeuser. He looked at the thick pine trees stuffed under Brian's semi, then pointed to a nearby stand of living trees. "Know what Weyerhaeuser used to call them trees?" he asked Danny.

"What?"

"Unemployed logs."

Harlan walked over and suggested they move to the town's southern barricade. Twenty minutes later they could see what Brian had contrived with his other semi and a few more trucks. Bob Williams was in charge. The setup was similar to the north road and would hold against a light intrusion but would collapse quickly in a major attack.

Another of Izzy's runners was there along with more sentries, among them, Pastor Voss. "What are you doing here Roy?" Harlan asked.

"Helping Bob. I've had a lot of people coming to see me. Thought I would pitch in." Danny knew Voss was a thoughtful man—literate, interesting, and a good listener. "People seem to want some mix of practical advice, confession, spiritual counseling, and help."

"What do you tell them?" he asked.

"Mostly, I just hear them out and, in a dozen ways, suggest they try to keep the faith. Couple of evenings, small groups have asked me to come to their homes and pray. They take comfort in that. Me too."

"What do you say?" Harlan asked Roy.

"I tell them I pray for hope because grief weighs heavy. I pray for patience in the face of hatred, and kindness because that's something God gave us. Too often the world overwhelms us. But every once in a while, light pours in, chips away at the darkness, and hope, patience, and kindness rise up. It's as if love tries to devour our wounded world."

"Thanks, Reverend. We could use more of that," said Harlan.

On the way to the river, Danny told Harlan that a Kashmiri he worked with in Srinagar gave him different advice. "It went something like, 'Pray to God, give the judge money, and remember to tie up your camels.'"

"Also sound advice in that part of the world," said Harlan.

They had two more visits to make, along the Big Green and at the top of the escarpment. Brian had also set up a thin line of barricade vehicles by the river: an excavator, the town's snowplow, one of Stinky's garbage trucks, a heavy duty D9, some haul trucks, a couple of Ted Cingcade's mixers from the cement company, and some motor homes they liberated from people who weren't around to object. They would stall the NADF but not stop them.

There were twenty armed men and women and some runners along the river. Tiny Porter came up to them with a pistol stuck in his belt, prattling away. "Hi, Danny. Hi, Harlan. We're ready for those guys and we're gonna give 'em real lickings. I know. I've been in fights all my life. People tease me about being a shrimp, but they know I can punch above my weight. Meanwhile, we have sandwiches and jugs of water. Want some?"

Watching Tiny jitterbug along the barricade, Danny didn't quite know how to tell him to cool his jets.

As they walked, Harlan scratched his head and said, "Our river stretch is long and thin. We are vulnerable there. If I were O'Reilly, I would forget the north and south roads, which are easy choke points. I'd concentrate on the river and the plateau above. They would have us pinned in a crossfire. Let's go take the trail up the bluff and see what Ian is facing."

The path followed the little stream that rolled over rocks and into the pond that gave the town its name. The top of the bluff was roughly eight-hundred feet up, steep in spots, but gently rising and flatter as they reached the top. On the plateau, a few men, women, and young runners from town were dug in. One of the runners was Julie Roth. Danny assumed a sexually-abused, battered person, man or woman, never fully recovers from that terror, but she seemed to be swinging back from her ordeal. He smiled and she smiled back. The Ars seemed so long ago.

"How you doing, Julie?"

"I'm good. People in Duck Springs make me feel welcome."

"I miss those nice coffees and cinnamon rolls you made at The Ars."

"Me too. Seems like a million years ago, doesn't it? It's good to see you, Danny. Everyone here has been wonderful, especially Clover. She's the big sister I never had and never knew I missed."

They talked to some of the team, then looked at the emplacements. After a time, Harlan said he wanted to head down and think. They ducked into the café. No other customers were around so they grabbed a table at the back.

Before she brought some rationed instant coffee, Danny pulled Clover around the corner to steal a moment of privacy. He gave her a long hug and an especially eager kiss. She laughed and said, "Down boy! See me later when we're off duty."

Harlan had been quiet on the way down the hill. The coffee, even though it was instant, helped them cogitate.

72

THE NEXT DAY, NADF SOLDIERS APPROACHED DUCK SPRINGS FROM THE NORTH FLYING WHITE FLAGS ON THE ANTENNAE OF A HUMVEE. As they climbed out of their vehicle fifty feet from Brian's barricade, a beefy, athletic-looking man in his forties waved another white cloth over his head and approached.

Brian Jankowski and Amos Arnold walked out from the barricade. Brian had a Glock tucked into the front of his jeans and Amos cradled his old rifle.

The NADF man said, "I'm Captain Daniel Willings, and I'm here to deliver a message to whoever your leader is."

"What's the message?" Brian asked.

"I need to meet with him personally," said Willings.

Brian looked at him.

"That's not going to happen. I'll deliver it and get you a reply. If that's not good enough, turn around and go home."

"OK, so be it. This comes from Lieutenant General O'Reilly. Tell your leader that if Duck Springs surrenders Marcus Longborn and Christopher Knox and agrees to new identity cards, our force will stand down. We also want you to turn over any NADF deserters who may have come to town. If you choose not to do these things, we enter town the hard way."

"Wait here," said Arnold.

Brian wrote out the demands and sent one of Izzy's runners back to deliver the message to Harlan, who happened to be at the community center talking with Mabel Wolff and Heather Hernandez.

"Excuse me folks," said the runner. "Sorry to interrupt." Harlan read the note from Brian, pulled out his own piece of paper, and penned a response.

Izzy's runner rushed back to the north barricade, handed the note to Brian and Amos, who read it and passed it over to the NADF emissary.

Willings studied it, folded it up, went back to his Humvee, and drove off.

"What did they want?" asked one of the defenders. Jankowski explained the NADF demand.

"What did Harlan say?"

Amos smiled and repeated what Harlan had written: "Not a chance."

73

THROUGH MEETINGS AND HUDDLES, DANNY GOT MORE AND MORE INSIGHT INTO HARLAN'S THINKING.

Sun Tzu, a battle-hardened commander, wrote *The Art of War* around 500 BC during an especially turbulent time in early Chinese history. Small warring kingdoms were constantly dueling for control. Sun Tzu was a mercenary general who was hired to teach discipline and cunning. He thought the big key was deception.

A few centuries later, a derivative essay called "The Thirty-Six Stratagems" appeared in something called the *Book of Qi,* allegedly written by a man named Xiao Zixian. The stratagems, Harlan explained, became proverbs that most Chinese students grow up knowing and applying to everyday political, business, and community matters as aphorisms. The underlying assumption was simple. Winning any high-stakes conflict is based on foresight and trickery.

Those same principles sat comfortably and side by side with the teachings of Lao Tzu and the Confucian idea of Tao and social accord. In fact, as Harlan saw it, Sun Tzu's work could be thought of as the Tao of War.

Harmony and disharmony are central, he said, which is just another way of saying night and day require each other, as do health and sickness, youth and old age, birth and death. One won't exist without the other. The yin-yang principle is foundational. It is like gravity, the third law of thermodynamics, and the speed of light. A given.

Yin-yang is not especially mysterious to most Asians. It includes tolerances, margins, and transitions. Still, yin-yang seems to vex Westerners who always want the comfort of absolute certainty.

The education Danny was getting from Harlan and Masaji was powerful. His old mentor Sam Johnson used to have *The Art of War* prominently displayed and always available on the shelf behind his desk. His copy was worn, dog-eared, and full of notes and bookmarkers. He also liked to make sure it could be seen when he invited opposing counsel over to have coffee and talk settlement.

Sam made Danny read it when he was making his bones as a baby lawyer at MCS. When he didn't understand something, which was often, Sam would call him a moron and then patiently translate the ideas into specific legal maneuvers for specific litigated and negotiated situations. The thirty-six principles applied to both.

The way Sam saw it, the stratagems were metaphors for tactics. For example, number one: "Cross the Sea by Deceiving the Sky" meant act in the open but hide your true intentions. Number seventeen: "Toss Out a Brick to Attract a Piece of Jade" advised you to trade something minor for something more valuable. And if you were in an unavoidable fight, use number thirteen: "Beat the Grass to Startle the Snake," which suggested stirring things up to cause as much confusion as possible.

But Harlan's interpretations were even better.

Having studied all of them, Harlan put them into his own play book, *The Sheathed Sword*. Echoing Sun Tzu, he wrote:

> The perfect fight is not to fight at all. Disciplined guerrilla fighters know this. Winning a conflict teaches you to rely on readiness and receiving the enemy in a time and manner of your own choosing. Winning without fighting is always best.

Danny read Harlan's book carefully and recognized the thinking:

> If you have to fight, vex the enemy, get them agitated, keep your own people calm, force your opponents to reveal what they really want, and keep your own intentions secret. Go left when they think you are going right and let them think you are weak when you aren't. And if you really are weak, avoid big confrontations and use small guerrilla hit-and-run moves.

It is what they had never done very effectively in The Sandbox Wars.

74

AT AN ESPECIALLY IMPORTANT HUDDLE WITH THE JEDIS, HARLAN LAID OUT THE PILLARS OF HIS DUCK SPRINGS DEFIANCE. Where his initial combat metaphor had been billiard balls and break shots, his thinking now was a three-platformed tic-tac-toe fight with O'Reilly. "We need a lot of Xs to line up, but now they can go three-in-a-row vertically, diagonally, or horizontally."

Everyone looked baffled. Finally, Meghan said, "Harlan, I don't get it. What does all that mean?"

Harlan laid it all out.

"It means, not now but *when* the exact moment is right, we have to do a lot of different things as close to simultaneously as we possibly can. It means a Cessna run with Molotov cocktails followed quickly with a charge across the Green in Strykers and a few armed trucks. While those are happening, we evacuate the last people to Bradford, and we will have mined and booby trapped as much of the town as possible. When the NADF rolls into Duck Springs it will be empty of people but as treacherous as we can make it."

Ian said, "What else?"

"Ian, you Masaji, and Danny have an especially challenging job. You are going to take a small, fast team on a roundabout route up into the hills across the river and try to catch O'Reilly and Matthews from above. These guys aren't the kind to lead near the front. They will be looking down and directing traffic from the rear. You capture or kill them. Just like the NADF decapitated our real government, we need to cut the heads off as many King Cobras as we can."

Masaji turned to Ian and said, "We could use Paul Chang with us."

"Who's he?" asked Danny.

"He came in from Superstition Pass. He's half Chinese and grew up in Vietnam. He is strong—trained in martial arts and knows small arms even though like me he prefers nonviolence. He told me he did a stint in the new Vietnamese army decades after Ho Chi Minh won independence. He said his father fought the Americans."

"Go get him," Ian said.

It all seemed logical and persuasive. But a few days before the raid, some NADF deserters made their way to Duck Springs. Among the pieces of information they provided was that General Eugene Brody was heading to Duck Springs with a thousand fighters but was still a few days away.

75

IN A BRIEF TWO-HOUR TIME OUT FROM PREPARATIONS, CLOVER, YOKO, SQUINTS, MASAJI, DAISY, AND DANNY COBBLED TOGETHER A PRIMITIVE PICNIC AND FOUND A PLACE JUST OUTSIDE DUCK SPRINGS THAT ONCE PASSED FOR THE TOWN'S PARK. There wasn't that much to eat: crackers, sardines, apples, some candy, a bit of the Miyamotos' huckleberry jam, and a few precious beers from Squints.

There was a rusty swing and a few paint-peeling wooden tables with built-in benches. Still, the sun was out, there was no wind, and they savored the moment, short as it was. Danny thought: *how fine, even if it is brief; no gunfire, no drones.* Clover sat on an old leather swing and he pushed her. Daisy sat on the other one and Masaji pushed her. Then came lunch.

Two raccoons poked their noses out of the bushes and waddled by, eyeballing the food, then ducked back into the brush. Before any of them started eating, Clover, Yoko, and Daisy began a long conversation about starting a little gallery if the summer people ever returned to Duck Springs. In addition to paintings and woodcarvings, it might have books and pamphlets by local writers, knickknacks, locally made jewelry, Miyamoto's jellies and jams, and maybe some specialty teas and coffees.

Yoko said, "We could call it Quack-Quack Arts."

Masaji, Squints, and Danny weren't part of the conversation, so they took a short walk on a trail leading off from the park. Their conversation skipped around but eventually, Masaji asked Danny what he hoped for if they lived through what was coming and things got back to normal. The question stopped him.

"Truthfully, I haven't thought about it. I want to be with Clover and I like it here, or at least I did before the fighting started. I've been trying to just find a place where I can live in some kind of peace with myself. My brother Josh is in Tillamook, but I really have no place to go and can't think of anywhere else I want to be."

"What would you do if you stayed?" Masaji probed.

"No idea."

"You could go back to lawyering," he said.

"I would need to reinstate my license . . . that is, if a state bar association exists and would let me."

"I think they would, given everything the country has been through. I could bring you some business and so would a few others," said Squints. "You know—land applications, permits, that kind of stuff. The only other lawyer up here is Peter Ashkin, and he doesn't really practice law."

"It's a thought," Danny said. Then he asked them the same thing: "What lies ahead for you if we get out of this pickle?"

Squint's reply was simple. "Back to the orchard. Fruits and jams."

Masaji's answer was more complicated. "I'm not sure. But I know I will need a long time of reflection to forgive myself for the killing I have done. War is addictive."

"What do you mean?" Danny asked. Despite periodic nightmares, he had never felt anything like that. Guilt, yes, revenge, yes, regrets for mistakes, yes . . . but no urge for atonement. War was what Ecclesiastes said it was: just a time to throw stones, a part of life and the life he had chosen.

"We will all need time to recover, including you, Danny. War is a bad habit."

That gave him pause. Maybe he was habituated, like with gambling.

On the way back, Masaji offered him a parable from Japan about a great samurai who had attained near perfection in his swordsmanship. He was a ferocious fighter, the best in Japan, and had killed many opponents, but he was more and more troubled. "All his life," Masaji said, "the samurai had heard references to 'heaven' and 'hell,' but he never understood what those things were. He yearned to know the truth of them.

"The samurai traveled up and down Japan engaging in fights and asking everyone about that perplexing business. Some people he spoke with told him to go and see a certain retired swordsman who lived in the North and kept to himself in a faraway valley.

"The samurai went to that valley and found the master drinking tea and arranging flowers in a vase. He said, 'Master, I have traveled hundreds of miles to have you tell me what the difference is between heaven and hell.'

"The old man said nothing. After a while, the samurai asked again, and then a third time. Still, the master ignored him and continued to putter with his flowers. It went on this way for a long time and the samurai kept repeating his request.

"Finally, he became exasperated and said, 'Old man, I am the most feared samurai in Japan. If you do not tell me the difference between heaven and hell this very moment, I am going to cut you in two.'

"The master paid no attention to the threat and asked if the gentleman would like tea. That set the samurai into a rage. He lifted his sword high in one of the many killing positions he knew. Suddenly, the master stopped his tea pouring, looked him in the eye, pointed a finger at his upraised arm, and said, 'That, noble samurai, is hell.'

"Startled, the samurai looked at the old man, lowered his sword, and slowly began to place it back in its scabbard. Then the master said, 'And that, sir, is heaven.'"

Danny said, "Masaji, it won't surprise me if you go back to Superstition Pass to rebuild the Parliament."

"I'm not an organizer like Shane was, but I would love to sit around, drink tea, and arrange flowers."

"With Daisy?"

"That would be wonderful," he blushed.

They ambled along and by the time they got back to the picnic, the weather had chilled. Clouds were rolling in and the wind had come up. Yoko, Daisy, and Clover were still talking about signage and wall hangings for Quack-Quack Arts.

76

MASAJI'S SAMURAI STORY STAYED WITH HIM. Danny wondered if anyone else with a lot of hand-to-hand combat experience was ever capable of finding that kind of heaven. Could Vernon, Ian, or Thomas ever really shed the habit of solving problems with weapons? His thoughts kept drifting to tea, *ikebana,* scabbards and swords. He also recalled something to the effect that peace is just a brief interlude when everybody reloads.

Danny knew wars take many forms: cold wars, border wars, cyber wars, psychological wars, civil revolts, and police actions. Most start with high-toned rhetoric and end with brutality. At some point, many pause, only to reemerge in different form.

Decades after the 9/11 attacks in New York and the subsequent Sandbox wars, America was in the middle of its second civil war with Americans pitted against themselves. Even now, in this messy business with homegrown terrorists espousing white supremacy and conspiracy theories, American troops where still all over the world in other people's fights.

Why are we like this, he thought. *Why so much cruelty? Why this endless succession of deaths that we keep inflicting on each other because we can't seem to solve problems any other way or make sustainable peace with each other?*

If there were a retired swordsman who could explain heaven and hell, he wanted to meet him. Or her. Or maybe he already had and it was Masaji or Harlan. America, he thought, needed something new and enduring, some fresh compact that could prevent the constant reloading. If he read him right, Camus yearned for that, too, and never reached it.

77

TENSIONS KEPT BUILDING AS PEOPLE WERE MOVED TO BRADFORD IN SMALL RUNS SO AS NOT TO DRAW TOO MUCH ATTENTION FROM NADF SQUADS. Return trips to Duck Springs brought back ammunition, MREs, and several more Strykers. Duck Springs now had fewer people left to receive fire or shoot back at the NADF and despite their precautions, Danny assumed the NADF would realize—if they hadn't already—that the town was migrating. Nonetheless, people grabbed moments of respite whenever they could.

In Srinagar, Danny's escape hatch was the twenty-four-hour mess tent where fighters clocked out after a patrol. Part of it was cordoned off for combat people, with refrigerators and cupboards full of beer and snacks. At Malcolm Crowley, the kitchen—with its nice lounge and modern, Scandinavian furniture—served the same purpose. It was a fine place to drink coffee, do some office politics, complain about Sam, and shirk real work.

The café had been their common relief valve in Duck Springs, but the community center became the main hangout after the veteran-organizing meeting. Now, with so few people left in town, the café was it again. That's when a major NADF snake struck Duck Springs.

A few people were inside the café drinking watered-down instant coffee from an urn. Ian, Harlan, Grant, and Chris were sitting at a booth, talking intently. Marcus, Bob, Paul, Alberto, Alyssaranda and others were standing around in front.

Suddenly, a man ran by the front of the building and threw a grenade. Most people were far enough away to receive only a few nicks and cuts. Marcus and Alberto were not so lucky. Alberto was nearly blown in half and died instantly. Marcus, who was standing behind and partly shielded by Alberto, had deep wounds on his face, chest, torso, arms, and legs.

Ian was the first one outside and saw the killer running toward the river. He pulled his pistol, fired from fifteen feet, and saw the man crumple with a bullet in his leg. It was Bennet Burton, one of the NADF deserters who had taken refuge in Duck Springs. He had been a patient infiltrator; stealthy, cunning, and intent on hurting the town when he could.

When Danny got there, Burton was moaning and writhing on the ground. At first, he thought it was a woman. Burton's hair was long and plastered around his face. Looking closer, he saw a skinny man with a shriveled, constipated look, holding his lower leg. Ted Cingcade came up behind Ian, pointed a shotgun at Burton, and prepared to execute him.

Ian put his hands on the barrel and lowered Ted's gun.

"This douchebag needs to die right here and now," said Ted.

Ian was calm. "We need him. We need whatever we can extract from him, then we can think about punishment."

"I'm not telling you nothing," Burton said.

Ian smiled down at him and said, "I guarantee you will."

"We need to kill this motherfucker," said Cingcade, his face contorted with rage. He and Alberto were close friends.

Cynthia and Mohan Das came running to the café and quickly examined Alberto. Mohan shook his head, then moved to Marcus and looked at his injuries. "The wounds are deep and serious," he said, "but I don't think they will be fatal. Let's get him to the infirmary."

Heather, Alberto's beautiful wife, took the horrible news at home from Harlan.

78

TED AND OTHERS WANTED PAYBACKS. They interrogated Burton, Pepper Wyle, Susan Patrick, and other NADF deserters. After repeated grillings, they concluded that Burton acted alone. Harlan, Ian, Peter Ashkin, and Danny all participated in Burton's interrogation. They were by no means gentle and told him flat out that they would withhold first aid and let him die of gangrene if he didn't cooperate. Other than that, they never crossed the line into active torture, though the temptation was there.

When Harlan asked Burton why the NADF assassinated Alberto, Burton admitted he was after Marcus and Chris.

"Our new country needs to eliminate all of you," he said with a snarl. "I'm only sorry I didn't kill Longborn, Knox, you, and a few others. Your old government failed. You are the disease. We are the cure."

Ian looked at Danny and rolled his eyes.

The bullet Ian fired had gone through Burton's lower calf and grazed his fibula. It wasn't life threatening, but it was painful. Professional as always, Cynthia cleaned and dressed his wound, and then he was chained to a bed in a cabin near the infirmary that had been converted to a makeshift jail.

Aided by two former corpsmen, Mohan, Laxmi, and Cynthia operated on Longborn and administered sedatives and antibiotics.

Harlan asked Peter to convene a trial when Burton could stand up. Under the rule of law, he would have his moment like anyone else.

Meanwhile, Harlan wanted to meet with as many Jedis as were available on short notice. They now needed to move fast.

79

EVEN BEFORE THE LOSS OF ALBERTO, THERE HAD BEEN A LITTLE GOOD NEWS. Electric power had been lasting longer. They would have several days before lights flickered off again. Someone was working to restore the energy grid and Duck Springs was recharging batteries.

Transmissions coming in from New York, St. Louis, Chicago, and Canada suggested St. Louis was the epicenter of a lot of fighting. The Jedis and remaining Ducklings greedily grabbed at every piece of information they could. Rumors, gossip, and free-floating speculation—a perpetual town habit—were gratefully received. Still, fact and fiction blurred into white noise.

The NADF was winning. No, they were losing. Willard and Brody were consolidating their forces and heading west. No, their alliance was falling apart. They were winning and taking control of huge swaths of the United States. No, they were retreating. Willard was on a plane fleeing the country. No, he was in Montana setting up a new capitol. Actually, he was dead. No, it was Brody who was dead. Actually, it was both.

Whatever was happening, they at least had more contact with the rest of the world. The only bad news—and it was bad—was Laxmi's report on Marcus. He had developed an infection that had spread to his lungs. His lips were cyanotic and his breathing labored.

80

THERE WERE SPORADIC SKIRMISHES, BUT DUCK SPRINGS NOW HAD ONLY A FEW PEOPLE LEFT TO RECEIVE FIRE AND SHOOT BACK. Most of the Jedis were still in town but Harlan figured the end game was close and they would all have to leave in another day or so. In anticipation, he asked Vern and some former combat vets who had been in special units to begin setting up C4 booby traps that they would trigger when they left.

"We'll mine the thoroughfare into town," Harlan explained.

Grant Terwilliger chirped in, "I know that one! The old pull-the-fat-guy-through-the-eye-of-the-needle trick."

"Exactly," said Harlan.

81

EVEN AS DUCK SPRINGS RESIDENTS PACKED OFF TO BRADFORD, THE NADF SENT SMALL TEAMS AGAINST THE TOWN'S DEFENSES. Though the NADF's store of armed drones was near exhaustion, they launched small ones. The town fought back picking off NADF soldiers and drone launchers whenever they could. Harlan counseled everyone to conserve ammunition and supplies while getting the NADF to waste theirs. He said one of O'Reilly's tactics would be to weaken them by forcing them to expend shells and bullets.

"How do you know that?" someone asked.

"Because that's what Sun Tzu advised, and what I would do if our positions were reversed. The NADF will have more fighters and ammo than we do."

The Duck Springs detachment on the plateau was dug in, but it was also the target of NADF sorties. O'Reilly had started to move his forces across from Duck Springs closer to the Big Green. Harlan had several Strykers from Bradford ranging along their side of the river firing occasional bursts at O'Reilly's people and, just as often, receiving fire.

Meanwhile, most radio reports were still amateur and infrequent, but gaining in number and, if they were even partially right, the NADF appeared to be now getting serious pushback. From what they could piece together, battles had broken out near New York City, in Richmond, Virginia, near Bethlehem, Pennsylvania, and in Canton, Ohio.

Assembling the strands of news, they surmised the NADF had created strongholds in Texas, Colorado, and South Dakota, and were now digging into their area in the Northwest. They presumed the NADF wanted to take Seattle, San Francisco, and Los Angeles—or at least cripple those cities and recruit more fighters.

The townspeople of Duck Springs were completely bisected. Most were now at Bradford while a small number stayed in town. Danny, Ian, and Harlan met with one of Izzy's boy-genius friends, a tubby kid nicknamed Smurf. He was doughy, with a thin mustache he was trying to grow. Danny never caught Smurf's real name. Amos Arnold, who seemed to know about electricity, was also in the huddle along with other Jedis.

"What do you think?" Harlan asked.

Amos said, "Our electricity used to come from hydroelectric generators along the Columbia River, but the grid is complex. Some of the juice came from Bonneville to Crockett City, some from a nuclear plant near Hanford, and some of it is pushed to outlying areas near Crockett City. "The thing about the grid is it has lots of interconnected transmission lines. That's what used to give everyone redundancy for shutdowns."

Smurf added, "The grid has been down for months, so it will take time to bring it back. It has to come online in stages or else the system fries. The good news is we should be able to get even more radios going and improve internal and external communications."

82

WHEN THE REST OF THE JEDIS ARRIVED, CYNTHIA SAID THE MEDICAL TEAM WAS TREATING A FEW MAJOR INJURIES AND DOZENS OF MINOR WOUNDS FROM THE BARRICADES. They had lost more than a dozen of the town's people. The medical people left in Duck Springs were working without X-rays, CAT scanners, or MRIs. The biggest danger was infections. Cynthia was eager to transport all wounded to Bradford, which had more beds available.

Pops reported that most of the usable food provisions had gone to Bradford. The rest were in a locked room at the community center. Their final stock of MREs was good, and they could get drinking water from the spring if they had to.

Reporting on the situation at the top of the bluff, Ian said there was sporadic gunfire from NADF patrols but no serious assaults. He said that, from his perch, the real action looked to be developing across the Green.

Meghan had moved three Strykers along the river. She said there were a lot of NADF troops setting up camp about a mile back from the Green's shore. Their team now had heavier vehicles and more people in black shirts and red scarves.

Harlan scratched his chin. He hadn't shaved for a few days and his stubble was white. "We need to deal with that. That's probably where their big assault will come from. I'd like to reinforce it and get more people by the river. Peter, how many men and women can we station there?"

Ashkin said, "We have thirty-two people there now. I think we can bring in another fifteen, but we will be tapping into local citizens who don't have much equipment or training, and most of them want to join their families at Bradford. And Bradford also needs defending."

"Let's strengthen the river, Peter," said Harlan. "But be ready to move out fast."

83

THEN CAME A BIG AND VERY PERSONAL LOSS FOR THE JEDIS FROM THE NORTH BARRICADE. A runner, Eric Abbott's boy Dexter, approached Danny at the café and breathlessly blurted out, "It was a sniper. He's been shot in the chest and it looks serious."

"Who?"

"Sorry sir, I don't know his name. Somebody told me to come here and find you, General Morgan, or Mr. Jeffers."

"Where is he?" Danny asked.

"He's with Cynthia and Dr. Das."

Danny raced up to the clinic as fast as he could. Cynthia looked at him and said, with exhaustion in her voice, "He just passed away. It was a massive chest wound. We couldn't save him."

Cynthia wasn't new to death from disease, car crashes, and hunting accidents. Danny admired her strength and competence more and more. She was wiping the wet from the corner of an eye. Behind her, Mabel Wolff was sobbing.

Brian Jankowski was dead.

84

AMID SPORADIC GUN SHOTS AND DRONE ATTACKS, BRIAN WAS BURIED IN A TEMPORARY GRAVE. There were not that many people left in town. Harlan had kept back as few as possible, enough to cover the retreat to Bradford and stave off the NADF. Some of Brian's old and new friends showed up. Diego Owens, the Catholic priest, talked about Brian and reminded everyone that there really is an unseen hand at work in the universe and a greater spirit that reaches down to touch us. Then he asked everyone to remember Brian and take strength from his generosity and courage.

Danny didn't agree with the Reverend. He felt nothing but an itch for revenge against the racists who were doing everything they could to kill them, stoke hatred, and extinguish decency. He kept his hunger for vengeance to himself.

Clover headed back to the café and asked Thelma if there were enough ingredients to do some baking. She said yes, and the next day Clover delivered yellow cakes with thick chocolate frosting and white letters that read: For Brian. They delivered cakes to each of the barricades and to the airstrip where Bob, Vern, Thomas, and others were fussing with the plane.

The moment was cheerless except for the dogs. They licked the cake pans clean.

85

HARLAN ESPECIALLY LOVED CHINESE STRATAGEM NUMBER EIGHT. "Pretend to Advance Down One Path While Taking Another Hidden One." There were many interpretations of what this meant, but the one he liked best was: We will appear to be arming Duck Springs for a confrontation while simultaneously evacuating and sending out a team to grab their leaders.

"I don't get it," said Peter. "We're thin on everything."

"Peter, remember, this is three-dimensional tic-tac-toe, horizontal and vertical action lines overlapping in time. We are at a precarious moment. We can stay bunkered here a little longer, evacuate, send out forays to give them some jabs, or try to strike a coordinated crippling blow." He reminded them, "We still need to do a bit of everything, carefully, and all at once when the moment is right."

"How will we know that moment?"

"I think the NADF is weakening but it will still be a big bet. Big moves are always big bets."

Harlan was ready to roll the dice using Sun Tzu's deceptions when conditions were as good as they could get.

"We know O'Reilly's main force is concentrated across the river waiting for its moment to cross the Green and storm into town."

Harlan paused, then said, "To put it simply, I want to complete the evacuation, hurt them when they enter town, capture or kill their leaders, and head to Bradford. It will require precision, coordination, self-control, and all of our remaining weapons. I'm also counting on the fast team to get over the river and capture or kill O'Reilly and Matthews."

"So that means that I go find O'Reilly?" asked Ian for clarification.

Masaji said, "I'll go."

Danny said, "Me too."

"I want you to try and catch him and bring him straight back to Bradford," said Harlan. "We are going to booby-trap buildings and mine the road in, the perimeter of trees, and the small buildings around it with as much C4 as we have left. Vern will take charge of that. Meaning, the NADF will run the C4 gauntlet, destroy the town, and sustain a lot of losses, but they won't be fatally crippled."

Ian said, "I can stay back if you want. Danny and Masaji are good at sneaking around."

"No. I want you to lead the team." Pointing to his map, he added, "Ian, before you go, I need to make sure you have good people up top and they understand this plan. Our people need to either get down off the escarpment in time for our departure or make their own way to Bradford. Same with your fast team."

Everyone was quiet. While everyone nervously absorbed the strategy, Harlan was calm and focused.

Even while Harlan explained his three-dimensional plan, Ian privately wondered if it was really possible. *We have to find O'Reilly and Matthews, grab them, get back to town fast enough to jump on the convoy and, if we miss the bus, make our own way to Bradford with the NADF chasing us.*

It was a risky plan and there was a lot of discussion about details. Vern and Thomas needed to make sure the remaining weapons and ammunition were rationed and ready. The C4 needed to be set in places at night when the NADF couldn't see them and the rest of the team needed to know exactly where they were set so they didn't kill themselves.

Amos, back from the army base, would have to thin out the north and south roadblocks but not leave them completely unguarded to make sure their people could also get back in time to leave.

Izzy had to ensure his runners fully understood what was going on. They would be essential. Injuries were inevitable.

Toward the end of the meeting, Cynthia and Mohan Das came in. She had a dark, vacant look, as if all the light in her world had gone out. Das, said in a soft tone, "We have very bad news. Marcus Longborn has died. He developed sepsis from the injuries he sustained by the community center. In the end, he went into septic shock." He bowed his head. "I am so sorry. We did everything possible, but we couldn't bring him back."

Izzy asked, "What is sepsis?"

Das said, "It's septicemia, blood poisoning. We thought we had fought it off with the strongest antibiotics we had left, but it raged out of his lungs and through his body, and over the last twenty-four hours, infected every major organ. Toward the end, he went into a delirium and thought he was young and playing with his friends here in Duck Springs by the river, building little rock damns and bicycling through town. Then he left us. It was peaceful."

The room fell silent.

"I am so sorry to tell you this," repeated Das. "He was a wonderful and great man."

Finally, Harlan said, "Dr. Das, Cynthia, thank you for everything you did for him and keep doing for all of us. Does his family know?"

"Yes, everyone was with him at the end, though he was no longer conscious."

Chris Knox arrived, tears on his cheeks but stoic as he could be.

Harlan turned to him and said, "Speaker Knox, you are now the president of the United States. We have no judge to swear you in, but you are the government and our commander-in-chief. If you have orders, we will follow them."

The room was still. Knox paused and looked at Harlan. Then he turned without saying anything. Finally, after a long silence, he said, "General, I know what Marcus would have said. He would not want a pity party, and he knew we wouldn't have time for it anyway. He would have said we have to win this."

Later, when the meeting broke up, Knox told a story to the few who stayed behind.

"I met an Eskimo leader once, a revered elder who came to Washington heading a delegation. He was visiting the Capitol to plead for funding for healthcare, schools, jobs, and ways to keep his people and their traditional culture alive in the face of the momentous changes engulfing them. I spent a long time with him, took him to dinner, and we talked at great length.

"He was a wise man. Somehow, the conversation turned from the centuries of indignities that had been inflicted on his people and mine to the future. I listened to him with great interest. Our ancestors came from different worlds, his from our northern-most icy region, mine from Africa. What we shared was the emotion of historical injustices that can never be fully understood by those with no experience of them. Neither can those wrongs be fully righted without first understanding what happened. But what he said to me next was profound."

Knox whispered. "Perhaps those lights we see in the sky on dark nights are not stars, just the openings through which our beloved ancestors look down to tell us they are happy and we must carry on. Their hope is not for us to wallow in sad memories; it's to live life."

Everyone in the room was absolutely still. Cynthia choked and cried.

"Marcus will be watching us tonight," Knox said with certainty.

Longborn was laid to rest beside Brian Jankowski in his own temporary grave. Reverend Voss helped the mourners say goodbye.

86

EVEN WITH URGENT PREPARATIONS UNDERWAY, ANOTHER DESERTER HAD COME ACROSS THE RIVER, A SENIOR CAPTAIN NAMED BYRON FORD, WHO SAID HE REPORTED DIRECTLY TO O'REILLY. He had evaded sentries, crossed the river downstream at night, made his way through the woods, and surrendered when confronted by a Duck Springs patrol. He was instantly disarmed and brought to Harlan's house with his hands tied.

Ian Jeffers, Peter Ashkin, Chris Knox, and Danny were summoned by Izzy's runners. The NADF soldier had been frisked and was handcuffed to a chair with his feet tightly bound.

Ashkin started the questions as if he were in court. "Captain Ford, you are a deserter from the NADF. Tell us exactly why you are here and what you want. And why we shouldn't hold you accountable as a war criminal."

His story spilled out. He was an experienced professional soldier who believed the existing United States government had become incapable of change. He ignored most of the racist ranting but thought Willard, Brody, and other new leaders might bring real order. He finally concluded the NADF was a group of hoodlums disguised as patriots.

“O’Reilly and Matthews execute people at will for any disobedience,” said Ford. “They encourage their people to inflict terror, plunder noncombatants wherever they find them, and kill civilians as examples. They allow rape, murder, and butchery, and punish their own troops for one crime: insubordination.”

“What were you hoping for when you joined?” Ashkin asked.

“I wanted a new direction. I wanted leaders in Washington to bring order and accountability. I wanted less taxation and more independent city and state governments that were fair and accessible. Instead, Democrats and Republicans were locked in perpetual electoral party battles in short political cycles that achieved nothing. They kept checkmating each other and taking more and more money without delivering much for average citizens.”

They questioned him and he kept talking. He was high enough in the NADF structure to have intel. He said the NADF had a lot of desertions and at last count, maybe three-hundred real fighters and another seven-hundred hanger-on types near Bradford. They had trucks with machine guns, some remaining drones, a few Strykers, and some anti-tank guns but more fighters and weapons were coming. Brody was moving a major force westward from the Midwest.

“Ashkin asked, “What does that mean?”

“They are coming by trucks and trains but are encountering serious resistance along the way. They want to occupy and fortify Seattle and then, city by city, move south and control the West Coast. They may have an appetite for Canada, but armed opposition groups have been forming everywhere and engaging in hit-and-run raids. Citizen guerrillas blow up tracks, derail trains, and gun down NADF vehicles on the road.”

“None of it seemed coordinated nationally,” he reported. “Anti-NADF resistance groups are balkanized and run by different local monikers like The New Peoria Government and

The Committee to Reestablish St. Louis. They are weeding out NADF collaborators."

Harlan asked, "Where does Duck Springs fit in?"

Ford said, "Normally, you would be incidental, but they know Longborn and Knox are here. They are determined to kill them since they are the last symbols of the old government. As long as they are alive, they risk insurrection against the NADF."

The longer they interrogated Ford, the more they learned. A long train full of fighters and munitions was blown up as it was crossing into Idaho from Montana. Same thing elsewhere. Attacks on the NADF were happening wherever convoys were spotted. The NADF command structure was now solely in the hands of Brody.

"What about Remus Willard?" Chris asked.

"Dead," said Ford. "Died of a stroke two months ago. Most people don't know that. Brody is in charge of everything. He always was."

Ian wanted to know what their plans were for Duck Springs.

Ford said, "They want Longborn, Knox, and will execute all of you. They need to take this town and make sure the world knows they killed you."

Ford went on for a while and was soon repeating himself. Danny's bullshit detector was up and he didn't trust Ford, but it was compatible with all the other news trickling in.

The NADF was at a turning point, perhaps on the run. They had been pushed back on the East Coast and shoehorned into the central Midwest. They still had strongholds in the South and Southwest, but resistance was emerging everywhere.

Chris Knox had been listening and finally spoke. He also asked the most penetrating question of all. "One of your people who came across talking like you was an agent who killed our leader and my good friend, Marcus Longborn. Why should we believe you?"

There was a pause, and then Ford said, "I'm sorry he died, but you need to believe me and if you don't and you tell me to leave, I will. I will try to run, but frankly, I'm ready to fight back."

"If we let you stay," Harlan said, "in fact if we let you live, which you shouldn't automatically assume since we are at war. Will you obey us?"

"Yes," said Ford.

"Swear it," demanded Knox, "and you better be believable. I've been in politics all my life. Like Lyndon Johnson used to say, I know the difference between chicken salad and chicken shit."

"I swear it on my mother's grave," said Ford. "Those men are monsters."

87

MUCH AS HE DISLIKED BEING CALLED "SIR" OR "GENERAL," HARLAN WAS UNQUESTIONABLY THE TRUSTED ORCHESTRA CONDUCTOR OF THE DUCK SPRINGS DEFIANCE. He had a profound understanding of how wars come in different sizes and are won at different moments—some of them simultaneous, some sequential, some asynchronous, and many of them unpredictable in size and ferocity. Even then, wars always resulted in carnage and collateral damage.

Harlan once told Danny the First American Civil War had 10,500 different battles. He said WWI, WWII, Korea, Vietnam, and The Sandbox Wars had thousands of specific sieges, ambuscades, tank fights, surface confrontations, destroyer and submarine chases, aerial dogfights, and bombing runs, often fought and refought over the same terrains by sailors or foot soldiers. Every clash had its own signature.

Harlan repeatedly said their biggest danger was hubris and overconfidence. Years ago, Sam Johnson and Myron Shapiro had said the same thing in different ways. Myron's style was intellectual. Sam's was blunt.

Harlan had examples he drew on. Bonaparte at breakfast with his generals on the morning of Waterloo reputedly said, "I tell you, Wellington is a bad general, the English are bad soldiers, and we will settle this matter by lunch." And General George Custer, full of monomaniacal thick-headedness, said "There are not enough Indians in the world to defeat the Seventh Calvary."

Harlan was what Danny's people called a *mensch*, a man of unusual wisdom and integrity. He was learned, brilliant, and brave and had a few specific behaviors that anchored his leadership. It took two more days for him to fully prepare for the big battle that was about to commence. Finally, he told everyone, "Tomorrow, we go."

88

WITH THE ADDITIONAL INTEL FROM FORD, HARLAN'S MULTI-PRONGED ATTACK AGAINST THE NADF BEGAN WHEN THE DUCK SPRINGS "AIR FORCE" LAUNCHED ITS AERIAL ATTACK ON THE ENEMY THAT WAS GATHERED ON THE EAST SIDE OF THE BIG GREEN. The grassy runway near Ogden Road was dry and the windsock barely moving, allowing Bob Williams and Thomas Quinn to take off in their creaky Cessna.

"It's really been an after-school project," Bob had originally told Danny with a grin. "A lot of WD-40, bailing wire, bubble gum, and duct tape. Sort of the way we did things in the Peace Corps."

It looked small, gawky, and lonely, as if the wings might need to flap up and down before it could lift.

"Does it actually fly?" Danny asked him.

"It's not quite an F-16 Falcon, but she'll get airborne. It's the landing I'm worried about. The airframe and landing wheels have a strong aversion to rockets, drones, and bullets."

This particular C-152 had originally been a flight school trainer outside Berwick in the 1980s. It was a gangly, sturdy creature with a tricycle landing gear, rickety-looking and ugly as a plucked chicken, but easy to operate and maintain. It had two seats and a small area behind them for bottles and guns. Bob was pilot, Thomas was the bombardier.

Diego, Roy, Chris, and a few other gawkers, including Clover, and Pops, came to watch. Clover whispered to Pops: "This is what Kitty Hawk must have felt like, people wondering which would win: gravity or a machine?"

She asked Roy, "Does Bob actually know what he is doing?"

Roy laughed. "He could fly a stove if we Scotch-taped wings to it."

Rosa Parks and Ladybird Johnson kept looking to see if the plane needed to be pulled as Thomas awkwardly folded himself into the copilot's seat. For a moment, the dogs whined and looked lost. Then they wagged their tails and lay down, heads on paws.

Bob wiggled into the pilot's seat, ran a few checks, and snapped his seat belt on. He turned the key, the plane coughed, fired up, rolled across the grassy runway, and took off. The peanut gallery clapped. When the Cessna landed forty minutes later, there were bullet holes in the fuselage.

"More duct tape and chewing gum work," said Bob.

They had flown low and straight over the NADF encampment and made a beeline for the armored equipment. Once there, Bob tilted the plane right and Thomas, loosely strapped in, opened his door and dropped gas bottles on Humvees, jeeps, and personnel carriers. Some of the hatches on the vehicles were open. They had caught the enemy off guard.

The Cessna banked, turned, did a second run and launched more cocktails into some tents, all the while taking fire. Bob and Thomas returned as happy warriors. They would become legends. Thoreau's buddy Ralph Waldo Emerson once said heroes are no braver than ordinary people, but they are braver five minutes longer.

Duck Springs had new heroes.

89

THE FIGHT ACROSS THE RIVER WAS JUST AS FAST, FURIOUS, AND DISRUPTIVE TO THE NADF'S GREEN RIVER TROOPS. Duck Springs had the Strykers they had brought back from Bradford. Strykers were a powerful deterrent since they could maneuver fast. Plus, Meghan, in the lead, handled hers like a highly trained horse.

There were losses: Otis, Stinky, and one of Izzy's runners, a kid named Joey but there were many more dead and wounded NADF soldiers and a lot of their equipment was destroyed.

90

THAT NIGHT, TWO THINGS HAPPENED. First, Clover told Danny she was coming with him when their team went off to look for O'Reilly and the other NADF leaders. She was unusually insistent and said, "You think I'm Duck Springs's star boarder? I won't sit around counting cans of tuna fish here or at Bradford."

Her idea was impossible.

"You're strong, Clover, the strongest, finest, and most amazing woman I have ever known, and I am deeply in love with you. But you cannot come. This is a military operation and Ian, Masaji, Paul, and I are trained for this."

He watched her jaw set and arms fold across her chest, full of pouty stubbornness. "My mind is made up," she said again. "I'm going with you. We are in it together. If you don't come back, I don't want to either."

"That isn't your decision to make, Clover."

Her face pinched up, her unblemished forehead furrowed with lines, her lips in as close to a snit as Danny had ever seen. "Whose is it then?" she asked.

"Our team's, and I know what they will say. Stay here, help Harlan with operations, and I'll see you at Bradford."

"You promise to come back?"

"I want to live. And I want to live with you and no one else. Forever. Finding you in the middle of this mess has been my blessing and calling."

"Huh?"

"My purpose, my job, the exact right thing."

"What does that mean?"

"I need to be of use in this world for whatever time I have left. I want to resist oppressors, be forever in love with you, and keep practicing both of those every day I am alive."

Danny saw the beginning of a smile. Close enough to a truce.

There was one other matter but no one, Danny included, had time for it. In the morning, Laxmi Das opened the door where Bennet Burton was confined to check on his leg. She found him in a pool of blood. Someone had snuck into the makeshift jail where he was tethered to a metal bedframe bolted to the floor and cut his throat. He had likely bled out in a minute.

91

DANNY ONCE READ THE HARDEST THING IN LIFE IS TO KNOW EXACTLY WHICH BRIDGES TO CROSS AND WHICH ONES TO JUMP OFF OR BURN BEHIND YOU. Now he knew.

Masaji, Paul, Ian, and Danny detoured five miles north of town to cross the Big Green. They waded through cold water over at a shallow spot and flanked O'Reilly's people. They assumed he and other leaders would be in the rear.

The morning was quiet and in the 40-degree temperature, the ground was muddy and the grass slippery from a brief shower. The Cessna was in the air again, and the diversionary fight at the river was underway as they moved on their mission. Clouds hung over Duck Springs, which worked to the benefit of their team counting on stealth.

Meghan's force was heading across the river with as much ruckus as they could generate. The NADF wasn't fully awake. Meghan's objective, along with the Cessna's, was timed to bust up the NADF's more lethal vehicles and weapons and get them to chase over the river and into town. Meghan led her Stryker team operating .30 and .50 caliber guns. Horace Gruber was her driver.

Local cop, Bucky Fontaine, drove another and Ted Cingcade one more. Former NADF lieutenant Byron Ford manned a gun.

Danny wasn't sure about Meghan, Ian, or anyone else, but when battles raged and he was killing, he felt nothing. The regrets came later.

Overhead, doing close air support, Bob, Thomas, and the Cessna 152 swept in low and dropped their remaining cocktails, then turned and ran. Some of the bottles hit vehicles, clusters of sleepy fighters, and stacks of munitions.

Once done, the river contingent turned and raced back to Duck Springs. Meghan's element of surprise was gone and NADF fighters scampered out of hibernation and fired back, with O'Reilly's people counter-attacking Meghan. The NADF stormed into town, crashed through the river barriers with their Strykers, and hundreds of men with guns rampaged through Duck Springs. Meanwhile, some of Brody's army attacked Bradford.

It was all unfolding.

92

HARLAN HAD DESCRIBED THE FIGHT AS THREE-DIMENSIONAL TIC-TAC-TOE. Danny thought it was more like a 10,000-piece puzzle with every piece vibrating and expanding or shrinking as someone tried to assemble it. It all made perfect sense and Harlan's porcupine offense was in play, all quills out. They were leading a strong fight even if by the numbers they were outmanned and outgunned.

The Bradford Roman Training Center where most of the townspeople were was far more defensible than Duck Springs. The base's larger concrete buildings were situated near the entrance. Offices, classrooms, the mess hall, maintenance buildings, the sickbay, and armory were in reasonable shape. The Cessna would have a small hangar where it could be repaired.

All the townspeople had found places to shelter. Ashkin was the logistics manager and had everyone on alert and organized into task groups for food, medical attention, and tactical fighting at places where they would inevitably be needed.

A dozen armored vehicles—Strykers, jeeps, and trucks—were fueled and roaming the inside of Bradford's perimeter giving and receiving fire. Thanks to reserve generators and longer periods of uninterrupted electricity, communications on the base and between vehicles were good.

Bradford's Duck Garrison was keeping the NADF at bay.

93

THE BLUFF CONTINGENT DESCENDED AND THE SOUTH AND NORTH BARRICADERS, MINUS A FEW VEHICLES, MOVED BACK TO TOWN AND HEADED TO BRADFORD. Tiny Porter drove his yellow bus that was parked by the café. Clover helped the remaining citizens load up. In addition to the bus and a dozen trucks and cars, Meghan and Horace were back from the river and their Stryker was stuffed with kids.

Luck happens when preparation meets opportunity, and it works against anyone who depends fully on it. That is what Danny knew from Kashmir, MCS, and gambling.

The last Duck Springs vehicles left minutes ahead of O'Reilly's force, which stormed into town. As they moved through the tic-tac-toe lines Harlan had choreographed, there was a lot of random small-arms fire and a couple of drones coming in. The last person to leave on the last vehicle was Harlan Morgan.

As his car sped away, C4 explosions started going off.

Vern and his team had done a precision job of mining the roads leading into town from the river. Dozens of NADF soldiers were killed and more wounded and clogging the road. NADF vehicles drove over them, intent on their targets.

94

WHEN IAN, MASAJI, PAUL, AND DANNY LEFT DUCK SPRINGS, CAPTAIN FORD, THE NADF DESERTER, HAD OFFERED TO JOIN THEM. They had drawn a lot of useful information out of him but declined his offer. Genuine as he seemed to be, after the loss of Alberto and Marcus, nobody fully trusted him for this kind of mission.

The intel he gave suggested O'Reilly and most of his people would be in a rear command post more than a mile and a half back from the Big Green and uphill. They would be using radios and couriers to send orders and, other than the force outside Bradford, they would be focused on Duck Springs straight ahead of them.

Ian's team made a wide berth away from town. It made sense even though it required them to move north, cross the river, bushwhack their way above the NADF command post, and come down through a thickly forested area behind them. They jump-started an ancient Toyota held together by instinct and rust. The starter finally caught and, after a lot of sputtering they got the old beater moving and drove north.

"This is a real shitbox," said Ian.

The Toyota's seats were ripped and moldy and two partially opened windows were stuck halfway up.

"I wish we had my Nissan," Ian said, "but it's at Bradford."

Masaji chimed in from the passenger seat. "This will take us time and we will want to zig, zag, and dogleg in wide ellipses.

"Why?" Danny asked him.

Masaji laughed and said, "Only demons walk in straight lines, not humans."

Danny liked that.

95

THEY DROVE NORTH ON C-18, ABANDONED THE CAR IN A DITCH ON THE SIDE OF THE ROAD, COVERED IT WITH BRANCHES, AND HEADED EAST ON FOOT TOWARD THE BIG GREEN AND THE HILLS ABOVE. They traveled light and carried minimal supplies: ammunition, MREs, first aid kits, ground cloths, camouflage Gortex, toilet paper, and binoculars. Ian had topographic maps in his pack.

They also had good weapons, all of which came from Bradford. In addition to pistols and knives, they had Army issue M4 carbines with extra magazines and Ian carried an M107 Barrett sniper rifle with a high-power telescopic sight. Once past the river, they headed uphill and then dry-camped in a cold swale.

That evening, Paul Chan and Danny talked. Paul was an introvert but his story unfolded.

"I'm half Chinese, half Vietnamese," he explained, "but I can speak both. My mother was Chinese and met my father at a diplomatic meeting during The American War."

"How did you become a Buddhist and find your way to Superstition Pass?"

"I studied engineering because my father wanted me to, though I had no heart for it. He wanted me to be a civil engineer or lawyer, but two things happened. Even though we were in a peace time," Paul continued, "I was drafted into the army and put in a detachment near Huế. It was an old city, and we didn't have much to do. That is how I started to connect with my Buddhist roots."

Masaji joined them. Soon, Ian came over. He had been scouting the hill above for about an hour.

Paul continued. "In Huế, I came across a temple organized by some Japanese priests, and I began to seriously study Zen. Zen made sense. Buddha said the trouble is we always think we have time. We don't. I understood that instantly and studied breathing, posture, and the letting go of thoughts, especially the ones I felt most attached to. I still struggle with that. Zen is demanding and full of many different paradoxes my teachers forced me to confront."

"I did the same thing," said Masaji.

Danny said, "I don't understand how to do any of this."

"Maybe when all this is over," Masaji whispered, "you'll find a similar path."

"But the one thing I tried to learn," said Paul, "was the way of the mindful warrior."

"When I think of religious warriors," said Ian, "I think of the Crusaders in the Middle Ages, who were actually a bunch of sadistic thugs."

Masaji then said, "In Japan, they were different. They were called *Sōhei* and were a brotherhood of Buddhist monk-soldiers charged with protecting their people and their branch of Buddhism. They had a big temple in Kyoto."

"I think Harlan is a warrior-monk," Danny said. "So tell me, how did you both get to Superstition Pass?"

Paul spoke first. "I met Shane at a temple in Hanoi after I was out of the army and he told me he wanted to bring together a small group of searchers someplace in the Pacific Northwest. I was impressed with his vision of living simply and trying to find harmony in our tumultuous world."

Masaji added, "I had a similar experience. Shane was one of the most remarkable people I've ever met. He talked at length about what he called 'crazy knowledge' I was hungry for it."

"When I left Seattle," Danny told them, "I felt nothing but death. I wanted to get away and empty myself out and disappear. Instead, I found Clover and Duck Springs, but I also have learned to keep my expectations in check. I know there's a fine line between hoping and hallucinating."

Ian had been quietly listening but then said, "I think each of us is some odd version of those *Sōhei*. We don't like fighting and killing, and we all struggle with right and wrong."

The talk trailed off and, after a time, they put down their ground cloths and wrapped themselves in Gortex.

96

THEY WERE MOVING BEFORE THE SUN WAS UP. As the sky got lighter, they could see the hills above were thick with firs, pines, and oaks. They followed a few game trails and ranged left and right to avoid Masaji's demons. After several hours they arrived on the ridge topping the Big Green River Valley. Then they turned east.

In the more open landscapes of the Kashmir Valley something as simple as walking used to tax Danny. He was always wary, moving slowly, scanning for that one small sound or sight that might ignite his amygdala and say snake.

Suddenly, Masaji stopped and raised his hand and everyone slumped to the ground. He pointed to a small NADF patrol ahead and slightly down slope. They scanned the patrol through binoculars.

It consisted of three men and two women. They were wearing NADF camo pants, red scarves, black shirts, and black berets and they were armed. Ian screwed a silencer onto the end of his sniper rifle, pulled down the tripod legs, and watched through his scope.

"Can we avoid them?" Paul whispered.

"I don't think so," said Ian. "Plus we might get information out of them and use their scarves and berets in case we need camouflage to get to O'Reilly."

Danny, Masaji, and Paul nodded. Ian fired five quick rounds that instantly took them down.

When they reached them, they were all dead. They inspected each of them. One man, who they guessed was the leader because of the insignia on his beret, was tall and thickset with a puffy, blood-smeared face. Maybe in his fifties. The other men appeared to be in their twenties. Both were sunburned and one had a severe case of acne. The women, a brunette and a redhead, looked a little older.

They stripped off some of their clothes and dragged their bodies into the bushes. They had made a mistake not to capture at least one of them alive for better information. Paul mentioned that to Ian.

He agreed. "I'm not the shooter I once was."

97

WHEN HE WAS TWELVE YEARS OLD, GROWING UP IN PORTLAND, DANNY LIVED IN A RUN-OF-THE-MILL NEIGHBORHOOD THAT HAD ONE SPECIAL FEATURE. They were a ten-minute bike ride from Forest Park, one of the largest urban green spots in the country. Forest Park's 5,000 acres of trails, meadows, and arbors were a perfect playground for the pack he ran with. There were lots of places to run around.

His mom didn't care for the kids he hung with. Some of them were Jewish, others Irish, some were German or Polish, and two were Mexican. None of them cared about any of that, but she would tell him, "Danny, lie down with dogs, wake up with fleas."

When there were enough of them, the game of choice was Capture the Flag, which they played in a large grassy area surrounded by trees. Back in the day there had been dairy farms there. This spot was a former pasture. They would divide into two teams and each would have its own base at least a quarter mile from the other. In the middle of each base was a flag on a pole. Old T-shirts and tall sticks were their only equipment. The whole idea was to creep around, avoid getting captured, snag the other team's flag, and bring it back to your own base. Loyalties were transitory. If you got tagged, or in their version tackled, you were conscripted by your opponents.

Boys in most cultures engage in similar games that prepare for manhood. Now, on the ridge above Duck Springs and looking down at the Green River, they were playing Capture the Flag with the NADF.

In the late afternoon, their long circle paid off. They were at a highpoint on the ridgeline above the Big Green and inched their way down so they could get a view. The vista below opened up.

Most of the NADF army was near the river preparing to assault the town, but well uphill from the fray there was a large tent with canvas sides, a cluster of smaller tents around it, and some vehicles that looked like vans, pickups, and ATVs. This had to be O'Reilly's command post. They scanned the area with binoculars and saw a dozen people. The man they presumed to be O'Reilly was standing in front of the large tent gesturing, pointing toward the river and talking to someone behind him and inside.

Ian reiterated the mission: capture NADF leaders alive. If that proved impossible, kill them.

Then they talked tactics. Ian and Danny would walk down to the tents as casually as possible. They would leave their long guns on the ground but close by. If anyone twitched, they would open up with pistols. Paul and Masaji would be right behind them and join in should firing start.

Ian grinned and said, "Don't forget to ditch the beret and scarf once we get to work. We don't want to shoot each other. Harlan would be pissed."

Then he turned to all three. "Rest up. We'll move after dark."

98

AS THE SUN WENT DOWN, THE SKY DARKENED, THE AIR COOLED, A NORTH WIND CAME UP, AND BOLTS OF LIGHTNING IN LICORICE CLOUDS MOVED IN ON FAST GUSTS. Then it started drizzling. As the squall whipped up, Masaji said, "This is perfect weather. They won't expect us."

Even though some of the clothes they appropriated were splotched with blood, they donned the berets and red scarves and started downhill. The grass was slippery and the going slow. As they approached the command center, there was surprisingly little activity. The five they had killed may have been sentries, but there could be others patrolling nearby. The side flaps on the larger tent were tied down and any remaining sentries seemed to be in their tents and out of the rain.

Masaji stood by two of the small tents, Paul by the others. Ian and Danny opened the door flap of the command center and went in. They saw five people inside: O'Reilly, Matthews, Brody, and two others. Matthews reached for a pistol. Ian killed him instantly. When two others started to move, Danny shot them. Then they heard gunshots from outside. Ian told O'Reilly and Brody to freeze and get down on the ground. That's when Paul and Masaji came in.

The NADF leaders were different from what Danny had imagined. Ned O'Reilly was paunchy and thick around the middle. He had a fat, liverish face with leaky eyes and an explosion of thin gray hair on the sides of his head. His nose was red and puffy the way serious drinkers look after years of boilermakers. He may have once had the trim and bearing of an officer, but the man in front of them was a sorry looking soldier.

"You fuckers will never get out of here alive," he wheezed and coughed, spewing out a string of epithets. "My people are gonna skin you."

Ian put the barrel of his pistol in O'Reilly's ear and told him to shut up. Once he felt the cylinder, he stopped talking.

Masaji tied their arms behind their backs, and Paul used the red NADF scarves to gag them.

Brody was silent, and also not what Danny expected. He was thin and hard-looking with jet-black hair and a wiry frame. Even on the ground inside the tent he appeared iron-jawed and in excellent shape for a man Danny reckoned to be well into his sixties.

Brody was a two-star, a major general who had seen combat, and had a long scar on his right cheek that he picked up in one of The Sandbox fights. Like his father, he was an academy graduate. He may have been an officer, but he was a traitor. Harlan suspected he was the central architect of the conspiracy from the start. Willard had likely been a front man, but Brody would have been the real brain behind the rapid decapitation of the United States government.

Danny stared at him. Brody said nothing but blazed with a look that seemed to say, *Untie me and bring your face over here so I can punch it.*

Ian and Masaji rummaged through various papers and maps in the tent while Paul and Danny dragged dead bodies outside and left them in the rain. They checked all the tents for weapons and examined the vehicles. Their next task would be to get Brody, O'Reilly, and themselves to Bradford.

The storm blew out as fast as it had rolled in. Ian said, "Just before dawn will be our best time. We'll stay here for a few more hours, then make our way downhill and cross the river into Duck Springs and head south to Bradford. We have to be prepared for resistance."

There was one large van that could hold all of them. When the rain stopped, the sky turned gunmetal gray and then inky with a few stars blinking in the wake of the storm.

Near midnight, O'Reilly cleared his throat of phlegm and tried to sit up. He looked at Masaji, scowled, and barked, "Hey, whatever your Jap name is, come over here and unhook me so I can go piss."

Masaji stared at him and said nothing. His stirring woke Brody, who said, "I need to do that too." These were the first words Danny heard from Brody. He had a voice and tone that was used to being obeyed.

"One at a time," said Ian, "under gunpoint."

A few hours later, the team put fresh ammunition in their pockets, loaded the van, and set off before sunrise. Ian drove and Danny was in the front passenger seat. Behind them were O'Reilly and Brody with Masaji and Paul behind them with knives and pistols out.

"Gentlemen," Ian said as he turned and faced them, "one wrong peep out of either of you and you both die holding your throats."

99

THEY DROVE DOWNHILL AND CROSSED THE RIVER AT A SHALLOW FORD THAT OTHER VEHICLES HAD USED. While they had been in the hills, Meghan's Stryker had probably been over this ford, as had the NADF's armored vehicles going the opposite way. They drove into Duck Springs on a slight prearranged zig zag of streets.

The buildings in the center of town were demolished, many of them smoldering. There were small piles of dead NADF soldiers. Even though they were at war with bad people, Danny was bone weary of so much death. *Never again*, he told himself.

They kept rolling, staring out the window. Masaji whispered a psalm. "As for man, his days are like grass and as a flower in the field, so he flourishes. And when the wind has passed over it, it is no more."

On the way to the intersection at Ogden Road, Danny noticed a few houses still intact. If luck held, maybe he and Clover could return to their painting and scribbling.

100

BEFORE THEIR MISSION STARTED, IAN HAD SAID THEY WOULD LIKELY ENCOUNTER NADF RESISTANCE ON THE ROAD SOUTH TO BRADFORD. The way was unexpectedly clear. They pulled up to the gate but kept their distance knowing it would be bristling with fighters. Ian stepped out of the van with his hands up.

"It's Ian Jeffers," he said. "I'm with Masaji Hiraoka, Paul Chang, and Danny Goodman and we have prisoners."

Izzy Watts stepped out, squinted, and his face erupted into a hubcap-sized smile. He was wearing fatigues, had a pistol in a shoulder holster across his chest, and a wicked looking hunting knife in his belt. His hair was a bird's nest—blond, kinky, and in need of a serious haircut. "Ian!" Then he saw Danny and out popped the old Izzy. "Dudes, who do you have there?"

Ian said, "Iz, let us in and send a message to Harlan and Chris letting them know we brought them some presents. That's Major General Eugene Brody, and that sad thing next to him is former Sergeant Major Ned O'Reilly."

When the gate opened, Harlan and Chris walked out to meet them. Harlan stood behind Chris, neatly dressed and composed.

Knox's eyes were blazing as he stepped up to the van. He opened the door and peered straight into Brody's eyes. He stared at him for a long moment, and then in that deep, sonorous voice said, "General Brody, I am President Christopher L. Knox. Welcome to the United States of America."

PART IV

101

IN THE FURY OF WWII, ALBERT CAMUS WAS A HUMAN RHEOSTAT, AN INSTRUMENT TO MANAGE THE FLOW OF RESISTANCE IN THE SERVICE OF LIBERATION. Being French and Algerian, he came from two worlds and yearned for authenticity, but his evolving discernments touched people who came in contact with him. He never did answer, with convincing logic, whether humans are inherently conniving and untrustworthy or intrinsically cooperative and generous. He seemed to accept we are both. His personal answer was his vow to be neither an oppressor nor a victim.

That is a challenging proposition and prone to slippage in either direction when confronted by people who want to kill you. In addition to physical threats, enemies thrive when fear wears down the edges of your soul. The Chinese say it is better to be a dog in peace than a human in war.

Izzy gave them a fast but thorough update. While they were hunting O'Reilly, Matthews, and Brody in the hills above the Green, Bradford experienced serious attacks from the NADF on the eastern perimeter. It was constantly under assault.

The NADF force outside Bradford appeared to be led by a lieutenant colonel named Franklin Rose Sherwood from Montrose, Georgia. Like most of Brody's commanders, he was a cool-headed fanatic who grew up two centuries too late for what he called "The War of Northern Aggression."

Sherwood had been deploying his fighters in small units in the hope of penetrating Bradford at three or four spots along the fence line. Izzy said the remaining NADF force was still dangerous but appeared dispirited. Desertions were increasing, but even the public execution of five people caught fleeing didn't make much difference. The fighting persisted.

"NADF snipers have been picking off some of our people and we have been shooting back and killing some of theirs," Izzy said. "We've traded a few drones but we are running out and I think they are too."

Small NADF squads kept hitting different weak spots on the perimeter, inflicting whatever damage they could. Duck Garrison people were returning the same. It was Capture the Flag.

Thanks to Peter Ashkin and The Lost Battalion's organization, the entire base was divided into quadrants with smaller grids inside each. The entrance to Bradford faced northwest. The hangar housing the Cessna and its small runway were on the southwest corner. The eastern side, north and south, was fenced, but it was also the weakest and hardest to defend. There was a lot of open ground with permeable fences. Some had been destroyed.

Danny could hear muffled gunfire and explosions coming from there. As Knox, Harlan, Ian, and the others marched the NADF prisoners off, he turned to Izzy and asked, "Where is Clover?"

"Danny, she's been hurt. She's with Cynthia and the docs at the infirmary."

Mann Tracht, Un Gott Lacht . . .

He turned and ran. When he barged in, Laxmi Das put her hand up and stopped him. "Danny, wait. You must listen to me."

He stopped. Laxmi, normally sweet and polite, was policewoman firm.

"Here's the situation," she said. "Clover was guarding the perimeter on the east side of the base with a small squad. Some kind of rocket or drone came over and landed on them. It killed Bob Williams and wounded Clover. She's sedated now, so please wait before you try to visit."

"What are her wounds?"

"She is concussed, has a dislocated shoulder, a badly shattered ankle, some cracked ribs, small lacerations, and a piece of shrapnel that punctured her left lung."

"Will she be OK?"

"Yes, but she needs time, and you have to give it to her."

Thoughts of Longborn's septicemia flashed through his mind.

"Mohan and I can treat the physiology and the threat of infection. It's the psychology afterward that takes time."

"She's tough. She'll recover," but even as he said those words, he felt threading doubt. He had seen this before in Srinagar. He knew how to immunize himself when it involved others. He had also seen combat-hardened soldiers who seemed immortal disintegrate. But this was Clover. She was different, the only fully luminous star in his sky.

He also remembered what Harlan and so many others had drilled into him. Hope is not a strategy. Neither is despair. They may be temporary stopping points on the road to somewhere important, but don't count on them.

Bob Marley, the old Jamaican muse with the lyrical voice and long dreadlocks, had it right. Everybody is going to hurt you. You just have to find those worth suffering for.

He sat down on an acutely uncomfortable plastic porch chair near the infirmary.

Laxmi said, "I'll let you know when you can go in, Danny. Be good and stay put."

When Mohan and Laxmi first landed in Duck Springs, he wasn't sure who they were or whether they were reputable docs. They turned out to be exceptional people. Both of them were from Madras—devout, high-caste Hindus who had gone to medical schools in both India and the United States, hated despotism, and had come to love America.

It wasn't just worry and fear. Suddenly, Danny felt completely drained. Not just exhausted, but lost. Military training and legal work prepare you for adrenaline and discomfort along with long, intermittent spells of boredom. Some of the preparation process is routine. You spent a lot of time getting ready for nothing. But combat and the loss of people close to you was different. He knew that from Srinagar, and Malcolm Crowley. And now, with an injured Clover.

Neuroscience proved it. The brain's limbic system is a fear regulator. Training numbed some of the panic, but in firefights it still surfaced. In the court system, even though the stakes could be high, anxiety reached an apex when you were in trial going mano a mano in a tough case with a highly skilled opponent on the other side and a big verdict hanging in the balance.

In everyday life, a car accident, a serious disagreement with your boss, a heated argument with your spouse, or a threat to your child suddenly changes everything. System 1 takes command and that ancient reptilian brain keeps hijacking System 2. Millions of nerve fibers stimulate adrenaline, which surges through your body, accelerating your personal horsepower. Breathing increases, muscles tense up, and blood pressure jumps.

The Marines tried to train all this out of Danny or at least attenuate it and substitute new autonomic responses. His drill instructor, the much-despised Sergeant Heenan, made everyone memorize his definition of panic and be able to recite it at any moment he might casually demand it. "Panic," he said, "is the sudden, unreasoning, overwhelming fear which attacks you in the face of real or fancied danger. Remember it. Recognize it. Keep repeating it."

Heenan's theory was that if you said it to yourself when alarm bells went off and coupled it with box breathing, it would become a muscle memory mantra. Snipers used box breathing to steady themselves for a long shot. You closed your eyes, breathed in through your nose, counted to four, held your breath inside, counted another four, and exhaled through your mouth for four more. Then you repeated the sequence.

Danny asked Masaji about this. He called it mindfulness and practiced it. He said, "That is why we chant *Om Mani Padme Hum* over and over. It's meditative and, after a time, it replaces endless mental somersaulting."

When he asked what the words meant, Masaji said, "It doesn't translate. They are six sacred syllables that have to do with a bead-jewel, a lotus flower, and enlightenment. But you don't need to know all that. You just do it."

Masaji said Zen practitioners sat every morning, trying to empty their minds and stop thinking. Eventually, the sitting meditation swallows everything and there is no day or night or right and wrong.

"What about practical things?" he asked Masaji. "What if you need to pee, scratch your ass, or fix a leaking roof?"

"There's an old proverb," he said with a laugh. "After Zen . . . the laundry."

"And after the laundry?"

"Why back to Zen of course!"

What Masaji didn't talk about is what comes after action—fatigue. Not PTSD, exactly, but the residual effect of decompression when adrenaline stops pulsing. The fatigue isn't only physical.

Clover was groggy when he was allowed in but was waking up. She had her arm, shoulder, foot, and ribs immobilized with casts and bandages.

"Hey," he said softly, kissing her forehead.

Her voice was hoarse and weak. "Hey yourself. How was the trip?"

"We got 'em," he said. "I'll tell you all about it later. You would probably have been safer with us than here."

"Doesn't matter," she whispered, "we're alive."

"Laxmi says you'll make a good recovery. Meanwhile, you look beautiful as ever."

Her eyes were half open and her voice was raspy. "Better talk to the docs and get your peepers checked, Goodman."

He sat and they talked in whispers. Mostly he held her hand until she fell asleep.

Then Laxmi came in. "Danny, go do other things. I'll send a runner if something changes. She is a very strong woman."

102

HARLAN HAD CREATED A COMMAND CENTER IN THE BUILDING BEHIND THE MAIN GATE AT BRADFORD. Danny knocked on the door and a voice said, "Come in."

Jeffers, Hiraoka, Knox, Ashkin, and other Jedis were there. As always, Harlan's office, even this makeshift one, was spare and tidy. A long table had maps, books, some Bradford manuals, and the papers they had snared on their fast team mission.

"Danny, I'm glad you're here," said Harlan. "You've been with Clover. She doing better?"

"Laxmi says she'll recover."

"She's tougher than you think," he assured him.

"That's what Laxmi says." *Why am I not fully believing it?*

Harlan turned to all of them and said, "Kudos. You folks did a terrific job. And, you all came back alive. Now we need to discuss what happens next with the prisoners."

Chris Knox added, "I want to say my thanks as well. You have given us the best, maybe the only, opportunity we have to end this fight and perhaps start to reconstruct the United States."

Harlan and Knox explained how they thought matters should proceed. Then Harlan asked one of the sentries to bring in O'Reilly.

103

O'REILLY WAS STILL FLESHY AND PUFFY AND HAD WHAT SEEMED TO BE A PERMANENT SNEER TATTOOED ON HIS FACE. His hands were tied behind his back and he was seated in front of all of them. After Ian untied his hands and cuffed him to the chair, he leaned in and whispered, "Don't be fucking around with us, O'Reilly. You're on thin ice here."

Then Peter Ashkin took the lead. A young woman took notes. She looked at O'Reilly with pure hatred. Her husband was killed by an NADF sniper.

"Sergeant Major O'Reilly—"

"That was my old rank. I'm a commander in the NADF now and that's how I want to be addressed."

Peter was his usual methodical and analytical self, but Danny could see he wasn't going to put up with phony courtesies.

"Mr. O'Reilly, you are in a still-active conflict zone and not a civilian court of law, so let's cut to the chase. President Knox and General Morgan have the power to put you to death."

O'Reilly tried to put on a brave face but was suddenly more attentive and a little less sassy.

"To be clear," Peter continued, "we don't recognize the NADF as a foreign country so your rank doesn't matter. As far as we are concerned, you are a traitor, guilty of sedition and mass murder. Under Article 1 of the Constitution, we are authorized to suppress insurrections. You can be executed."

O'Reilly physically sagged in his chair as Ashkin stared at him and started in. The questions came fast, and everyone listened and took their own notes. Ashkin's examination was another clinic in cross-examination. The more Peter dug into him over the next few hours, the weaker and more pathetic O'Reilly got.

Why did you join the NADF? How did you become a leader? What was Remus Willard's role? What happened to him? What was Brody's role in planning the coup? Who ran Pharaoh? Who were the other NADF leaders? How many fighters and units remained? Who is in command? What kind of heavy weapons do they have?

Every question led to follow-ups. Ashkin pressed harder and harder for details and slowly squeezed them out of O'Reilly. After three hours of answering questions, O'Reilly asked, "Can we take a break and can I get some water?"

Ashkin glanced at Knox who said, "Maybe later."

O'Reilly, rattled, wilted even more.

What they learned at the end of five hours was that the NADF was in tatters. They were dealing with their last remaining effort. Danny thought: *Not only is hope not a strategy, it is a very lonely emotion.*

The big NADF idea was to unify their army in the Midwest, then head west. The push through Duck Springs was supposed to have been an easy detour and a way to finish their decapitation of the government by killing Longborn and Knox.

The NADF had collapsed on the East Coast and in the Midwest. A big battle was underway in St. Louis and isolated units were fighting in the South and the West, mostly in rural locales where specific paramilitary groups were entrenched.

If accurate, the NADF was running low on people, equipment, and munitions.

A break was declared and the sentry returned O'Reilly to his locked room.

When they were alone, Knox said, "Gentlemen, I'd like your thoughts."

"Peter, you did a great examination. We got a lot of information," Harlan said, pausing, "assuming what he said is true and confirms the reports coming in by radio."

Ian said, "I think it is. Everything tells me the NADF is weakening even though they keep trying to get at us here."

Ashkin said, "We will verify what we learned when we get to Brody."

Masaji had been quiet, but now, in his mannered way, he said, "Our meeting with Brody could be a pivot. Chris and Harlan, what's the outcome you desire and what do you want to do with him and O'Reilly?"

Harlan said, "We have choices. We can put them through a formal trial by jury, which will probably lead to death sentences. We can also hold them until we are done fighting. I think the end is near anyway. Chris?"

Chris was silent for a moment, then said, "There's a part of me hungry for revenge—for my family, for those who were killed in DC, for Marcus and Alberto, and for everyone who died or was injured in this disaster. It would feel good to execute them and intimidate the NADF into submission. The problem is that it may make them into martyrs and drive them underground."

He paused as he thought out loud. "There are a few options. When it's safe, we could organize some kind of commission to determine a sentence, but I don't care for that. We need to determine our own fate and not rely on committees."

"I don't like that either," said Harlan.

"The other thing I have in mind is some kind of negotiated surrender that ends things so we can set up a reconstruction."

Danny stayed quiet during this exchange but listened carefully. Then Knox turned and said, "I'd like to hear from each of you. Masaji?"

"One way or another, we need a peace that has a chance of lasting. Even if it's not a full reconciliation, we need an end to hostilities."

Ian stood up and said, "We need to do what Masaji says. Bring this to an end even if it's distasteful and unjust for these murderers. They are real scum, but it's the long term I'm thinking about."

Chris turned. "Danny, you have a thought?"

"My mentors at the law firm trained me to win in court, but they also said that negotiating a reasonable outcome that's good for your opponent but better for you is also winning."

"I like that," said Ian.

"And if negotiations fail," he added, "we still have our combat options."

After they adjourned, Danny headed back to the infirmary to see Clover. She was still drowsy from painkillers. He sat there for a long time until Mohan, Laxmi's husband, said, "Danny, go get some food and rest."

Going out the door, he could still hear occasional gunfire coming from the east side of Bradford.

104

WHEN THEY CAPTURED BRODY AND TOOK HIM DOWNHILL WITH A KNIFE AT HIS THROAT, BRODY HAD SAID NOTHING. Danny thought that he would continue to stay sullen and tightlipped. He didn't. He glowered at everyone but was unexpectedly candid.

Brody's hands were uncuffed and he sat on a hard wooden chair. With the exception of Knox, everyone—including the sentry at the door—had sidearms at the ready. Danny took his own copious notes.

Peter Ashkin started with the same opening statement he gave to O'Reilly. The essence of it was Brody was a criminal and could be put to death for treason and murder. Unlike the day before, Ashkin then sat down and let Harlan conduct the examination. The thinking was a general-to-general discussion might be more productive.

Harlan started in. "General Brody, good morning. We are going to be here for a while. We will break midmorning and again for lunch, so before we start, can I get you anything? Food, water, coffee?"

"I had an MRE but yes, I would like strong black coffee and some water."

Harlan asked the sentry to bring both.

"General, what made you decide to overthrow the United States government?"

"I, along with a majority of Americans, were convinced the United States had descended into an irreparable condition. We had hit bottom and the current political regimes in all three branches of government couldn't be fixed. It needed to change. It still does. We need a country led by white Christians, the way our founders intended."

"How did you go about planning the coup?"

"Willard had been arguing this for years and had the support of the Hammond brothers and other businessmen. He also had the support of many in the military. As you know, my father and I both thought the country was sinking with no prospect for righting the ship of state."

"Where is your father? I knew him slightly at the academy."

"He died."

"I'm sorry, I didn't know that. What happened to Willard and the Hammond brothers?"

"Remus had a massive stroke while he was having dinner. So far as I know, the Hammonds are in the Caribbean."

"Were you the architect of the coup?"

"Yes, I want to think so, and I have no regrets."

"Why wasn't Remus?"

"He was our spokesman. Frankly, he was everybody's jolly uncle, but he had no mind for strategy, tactics, and logistics. General, you know as well as I do, it always comes down to operational execution."

"What was your strategy?"

At this, Danny thought surely Brody would clam up or change the subject. He didn't.

"We needed to delegitimize the existing United States government and take down the current leadership in all three branches of government. It had to be fast and complete." Brody turned to Knox and said, "Mr. Speaker, it was never personal. We were, and still are, patriots."

Knox stared at Brody with disgust. Danny could feel Knox's rage at the memory of all the deaths. His wife and children. President Chavez. Vice President Longborn. So many friends and colleagues. And tens of thousands more, dead. He stared at Brody but said nothing.

"What was your plan, General Brody?"

"I wanted to start in DC, then truncate as much resistance as possible in the major cities and let the NADF's regional groups gain control of smaller cities and towns."

"Who was Pharaoh and how did it operate?"

"Pharaoh was one of the smartest tactics we employed to connect and unify underground groups. We used the cyber strategies other countries had used against us and pointed them toward rightfully angry white people. They might look like crazies to most people, but believe it or not, many of them were actually very intelligent and primed for what we felt needed to be done, even if they hated each other."

"How did Pharaoh work?"

"Pharaoh was based on an older group called QAnon during President Donald Trump's takeover of the Republican Party. Trump's second term, and his final inglorious denouement didn't change anything. It just compounded the problems." He paused, drank water, and continued. "Pharaoh was basically an underground operation. Rather than send direct messages, the whole goal was to create deep doubt and make the United States government's paralysis obvious to everyone."

"It worked?"

"Completely. Along with our own communiqués, it helped make transparent the total inability of the United States government to do anything constructive."

"Wasn't it a propaganda machine to tell lies and encourage conspiracy theories?"

"That's your interpretation. We always believed it was the truth with our own views added in. Frankly, I underestimated the power of it. Pharaoh had more than two hundred fifty million followers, more than half the country—far more than I ever imagined might be possible given the leftist proclivities of the media. Bottom line: it worked."

Harlan's examination continued, tough but civil. At noon, they adjourned until 2:00 p.m.

105

DANNY STOPPED AT THE MESS HALL TO GRAB SOME FOOD. Army high-calorie MREs tasted like flavored cardboard, but Julie Roth, Amos Arnold, his wife, and a couple others had made a giant pot of soup that smelled great.

"Chicken noodle," said Julie. She looked so much better than when she first came to Duck Springs. And Danny recalled Clover saying she had a boyfriend.

Julie packaged up two take-away bowls and he headed over to the infirmary. Laxmi Das and Cynthia were sitting in the little room that passed for a lobby. "How is she?" he asked.

"Better," said Cynthia. "but still weak. We are going to have to rebuild her ankle later. but she is mending. Alert and getting hungry."

Laxmi added, "That's a good sign. She's in pain but managing it. Mohan and I are convinced she will make a strong recovery."

When he tiptoed in, Clover smiled. Strands of strawberry blonde hair were plastered on her forehead and she looked tired and in pain, but she said, "Hey Jarhead, come sit here." She patted a place next to her on the bed with her free arm.

"You look beautiful."

"You say that to all the chicks, but I'm glad you're here and I'm happy to be alive. My lung is still pumping up but I can't take deep breaths yet. My shoulder, ribs, arm, and ankle hurt a lot, but Cynthia and the docs tell me I'm healing. There will be scars and some foot issues, but I'm coming back to life."

"That's what I'm counting on. When you get healed up and this goddamned shitstorm with the NADF is over, I want to make plans."

One eyebrow arched up. "Plans?"

"That's for later."

"How goes the meeting with the NADF leaders? What are they like?"

He told her about O'Reilly and Brody but really wanted her to talk. He asked what she remembered about getting injured, hoping it was not too soon to go there.

She said, "I'm still reliving what happened, though there are blank spots."

The story sounded exactly like battles Danny had been in, especially when he was wounded and the whole world was consumed with noise and smoke and he had a constant ringing in his ears.

She said, "I was on a patrol along the eastern fence line with Bob. A couple of Strykers had been moving up and down. We saw a small squad of NADF fighters on the other side edging toward us. Then there was an explosion."

She described a weariness pressing down as if a great weight had been dropped on her, and then she just closed her eyes. Later, things stirred but she wasn't fully conscious.

"Laxmi told me I was in a dream state. She said it was common and told me I called your name. Then slowly I swam up to the surface and opened my eyes and was staring at a ceiling light and had bandages on my head, arms, legs, foot, and torso and a saline drip in my arm. Cynthia was leaning over me and Mohan and Laxmi were there. I remember Cynthia saying, 'Welcome back to the world, Clover. You'll be a little more mobile in a few days though you will still have a lot of pain. You need to take it very slow.'"

Danny urged her to have Julie's soup. "Chicken noodle soup was the cure for everything at my house," he told her. "Ma Goodman said it's Jewish penicillin."

"I don't want to know where they got that chicken," she said. She was getting perkier and sassier, and her eyes were recovering some sparkle. He stayed with her for an hour, then kissed her and headed back for the afternoon session with Brody.

106

AT THEIR NEXT MEETING, HARLAN PROBED FOR INFORMATION ON THE NADF'S REMAINING STRENGTH. Brody wouldn't get specific.

"We will replenish our fighters and supplies. Contrary to what you think, we aren't finished."

Harlan gave him a skeptical look. "General Brody, victory for the NADF is a bridge too far, so let's get down to what happens next. Candidly, we have information that you are losing in virtually every part of the country and your group outside Bradford is breaking up and filtering away. What you have left are remnants and without the strong leadership you provided, they won't keep together." He paused and looked Brody in the eye.

"You and I are soldiers. We both know militias and renegade locals don't maintain long-term discipline. You have a problem. Your troops have been abused by your own commanders. Many of them want to be done with this and go home. Bottom line: we don't believe you can succeed and we think it's time to end all this so more people don't die needlessly."

It was clear that Brody was listening. "We have the money and backup to carry on," he said.

"I think not. In fact, I'll bet on it."

Brody went quiet, then finally said, "What do you have in mind, General Morgan?"

"We are at Appomattox."

"Why do you think that?"

"Because all of us are exhausted from fighting, your people are fading, and citizens everywhere are rising up and fighting back. You may want to make some final attempt for history, but you can't win."

Both Morgan and Brody knew the American Civil War in detail, the battles, the personalities of the generals, and exactly how it ended at Appomattox in 1865 when Lee and Grant met to talk turkey.

Brody fell silent for a time, then repeated his earlier question. "What specifically do you have in mind, Harlan?"

It was the first time Brody had used Morgan's first name. Harlan reciprocated.

"Gene, you need to issue an immediate national ceasefire starting here and now. Very shortly after that, you will broadcast your announcement of the NADF's unconditional surrender and acknowledge Christopher Knox as the rightful president of the United States."

"Those terms are impossible," said Brody. "My people would never agree to them."

Harlan wasn't done.

"In that same communiqué you will explain that the NADF has agreed to give up its coup and work peacefully to rebuild the country."

"You are demanding complete capitulation."

"Absolutely. Complete and total capitulation. We will also hold accountable some NADF leaders in different parts of the country, yourself included, for atrocities. You, O'Reilly, and others will stand trial."

Knox, Ashkin, Ian, and Danny were transfixed.

"If we were to do any of this, and I'm not saying we will, we will have conditions of our own."

"State them clearly, Eugene. This isn't going to be some Solomonic splitting of the baby. The baby is the whole USA. We are at Appomattox, Versailles, and every other moment in history when opposing forces sat down to try to end hostilities."

Brody said, "Give me tonight to think about all this, and I'll come back with a response."

"Agreed," said Harlan, "but I want you to send a message to the head of whatever NADF force is still attacking us on our fence line and command them to stop. If you write out the message, I will make sure it is delivered under a white flag. Then we can talk tomorrow."

"His name is Colonel Frank Sherwood and he will honor it. He's a good man."

The message to Sherwood was delivered by Meghan and Samantha with Tiny driving and waving a white flag. If Sherwood hesitated, Tiny might talk him to death, but in short order, the NADF stopped their attacks.

107

THAT EVENING, AFTER A VISIT WITH CLOVER, DANNY MET IAN, PETER, AND MASAJI IN THE MESS HALL FOR DINNER. They talked about what had transpired and the status of the negotiations.

Masaji smiled and said, "I'm glad we have a watering hole."

"What does that mean?" Peter asked.

Masaji said, "In Africa, I once saw a lot of animals come down to drink at a big pond. Birds, monkeys, elephants, wildebeests, even bad-tempered lions and hyenas."

"I'd like to see those critters," said Ian.

"I wish we had more watering holes where we could talk things out instead of murdering each other. We need places to meet our enemies. Our negotiation table is a watering hole."

Danny loved Masaji Hiraoka. He was a monkish poet, a reluctant warrior when he needed to be, and a man who could fight like hell even when he hungered for peace.

Ashkin chimed in. "Watering holes are dangerous places. There may be crocodiles watching, waiting, hunting. Big cats can make an easy pounce once they have quenched their thirst. It's potential easy pickings."

Danny said, "My old law mentor Sam Johnson used to say if you're not at the table you may be on the menu."

Ian said, "You guys are both right. We just need to end the war."

108

THE NEXT MORNING THEY MET WITH BRODY AGAIN. Harlan started off.

"Gene, we need to hear your proposal and I hope we can find an amicable resolution."

"Thank you. I was up much of the night thinking and I agree. We are at a window of opportunity. Windows open, windows close, but the costs to get to the next one always go up. Here is what I propose."

Knox leaned in and cupped an ear.

"We will agree to a truce that spells out the conditions for dropping our war but also calls for a new constitutional convention. America needs real revision if it is to continue."

Harlan turned to Knox.

"Chris, your thoughts? You're the president. And as a backboard for all of this, let's assume that, while we are having this conversation, all formal hats are off. We are all free to explore options without the slightest assumption of commitment. In other words, nothing is decided until we decide it."

Chris pulled a chair to the table where Morgan and Brody were sitting. He thought for a moment, then said, "No, that is not a decision we will make here. The United States Constitution has provisions for its own amendment. The first order of business has to be to get government functioning. Only then can we talk about amending the Constitution."

Brody looked at Knox and said, "Would you personally endorse the idea once a working Congress has been restored?"

"I would consider it, and I would be willing to appoint a fast-acting group to suggest a list of issues should the Congress and the states approve it."

"Can some of my people be on it?"

"I won't make any promise to specific names. Hell, I don't even know who is alive, but I will commit to creating a balanced set of views representing Republicans, Democrats, conservatives, liberals, progressives, independents, libertarians, and others. If some of those are former NADF people after you have surrendered, that won't be an issue unless they are convicted of war crimes."

"Will the NADF formally be part of your new administration?"

"No, it can't be. Your organization has to be dismantled and the same principle applies. If they aren't accused of personal war crimes, they are citizens with the same restored rights as other citizens."

Knox paused, then stared at Brody.

"Frankly," he continued, "I don't care whether all your people crawl back into their holes, but we sure as hell are going back to the basics of United States democracy."

"What specifically do you mean?"

"We have laws, rules, regulations, and policies that evolved over three centuries," Knox continued, "but all of them follow core principles. We live under the rule of law, and our political existence is powered by elections and peaceful transitions of power. Everyone is equal under the law, including all the people in your army—before you tried to change that."

"What else?"

"Checks, balances, fair hearings for grievances, and simple transitions when new leaders are elected," he said. "Three branches of government, separation of powers, and procedures that keep the balance."

Brody was taken aback at Knox's vehemence.

"Tell me how you think the disbanding of the NADF will work," Brody asked Harlan.

Harlan responded, "Each unit and every individual has to swear allegiance to the United States in a verbal oath and sign a written pledge."

"What?"

"They have to take the same oath new citizens take when they immigrate. Frankly, I would love to give them the same citizenship test, which I think most would fail. We won't do that but they must support the Constitution, renounce fidelity to any other sovereign, and agree to defend the laws of the United States against all enemies, foreign and domestic.

"That's insulting. My people aren't foreigners."

"They are right now," said Harlan. "They chose that."

"What about their weapons?"

"Each man or woman who signs the oath can keep a pistol and hunting rifle. Every military-grade weapon is turned in or confiscated. Those leaders who have allowed or encouraged war crimes defined by the Geneva Convention will be prosecuted and brought to trial if there is sufficient evidence to indict them."

"What about the Second Amendment?" Brody asked.

Knox was angry now. "You abrogated the Constitution and its amendments when you killed our elected and appointed leadership."

Then, in a slightly softer tone, Knox added, "General, we need to heal the country. I plan to establish a nationwide truth and reconciliation process with skilled moderators and mediators that will encourage people on all sides and in all parts of our country to come forward with their stories. Political and legal motives aside, and painful as it will be, we have to let people tell their stories, make their declarations, and create a record for future generations."

Brody said, "I suppose there will be trials like at Nuremberg at the end of WWII. Some of the Nazis got life sentences and some were hanged."

"I'm not going to prejudge what will happen and neither should you. What we can say is it will be legal, everyone will be represented, and there will be a proper examination of witnesses and evidence."

"Mr. Knox and General Morgan," said Brody after a pause, "before I submit to any of this, I want to bring some of my senior NADF officers here. If this is supposed to be Appomattox, I want some of my people here like you have yours."

"We will do that Eugene. Tell us who you want and we'll get them."

109

THAT EVENING AFTER DINNER AT THE MESS, DANNY VISITED CLOVER AND THEN TOOK A LONG WALK. Danny was a pragmatic man but the negotiations felt surreal, as if they were taking place on another planet. They seemed completely devoid of the deep reckoning that was so needed. Vengeance? Yes, that's what he wanted. All the talk of terms felt other-worldly. What about all the blood that had been spilled because renegade nativists wanted to turn the clock back?

Morgan must have been restless too. He was out walking and they stopped and talked.

"Harlan, these negotiations are conjectural and abstract."

"They are," he admitted, "but they are necessary. We have to end this. We can win in the long run but Brody is right. The costs will go up. We need a negotiated end that will stick."

"You have doubts?"

"I do," he said. "It's easy and tempting to talk abstractly about morality and ethics. I would like to do that and I'm guessing Brody might also. We can compare cruelties and injustices forever, but we have to make decisions in real time. You know that, too, Danny. You know it from combat. We have to find tractable solutions right now. Peacemaking and war making aren't that different. They are both messy."

"I feel like we are the dog that just caught the car it had been chasing for years."

"In the end we are fallible creatures. We will sift ideas and create new ambiguities that replace old ones, hopefully better expressed, and perhaps sounder than the ones that broke us apart."

"Are you tired, sir?"

"I am. I'm too old for this. But Danny, I want to thank you for all you've done. We all have to live with our monsters. I remember some proverb that says if you dance with your demons long enough, they become angels."

They shook hands and then he added, "And what did I tell you about that 'sir' business?"

The sun was setting and the sky was vermilion. They walked back to the barracks together. Off in the distance, they heard music and finally came across Masaji and Paul playing some kind of duet on wooden flutes.

"Actually," he told Harlan, "we are indebted to you and Chris. You carried us to this moment. If not for you, we would all be dead."

"We may still be if we don't get this done."

110

THE ROOM, NOW REASSEMBLED, HELD IAN, PETER, MASAJI, DANNY, CHRIS, HARLAN, BRODY, SHERWOOD, O'REILLY, AND TWO OTHERS THAT SHERWOOD HAD BROUGHT ALONG, CAPTAINS NAMED WILFORD AND THOMPSON. Most were audience. At the table were Harlan and Knox on one side and Brody and Sherwood on the other.

This particular room had no electricity but another table in the corner had a usable manual typewriter from Maynard's collection of legendary gizmos, pads of paper, and pens. It was time to get down to business.

In every negotiation of any consequence, comes an apex moment when matters either tie together or collapse. They were at that crossroad.

Danny knew this was the exact time when some negotiators pulled out bargaining tricks in the hope of gaining last-minute advantages. They used tactics they had kept in their back pockets: feigned anger, insults, flattery, red herrings, false demands, and phony deadlines. They might create unrealistic low-ball offers, sudden new preconditions, sham walkouts, or a bogus insistence of not having authority. Danny had seen every ploy at the courthouse.

If there was any viable way to end the bloodletting and rebuild the country, both sides needed to look beyond the entrenched positions of the other and consider the deeper interests at work. The NADF needed some kind of recognition as Americans with serious goals for the country. The question in Danny's mind was good faith. Could they trust them? Was this a handover, a take-over, or something mutually acceptable between extortion at one end and bribery at the other. Negotiation, he knew, is a delicate dance and bargainers use many tactics, but any tactic that can be recognized and named by your counterpart immediately loses some of its punch.

Brody was also thinking several steps ahead. He began by saying, "Chris and Harlan, subject to two conditions and some details that we can discuss, I'm ready to try and find terms."

"What are your conditions?"

"This will be a treaty and not characterized as a truce or a surrender. For my people, these optics are critical. The treaty will meet your conditions and not presume we are an independent nation or include wiggle room for future litigators to quarrel over. It will be a treaty that obligates us to defend the United States Constitution.

"No," said Chris slamming his hand on the table. "It won't be a treaty. It won't be a truce, a contract, or some weak-assed memorandum of agreement. You must surrender and we need to embrace your concessions and capture the mutual obligations we've discussed. It has to be as airtight as we can make it and clear as a bell to anyone who reads it now or in ten years."

Brody stiffened. "What we call this is critical for my people and yours. Names are important."

Harlan let them argue, then floated his own idea.

"Better to not let the perfect defeat what is good enough. How about if we called it an accord, the Duck Springs Accord?"

"What does that mean?" asked Brody.

"It means a pact or agreement arrived at by people sitting around a table. An understanding. We can let our lawyers do the drafting to make sure it has all the right whereases, gives, and takes. We can review it and correct it until it says precisely what everyone agrees to, then sign it, issue it, and bring this goddamned shitstorm to a close."

That was the first time anyone had ever heard Harlan curse.

Harlan paused to let his idea marinate, then turned to Chris. "Could you potentially live with that if General Brody was agreeable and if all the terms were right?"

"Not what I want, but subject to review, yes."

"General Brody?"

"The same. Not what I prefer, but I could live with it."

111

THAT NIGHT AFTER VISITING CLOVER, DANNY ASKED HARLAN AND CHRIS IF HE COULD VISIT WITH BRODY ALONE. They looked puzzled and asked why. He told them he wanted to understand what made Brody tick, grasp his worldview, and put notes together for a record. Chris nodded his agreement and Harlan scribbled a note that would get him into Brody's quarters.

Chris said, "Take good notes. History will want them."

Once past the sentry, he knocked and Brody said, "Come in."

Brody was more haggard and withered from the time of his capture, the drive south to Bradford, and the long meetings. He was arrogant and hard then. Now he had dark circles under his eyes, had stopped shaving and looked like he may have stopped sleeping and eating. Once trim and sinewy, he looked eroded.

He was sitting on a bunk with his chin resting on one hand, deep in thought. Danny realized it was the same posture as Rodin's *Thinker*, body angled forward as if his head weighed too much and he needed to hold it up so he could cogitate.

"General, may I take a few minutes of your time? I'm Danny Good—"

"I know who you are," he said, looking up. "You were part of the squad that killed Matthews and captured O'Reilly and me. What do you want?"

"A conversation, sir. There are some things I'm curious about, and I suspect others will also be when this is over, including the thousands who joined you and will ponder it for the rest of their lives. I've been keeping a journal since I came to Indian Creek and Duck Springs. I want to try and write down some of what has gone on before it all gets lost and the academics start interpreting."

"I'll answer your questions, but maybe not everything. You were in the Marines, weren't you? I think I recall hearing you were in Srinagar and the Vale."

"You had good intel, sir."

"More than you know. You don't have to call me 'sir.' My name is Gene and we are both out of the military."

"That's what Harlan keeps saying. He says to stop calling him 'sir,' 'General,' or anything other than Morgan or Harlan. The way I respond is 'Sir, yes, sir!'"

Brody laughed but he had a chest cold. It came out with a wheezy cough.

"Harlan is a good man. I wish we had been on the same side. He's a fine general and a thoughtful scholar. What do you want to know, Goodman?"

Brody sat on his bed and Danny sat close by in a metal folding chair, pen and note pad ready. He assumed Brody's normal persona was brooding and pensive, but he warmed to the conversation.

"There are things I never understood about your war."

"Like?"

"I don't understand what your vision was for the United States once the coup was over. It's never been clear, and in my own mind, I'd like to know what the NADF would have done had you been victorious."

Brody went silent for a few minutes. When he finally talked, his voice was low and he groped for words. Danny wondered if he might have some kind of aphasia.

Now in the bare cell with no windows, Brody seemed a beaten man. But then he stood up, looked at Danny and said, "He who among you finds by spear thrown or spear thrust his death and destiny, let him die. He has no dishonor when he dies defending his country . . ."

"What does that mean?"

"It's from Homer's *The Iliad*, the speech by Hector before Achilles kills him. You know *The Iliad* and the Trojan War?"

"Not really," said Danny. "I think I read some of it in high school, but I don't remember much."

"Read it again. Achilles, the greatest warrior of his day, is completely crazed over the death of Patroclus, his friend and lover. Even though he detests his own king and doesn't want to fight for him, he kills Hector, then he drags his body around behind a chariot. The fight was personal. He wanted revenge."

"Down on the ground, it's always personal, but I don't follow where you are going."

Brody explained that even in defeat, the NADF was still a righteous cause. And it was personal. Remus, the Hammonds, and other NADF leaders had made elaborate plans for transforming the United States, not just how government would work, but also how the entire geography of the country would be changed. Brody and his co-conspirators wanted much more than the sheer removal of federal officials.

They hungered for a fresh system of governance that would permanently install white supremacy. New rules and laws. New arrangements. "We knew where we were going," he said. "It would be the rebirth of America. We wanted to seal the borders and end the influx of undesirables."

"Who were you wanting to exclude?"

"Mexicans, Muslims, Africans, Asians. Anyone from the countries we had fought in The Sandbox. Anyone not Caucasian and Christian."

"Why? So many of those people helped make the country strong and vibrant. They contributed a lot. Why exclude them?"

"They replaced legitimate white United States citizens, Goodman. I know you are a second-generation American and a Jew, but when the United States was founded, it was for Christians and whites. We made a profound mistake importing Blacks. Look what happened—they've become the real racists demanding extra financial entitlements, reparations, and special privileges. It never ends."

"What about mixed-race people?"

"We would have to figure that out . . . maybe with blood quantum tests."

"How would you have restructured government?"

"Far greater regional and local autonomy, fewer constraints on individual freedoms for whites, and much greater efficiency in policy and planning."

"How would you have done that?"

"We know it would have taken time, a decade or more, but the NADF had a blueprint and roadmap, a Yellow Brick Road . . . to use an old phrase."

"What were the steps?"

"Our first big move would be to organize a new constitutional convention with ordinary white people serving as delegates. We had a Jeffersonian vision of this. No professional pols. No K-Street lobbyists. Instead, there'd be farmers, doctors, and plumbers. People from big cities and small towns, young and old, all good white men and women who could trace their heritage back to Northern Europe."

"What about Blacks and Hispanics and their sons and daughters who have been here for generations?"

"Given our long-range goals and the composition of our supporters, that would be counterproductive. Those people wouldn't have a vote or citizenship."

"Where would they go?"

"That would be up to them."

"What would you have for basic liberties?"

"Redo some of the fundamentals and fine-tune others. Human rights with limits. Freedom of speech with guard rails."

"That doesn't square with your Pharaoh project."

"That was only a means to an end."

"Yes, but a vicious one. Did you sanction all those distortions, lies, and dirty stories they put out?"

"No, that was Remus and the Hammonds. It did help us unify the paramilitaries and create the NADF. I also know most people don't have the patience for the truth. Truth is always nuanced and multifaceted, a matter of margins and degrees. Most people prefer one big delusion to complex realities."

"You had a lot of loose cannons and wingnuts in your army."

"We had enough real soldiers with combat experience to get the weekend warriors trained in remote places and set up drills and war games. Personally, I would have liked more professionals."

"Back to your post-takeover aspirations and your plan for a new United States."

"We would have arranged the fifty states into five regional confederations:

West, Northeast, Midwest, Southeast, and Southwest. Each region would have its own constitution so long as it stayed in alignment with the national one."

"Who would be in charge of the country? Who would manage international relations, interstate commerce, and protection against the excesses of local or regional leaders?"

"You're asking smart questions, Goodman. We could have used you."

"You wouldn't have liked me. My ex-wife, Kirsten, once told me I was one of the better minds of the tenth century."

Brody cracked a smile. "To your question, initially it would have been a small cadre of generals and business leaders that would carry the burden."

"A military junta?"

"I've never liked that phrase but yes, a committee to organize the transition from old to new. That's how these things are done."

"I'm still not clear how a national government would function."

"There would still be three branches of government but they would be different." He paused. His body seemed to slump and he lowered his head. He looked weak. Then he continued.

"Ultimately, we would have had a new executive branch, and a council made up of five leaders, one from each of the five new region-states. There would be rotating presidencies and regional elections every seven years. There would have been a unicameral Congress with ten legislators from each region. They would be initially appointed on an interim basis by the committee but eventually voted in through elections."

"All white?"

"Of course."

"What about the judicial system?"

"Simplified. Local justices of the peace in every community and neighborhood, and two higher tiers of courts, one in each region and one nationally."

Brody was tiring but the talk seemed cathartic.

"A few more questions, General. What is it all the NADF groups, you, and the leaders were so afraid of?

"The truth? My people are afraid of foreigners who have flooded in and are taking the homeland away. Our jobs, our land, our women, our children. You ask about fear? I'm afraid of people taking away our guns, our history, our flags, statues, and street names. I'm afraid of folks like you, Knox, and Morgan canceling who we are."

"Another question. Why so much bloodshed? Why all the excess killing in DC and the state capitols, and the obsessive chase for Longborn and Knox?"

"Regime change is hard, Goodman. Lawrence of Arabia said it was eating soup with a knife, slow, messy, and ugly when you spill it on yourself and others. It always has been, always will be. You know it yourself, Goodman. America has been crumbling. Our choice came down to a swift exorcism, or the long, slow descent into chaos."

"Isn't this all just tyranny?"

"I think of it as something necessary for something better."

"That may be your greater good. For everyone else, it would be oppressive."

"Well, as someone once said, beliefs have a right to differ and scrambled eggs start with broken shells."

Danny wanted to argue, but he didn't.

They talked awhile longer, during which Brody shared more personal information about his family and growing up. He had no wife or children. His mission, inherited from his father and nourished by the Hammonds and a few others, had been his passion. His voice began to trail off.

"General, thank you for your time. Perhaps my notes will be helpful for you. I'll clean them up and get you a copy."

"That would be appreciated. By the way, have you kicked your gambling habits?"

How does he know about that?

He could see Danny wondering and gave him a tired wink. "Good intel," he said.

112

FOR THE NEXT TWO DAYS, PETER ASHKIN, FRANK SHERWOOD, AN NADF LAWYER NAMED CY SWANSON, AND DANNY WORKED ON THE DETAILS OF THE PROPOSED DUCK SPRINGS ACCORD. For the most part, the process was cooperative, but Goodman had forgotten what it was like being in a room full of lawyers picking nits.

They had their disagreements and set aside certain thorny matters for later, but Sherwood and Swanson were experienced attorneys. Sherwood had gone to Baylor Law School and was in private practice. Swanson was a law-trained graduate of Duke and had concentrated his legal work on a large interstate family business. Like everyone else in the NADF, they were white.

Peter Ashkin, Danny, and Harlan caucused numerous times to think through the wording of certain terms. Peter brought his detailed eye to the task. Danny's contributions were defensive. His clients were Knox and Morgan, and he wanted to make sure they had the best ammunition available for the inevitable lawsuits that would follow.

Someone once said litigation is the nearest thing to eternal life on Earth. The lawsuits springing from this would still be around when they were all under the grass.

The legal beagles finally delivered a strong draft to their leaders, who studied it overnight and were fully prepared for what would be a final settlement discussion.

All the lawyering made Danny think of stories he wanted to tell Grant Terwilliger. When he was at MCS, he relished lawyer jokes even if he was making fun of himself. He would love to tell Grant a few, but sadly, Terwilliger had been killed defending the town in a gun battle on the tableland above Duck Springs, one of many good people the town had lost, including Bucky Fontaine, the cop; Bob Williams, Willy Cazimero, and Smurf, the electricity kid; Crazy Mary, and Ted Cingcade. Thomas Quinn and his dog Ladybird Johnson both perished when an armed drone landed on them near the fence line. Alyssaranda Gibson from the Parliament of Owls was shot by an NADF intruder. Many others, people he hadn't met or didn't know very well, were gone.

The next day, after last-minute haggling and wordsmithing, the final version of the agreement was typed on a restored computer and signed by all parties. There were handshakes—tentative and fragile—but the Duck Springs Accord concluded the Second American Civil War.

It was also Eugene Brody's final testimony. The night he signed it, he went back to his room and hung himself.

113

RETURNING TO TOWN, THEY SAW THE DESTRUCTION. The Anthony C. Holbrooke Community Center was gone. The café was gone. Slim's grocery store and Mo's bakery were flattened. Harlan's house, along with all his books, including Danny's *Carnets*, were destroyed. Mabel's post office and Ian's Forest Service offices were destroyed. Grant Terwilliger's fire station was burned to the ground. Cynthia's infirmary and Vern's gun shop had disappeared. Somehow, no one bothered with the Miyamotos' house and farm.

In the weeks and months that followed, life slowly crept back but it was, as everyone knew it would be, very different. All wars have afterlives with scars and memories that are embedded but which always find a way to haunt each person in their own way. They become new ghosts.

In a place like Duck Springs, no one who had lived through it could put the past fully behind them. When others they all knew died, parts of everyone else died with them. Still, those who had lived the NADF fight every day knew their fight was important, but so, as they came to learn, were clashes in Annapolis, Little Rock, and a half dozen other places. Critical as Duck Springs was, the decisive body blow against the NADF happened in the Battle for St. Louis, where huge numbers died.

The rebuilding of Duck Springs started slowly. Dozens were formally interred in the town's new cemetery on Ogden Road. Peter Ashkin became the new mayor and began reconstruction. Cynthia, Mohan, Laxmi, and Maximo continued to work on injuries, lost limbs, and burns, while Diego Owens and Roy Voss tried to heal inner wounds.

Clover recovered. She was stiff and slow and constantly in pain at the start, but irrepressibly eager to be back in the world. She and Danny moved into her slightly damaged but still-intact house. The porch was burned, but her studio and the large triptych picture of the garden in her mind were miraculously unscathed. The surface of Danny's writing desk was hidden by clutter, but little by little he started mining his journals and notes on scraps of paper for the long story about Duck Springs that he wanted to put together.

Pops and Thelma began to rebuild their café, making it a bit more stylish and modern. "Always wanted to upgrade the joint," Pops said over coffee.

Squints and Yoko Miyamoto restarted the orchard and renewed their lifelong quest for the perfect berry jam. Paul and a few others returned to Superstition Pass to resurrect the Parliament of Owls. Masaji and Daisy decided to stay in town.

Eighteen months later, Clover, Daisy, and Julie opened Quack-Quack Arts and began selling books, pamphlets, paintings, and photos to a trickle of tourists who started to come back. While they were browsing, they could enjoy Julie's cappuccinos and lattes, along with muffins and slices of Clover's peanut butter pie.

Izzy and Penelope moved in together, and Penelope found new combinations of hair colors. Last time Danny saw her, it was a blend of chartreuse and blue. Meghan Turnbull became the new chief of police. Mohan, Laxmi, and Cynthia planned to create a regional medical center, and Chris Knox made his way back to Washington and was officially sworn in as president, along with forty-one new senators and a herd of energetic young house members.

NADF leaders from different parts of the country were put on trial. Some juries called for executions, but President Knox commuted all NADF death sentences and instead brought them before Truth and Reconciliation Commissions chartered by the federal courts. O'Reilly died awaiting trial.

Izzy asked Danny to help him restart the *Duck Springs Chronicle* and offered him part ownership. Everyone, it seemed, was hungry for news and gossip, but Izzy had ideas about a national publishing venture. He and Danny got the *Chronicle* up and running, and then Danny put out a shingle to do some work when occasional legal or administrative matters popped up. For some reason, probably to aggravate him, Izzy still called Danny "Dude."

Like Masaji and Daisy, others found love. Julie Roth lived with Billy Rankin, the young fighter she met when they were doing a rotation in the Bradford kitchen.

Harlan rented a house and was writing a history of the Duck Springs battles. He used some of the notes from Danny's journals and interviews.

Some evenings a few gathered over food and libations, and indulged in more discussions on the nature of life. Roy Voss joined them as did Clover, Masaji, and Daisy.

Life in Duck Springs would never be the same as Danny Goodman experienced it when he first came to Indian Creek looking for redemption or death, but he was different now, even with new memories and new ghosts of people lost in the fighting.

Clover, the great love of his life, said "What took you so long?" when he asked her to marry him. Life, with all due respect to Camus and the other existentialists, was not absurd after all. It came down to whatever possibility and purpose any of them could make.

PART V

114

COOLER WEATHER IS COMING. Everyone feels it. It's late morning and a few townspeople drift in. The overhead sun is still bright, radiating warmth through the pines and onto the swath of grass that makes for the new park.

Danny feels a whiff of coolness coming but none of the leaves have gotten the message. They are still green.

Albert Camus's predecessor, Søren Kierkegaard, nailed it in his diary: the real meaning of a journey only comes clear when it is behind you.

That time in the old park before the final battle—he still remembers the sardines, crackers, and swings. Today, the spread is slabs of tangy barbecue, pots of beans, loaves of sourdough bread, salad, bowls of coleslaw and fruits for the vegetarians, and a table full of sweets, including Clover's fully perfected peanut butter pies. The coolers are filled with beer and ice cream.

Roy Voss will do the ceremony. He huddles with Diego, Mo, Peter, and Slim, all of them chuckling. There are other scrums of conversation going on.

Izzy, Penelope, Julie, Cynthia, Billy, Gloria, and Amos are gathered around Masaji and Daisy. Mohan and Laxmi Das are smiling. Paul Chang is conversing with Chris Knox, who made the trip from DC. A flock of little kids are running around like chickens and three teenagers are sneaking into the beer cooler.

Josh and Sharon drive up from Cape Meares on the Oregon coast in their Toyota SUV that still has bullet holes in the back. It's pure joy to see them. Turns out they were part of a local partisan group fighting the NADF near Tillamook.

"I know why you came back," says Danny, wearing a grin. "You want your Karmann Ghia!"

"Nope, it's yours," Josh says. "Wedding present, along with all this other stuff."

Josh and Sharon have brought cheeses, homemade beef jerky, and Sharon's wonderful cookies and breads.

Something brushes Danny's leg. He looks down and sees the funny-looking mutt Clover and he adopted to join Rosa Parks, Thomas's surviving dog. The little guy is reddish-brown, runty with a ratty-looking tail, a dog-and-a-half long, half-a-dog high, and some unknowable mix. He was found abandoned, injured, and terrified in Duck Springs when everyone came back from Bradford.

Most everybody was similarly freaked out but for most, memories are slowly tucking into everyone's private netherworlds.

He looks into the dog's shiny eyes. *I hope he eats soggy vegetables.*

Pops comes up and says, "What's your dog's name?"

"Elvis."

"Why Elvis?"

"Because he's cool, plus my first wife wouldn't allow that name with a cocker spaniel we had."

Izzy listens to this, drops down and pets Rosa and Elvis, who wag their tails and lean into him with obvious pleasure.

"You should have named him Dude," he says with a wink.

"I almost named him Izzy!"

Harlan comes over and shakes Danny's hand.

"Congratulations." He beams. "God bless you both, assuming there is a god. Either way, you and Clover deserve every happiness."

Clover is radiant even with the limp from her slow-healing ankle. Her honey-blonde hair is long again, her lacerations and lung puncture are healed. She wears a lovely white dress with a delicate turquoise necklace and matching earrings. She pulls Danny away. "Nice party, soldier. You ready for this?"

"For you? Yes, completely . . . always! For all this fuss? Not really, but here we are. Me in my most hygienic jeans; you in this dress, looking ravishing . . . along with all those peanut butter pies you, Thelma, and Daisy made."

"Pie is the way to a man's heart. Thelma said that."

"We didn't do all this for nothing, so we might as well finish it . . . unless you chicken out."

"Not me. You're the guy who likes to run off and be a hermit."

He hugs her. "Not anymore."

Others show up. Clover's sisters, Zephyr and Meadow. Eric Abbott and his family. Peter Ashkin, Amos Arnold, Tucker Jones, Louis Bennis, and a few others from The Lost Battalion. Vern comes by with the dog he adopted named 'Ammo T.Q. Craft,' he says. "The t and q are for Thomas Quinn. I miss my friend and partner."

One part of Danny is sliding back into monkey-mind mode. He can't help it. His thoughts turn to fat trout near underwater rocks rising to snap at flies. Tomorrow, he and Clover will head to a cabin on a river near Wild Wind Pass. They will catch fish and laze around, read books, and just be together.

Then, his monkey-mind road race launches. When he gets back, the *Chronicle* will need reporting and writing, the toilet needs a new flapper valve, and Clover will want him to frame her big garden picture. *After Zen, the laundry. . .*

The ceremony is blessedly short. Harlan walks Clover down a makeshift aisle and Masaji stands with Danny holding the ring. Voss keeps it short and follows Mark Twain's advice that no sinner was ever saved after the first five minutes of a prayer or sermon. There is food, music, good-natured toasts, and presents, even though people were asked to skip them.

Clover throws a tightly knotted bouquet over her shoulder. Julie catches it and giggles.

Late in the cooling afternoon, the park is cleaned up and the pines start to sway in a rising breeze. Harlan is the last to go. He hugs Clover, and she gives him a framed painting of a flower, a rich red Indian paintbrush. He hands the two of them an envelope. Clover opens it and smiles. In his careful handwriting, the note says:

In the midst of winter, I found an invincible summer.

—Albert Camus, 1954

That was Camus's answer to the big paradox.

"Mann Tracht, Un Gott Lacht," Danny's grandfather said. Man plans and God laughs—but sometimes it may just be out of contentment.

Driving back to their house as the sun sinks, they pass by the little spring at the bottom of the waterfall. Four wild mallards have dropped down and moved in.

ACKNOWLEDGMENTS

In the place where I live, I am required to acknowledge everyone else for anything that helps accomplish something important. My thanks go to those who read, encouraged, or helped with this. My serious author/editor comrades: Lucy Moore and Jana Wolff. Dick and Matt Harris, Hollis McMilan, Ted Riley, Chip Hughes, Frank Haas, Tom Adler, Howard Gadlin, Tom Corbett, Jan Ten-Bruggencate, Helen Nakano, Rich Wilson, Tom DiGrazia, John Barkai, and Bill Tam who all cheered me on. To my military buds who helped me since they were in kinetic battles while I was building little schools and raising chickens in the Peace Corps: Staff Sergeant Victor Craft, Captain Michael Lily, Captain Ken Kupchak, and Commander Cody Acuna. And to the people who helped me navigate the turbulent world of publishing: Arnie Kotler, Tom Peek, Liz Trupin-Pulli, and David Wilk, Jeremy Townsend, and Candace Shaffer at All Night Books.

And deep apologies to anyone I forgot.

ABOUT THE AUTHOR

Peter S. Adler, PhD lives in Honolulu. He is a planner, mediator, and consultant specializing in cooperation strategies for complex public policy issues.

In the late 1960s, he was a Peace Corps volunteer stationed in a village halfway between Mumbai and Goa. He and his roommate built schools, killed rats, and helped farmers start poultry businesses. In the 1970s, after finishing graduate studies, he was an Outward Bound instructor and associate director of the Hawai'i Bound School. In the 1980s he worked for the Hawai'i Supreme Court before becoming President and CEO of The Keystone Center in the 1990s.

Adler is the author of five previous books: *Beyond Paradise* (Oxbow Press1993), *Oxtail Soup* (Oxbow Press, 2008), *India-40 and the Circle of Demons* (Xlibris, 2017) *Eye of the Storm Leadership* (RIS, 2008), and *Calming the Storm: A Leader's Handbook for Managing Unproductive Conflicts* (Roman and Littlefield, 2024).